COP 1

FIC

Leavitt, Caroline.
   Meeting Rozzy halfway / Caroline
Leavitt. 1st ed. New York : Seaview
Books, c1980.
   p. cm.

RCN 80-52421-7

  I. Title.
PS3562.E2617   813.54 19   80-52421

MEETING
ROZZY
HALFWAY

MEETING ROZZY HALFWAY

Caroline Leavitt

Seaview Books
NEW YORK

Portions of this book originally appeared in *Redbook* magazine.

Library of Congress Cataloging in Publication Data

Leavitt, Caroline.
    Meeting Rozzy halfway.

    I. Title.
PS3562.E2617M4   813'.54   80-52421
ISBN 0-87223-684-X

Design by Tere LoPrete

PRELUDE

When I was writing my usual Christmas letter home, I noticed that the shapes of my letters were changing. They looked something like Rozzy's, like my sister's scrawl. I thought about tearing that letter up and typing the damned thing, but something stayed my hand.

Nothing changes. Once again I feel that bright flame, that responsibility, and the blame. My sister Rozzy's story was always one I felt compelled to tell, as inescapable as my own heartbeat. I keep thinking that if I tell her story enough times, I'll finally be able to accept the way things worked out.

I hadn't yet been born for pieces of this story. I wasn't around for others. But I've heard it all; I've felt the emotions and lived out the incidents in my mind, so many times, and so strongly, that they have become mine, they have become part of me. The brain doesn't know the difference. You can tell a person under hypnosis that he's touching fire, and right away a red angry welt will flower up on his skin, as if the flame was real.

Rozzy's story begins before she was born, made up of the background noises that both shaped and tormented her. To really see my sister, you need to hear those noises, because you can't take people in a vacuum, especially not

Rozzy. You need to live a part of some other lives before you can touch the threshold of hers.

PART ONE

CHAPTER ONE

It begins like this. With my mother's stories of the fifties, back when she was Bea Natalie Simpson, twenty-five and single, and living in Detroit. She was beautiful, with black eyes and olive skin and that rippling of shiny black hair that she would later pass on to Rozzy, the one true gift Bea ever really gave her. Bea could have married many times. There were always men hanging around her, sugaring the air with their talk full of shadows and stars and their hands full of blooms, but Bea was fussy. She kept a mental scoreboard on every man she dated, and no one ever quite measured up. They were too shy with her, or too bold. This one made her pay for her own lamb chop at dinner; this one screamed at her in public when she slid a rose into the buttonhole of a waiter at the Regency Diner. Besides, she was a great believer in destiny. She was looking for signs, for omens. She didn't think she really had to worry about choice.

Her parents chided her. Her mother kept reminding her that they could get the old Unitarian church for a wedding, but only with plenty of advance notice. Bea didn't care. She had stopped going to church a long while back, and she had stopped hearing her parents, too. She moved out of the house and shared a cramped apartment with another

girl, a nurse who slept days and worked nights. Sometimes
the two roommates didn't see each other for weeks. Bea
didn't mind. She liked being alone.

Bea hated getting up in the morning to drag herself into
work. She was too tired to make herself a lunch, so she
frequented a tiny vendomat nearby and had an apple and
vanilla pudding from a tin and a waxy carton of lukewarm
milk. Evenings, she ate Italian food from cans. She was a
perfectly good cook—a gourmet cook, in fact—but it was
boring to cook for herself and she wouldn't cook for a man
unless she felt he was worth it.

She worked at the Champion Book Market, a small,
messy, two-story place run by an overweight old Italian,
Mel Torrino. Mel spent most of his time across the street
at a pizza place, eating slices of pizza and forgetting the
store. His wife Deena came into the shop almost every day
to check up on things and to pick up some new hardbacks
to take home and read, inevitably returning them a week or
two later, the corners of the pages turned down. Bea was
startled when she first saw Deena. Deena was as blond and
bland as a baby, and as overweight as a steer, but she insisted she had danced with the New York City Ballet. She
still wore her frizzled hair in a bun, but she waddled rather
than glided, and she was always telling Bea to stand up
straight, to get her rib cage over her feet, to stretch up. She
had two poodles with lambcuts. Deena took her dogs to a
psychiatrist to find out why they weren't mating. She even
gave them special yellow pills. "Here," she would order
Bea, "walk my babies." She handed Bea the leashes, while
the twin animals struggled at the ends. Bea loved walking
the dogs. It was nice being outside, the dogs were a conversation piece, and it beat working the cash register, where
Mel wanted her mornings.

People treated Bea as if she were part of the machine.
They shook their heads in disbelief when she handed them

the wrong change; they tapped their fingers on the counter while she penciled out some sum or another. No one had ever bothered to explain to her how to count up change. One man was so annoyed with her jumbled math that he strode past the counter and reached into the register himself. Bea thought he was robbing her, but he just took his change, pocketed it, and walked out muttering.

In the afternoon, Mel came back to the store and let her shelve all the new books. She began learning, getting a varied education despite herself. She sampled art books, religion, history, science, and anthropology. She kept a watch out for Mel, leaning against one of the heavy wooden shelves and reading away the long afternoons. When the shop was busy, she was supposed to ask people if she could help them. She hated that. People were so thickheaded. She had to resist making a sour face when they asked for some pulpy fiction or when they mispronounced a name. ("Never correct a customer," Mel had once scolded her. "They won't buy a book they can't pronounce.") The college students annoyed her. She'd get excited when they asked for a title she knew; she'd want to discuss what she had read, but they weren't interested, not really. She could tell by the way they took the book from her, by the stormy indifference in their faces. But kids were the worst. Kids came in with remnants of their lunches on their hands, mustards and relishes and chocolate, and they quickly transferred them onto the clean white book pages. They plopped on the floor and cracked the tight spines of the books and they never bought one thing. She wanted to jerk their hands away. She was curt to their mothers and felt a special satisfaction when these women looked sloppy and harried, or when their husbands trailed after them, indifferent. Mothers got what they deserved. Bea told Mel that the kids' books didn't sell, hoping he'd order less and less, until the entire children's section disappeared. She misplaced a lot of the books, stacking them behind the philosophy section. But Mel loved kids. He even bought two little red leather chairs and a brown wood table and set them up by the children's books to encourage reading.

Bea had been working for two years when she began to get restless. Her roommate was serious about some doctor and began sleeping her days away at his place, so Bea really had the apartment all to herself. There wasn't even the clutter of her roommate's clothing to reassure her. She began dreaming in the shop, counting the people who wandered in, suddenly feeling that the twentieth would be someone interesting.

Bea told me that she didn't even notice Walt when he came in. She always insisted on that detail. He was so small and squirrelly, with that dark hair that he slicked back as if he were some sort of dandy, that smooth hairless face. He was a book salesman anyway, and had nothing to do with her. He jerked out a flat white hand to Mel, letting his eyes slide around the shop, settling on the book titles from his publisher.

It was several weeks later, when she was dusting the bottom rows of books, on her haunches, swearing and sweating, that Walt reappeared. He tapped her on the shoulder. "Come have some dinner with me," he said. Bea blinked at his hand stretching out to her. She took it; she let it lift her up.

"Right now," he said. "It's nearly closing time, isn't it? You don't even need to change. You look delicious."

"Why should I go out to dinner with you?" said Bea. "You've never said a word to me."

"Sure I have. In my mind. We had whole conversations. Weren't you listening?"

Bea leaned against a shelf, watching him.

"Oh, come on," he said. "I'll be off on another round of business in two weeks, so if you decide you don't like me,

I'll be gone." He grinned. "For a while anyway. I'm based right here in town."

She had expected an ordinary dinner at a small restaurant, but instead they went to the supermarket and bought boxes of Cracker Jacks and packages of yellow cheese, and they walked around town eating and talking, pulling off sections of cheese and feeding it to the birds. He brought her home early, kissing her hand, slipping something inside her palm. When he was gone, she uncurled her fingers. It was a cheap yellow ring from the Cracker Jacks, and she took it as her first omen.

They had a funny kind of courtship. Bea told me she had never met anyone so unpredictable. He would show up at her door with two sets of brilliant parrot-green skates strung around his shoulders, or he'd get tickets for the Mr. America contest at the Y. They went to the zoo or the circus, or they stayed home. "Those were the best times," Bea said. "We were like two old marrieds, sitting around in our socks watching TV and talking, two dyed-in-the-wool homebodies."

Walt worked out of Detroit, but once a month, he hit the road to sell books. He hated it. "Those stupid traveling salesmen jokes. Sometimes when people ask me what I do, I lie and say I'm in real estate. What do I need traveling for? What's there to see? All those places look like the inside of a hotel room to me. I want to stay home. With you." He always brought her back souvenirs. T-shirts with the names of the cities stamped on the chest. If he couldn't find the shirts, he bought them in plain white and scribbled in the city name himself with felt pens. Bea wore the shirts to sleep in. They ran in the wash. Even when she did them by hand, the ink tinted the water blue.

Walt was as superstitious as she was. One hot sulky day they were prowling around the city edges when a little girl with curly black hair, dressed in a pink smock, tugged at Bea's hand. She gave Bea a slip of paper, an advertisement for palm reading. "Upstairs." The girl pointed. "My mother does it and she's pretty good. You should go on up. You need it. I can always tell."

"Are you a gypsy or something?" asked Walt.

"English," said the little girl. "It costs ten dollars. Each."

They went up four flights of polished stairs into an ordinary living room. "Ma," called the child, and a middle-aged woman in shorts and curlers came in. "Thanks, Ceci," she said, ruffling the girl's curls and making a scooting motion to her. "I'm Mona Killington. Excuse the curlers and have yourselves a seat."

She immediately took Walt's hand. She studied it for a moment and then she shook her head. "Nope, I won't read this." She gave him back his hand, brushing her own off against her shorts. "Two lifelines."

"So?" said Walt, leaning forward, curious, but the woman was adamant. She wouldn't even look at Bea's palm or take their money. She stood up. "Ceci," she called, and the little girl skipped in. "Show these nice people out, would you, love?"

"I don't understand—" began Walt, but the little girl was clacking down the stairs, impatiently glancing back at them. When they all reached the bottom and the bright sun, Ceci said, "Aren't you glad you came in like I told you? My mother's good, isn't she? I told you."

It bothered Walt for days. He kept staring at his palm, tracing the twin outlines, studying them against Bea's cool white hand.

"She's not the only palm reader in this town," Bea told him. "We can just go out and scout us up another." They spent an entire Saturday combing the streets, looking for the shabby signs that advertised "Reader," "Adviser," "Spiritualist." It was always the same though. No one would tell them anything. Faces folded up like telescopes, eyes deadened. Normally boisterous women became silent and stiff, polite. It wasn't until they wandered into an occult bookshop by the park that they found someone who would talk to them.

She was very young, about fifteen maybe, and she was sitting in a corner by the door, leafing through the books on palmistry. She twirled one long strand of her hair in her fingers, and she chewed gum. Bea nudged Walt.

"Uh, you read palms?" said Walt, digging his hands into his pockets, hiding the lines as if they were stains.

"Yup." The girl looked up, squinting. "You want it done?"

"I have two lifelines," said Walt.

"Like fun," said the girl, plucking out a wad of gum and tucking it into a piece of tin foil. He held out his hand and she took it, pursing her lips.

"Jeez," she said.

"I told you. What's it *mean?*"

"No one will tell us," said Bea, drawing closer.

The girl traced Walt's double line with her index finger. "Two lives," she said, looking up at him. "Maybe you were born dead and then got yourself revived. Or maybe you're going to have some sort of accident and get yourself killed and brought back to life again. It could even mean you got two people living inside of you, like two personalities." She shook her head. "I don't really know for sure."

"Who does?"

"No one really. That's probably why they don't want to read your palm. No one wants to look like a jerk, do they." She smiled, showing gap teeth. "But look at it this way, look at it as having two chances where everybody else gets stuck with just one. What are you worried about?"

"Read hers," said Walt, taking Bea's hand and placing it in the girl's. "Please."

"We'll pay you," said Bea. "Is ten dollars good?"

"OK," said the girl.

Bea's fate claimed Walt; it calmed him down. She was to marry very soon (when he heard this, he placed his hand on Bea's shoulder and she twisted around to smile at him) and she would travel. Walt dug out a ten-dollar bill from his pocket and paid the girl. "Any time," she said.

But it took Walt weeks to get the twin lines out of his mind. He kept feeling the weight of them, wondering what exactly it was that they might be etching into his life. He drove Bea crazy. "Would you please relax?" she said. "I think it's kind of special. Interesting." She rubbed his forehead where small lines were deepening. "Come on. I like that about you. I've never met anyone with two lifelines before."

It never stopped bothering him, but something else, some stronger emotion, was usurping his worry. Four months later, he proposed to Bea. They were sitting in a booth at Frenchie's Deli, eating corned beef sandwiches and slugging down red cream sodas. Walt pried his gold pen from his front pocket and began scribbling something on one of the yellow napkins.

"What are you writing?" said Bea, but he ignored her, shielding the napkin with his hand.

Walt stopped writing and looked up at her, smiling. "You got some mustard there," he said, laughing, grabbing the napkin and dotting it on her chin. Bea kept her eyes on his face as she unfolded the napkin. There, smeared with mustard, was a wedding announcement—their wedding announcement. "How does December sound?" said Walt, reaching for her hand. Bea couldn't stop smiling. She tucked the napkin into her purse. Her purse smelled of mustard for days. Later, she would keep undoing the click lock to inhale the memory, to relive it.

"So what happens now, do we do the parents bit, set up dates, or what? I have just one more trip to make, and come next week, I'm going to try to find some other line of work. Maybe one of those paperback stores, maybe I could manage it. I'll call you every single damned day I'm gone, and when I get back, we'll firm things up."

They began planning out their dream house, etching it into Walt's faded carpet with their nails. "You want kids?" Walt asked abruptly, not looking at her. Bea drew a wobbling line across their kitchen.

"But you're not all that set on them, are you?" said Walt. "I guess I'm just selfish. Kids do things to a marriage, though, don't they? I've seen it happen, and I can tell you, I understand. It's kind of like a rejection, like a slap in the face. I couldn't help feeling that a kid would mean that I wasn't enough for you, that you needed more." He searched her face. "Sick, right?"

Bea swung her arms about his neck, grinning.

"I've got to always feel that I'm number one, Bea. I bet I couldn't even cope with a dog."

"I'm allergic to dogs," said Bea.

From then on, they had a shared joke about kids. They made faces at one another whenever they saw some kid hanging on to the back of his mother's dress and whining, or some mother pivoting furiously to whack her offspring half silly. Walt labeled all pregnant women beach balls and stroked Bea's hard flat stomach in admiration. "It's a deficient relationship that needs kids," he told her. "We'll never be like that."

Walt left on a Thursday, and Bea's life immediately cracked open with loneliness. She called her folks and told her mother she was getting married, and her mother cried, which irritated Bea.

Walt didn't call and she began to worry. At first she told herself that he was just busy, but then she started to panic, imagining him in some terrible crippling accident, losing his memory and wandering forty years in some tiny unfindable country. She kept having dreams about him. He was transformed into a giant bird with huge red flapping wings. He'd swoop down and catch her in his talons, but then he always released her, sending her helplessly floating down in an endless expanse of gray sky.

She waited a week and then called his Detroit office, where a breezy secretary told her that Walt was no longer with them.

"What?" said Bea.

"Fired," said the girl.

"For what?"

"Can't tell you that," she said. She couldn't tell Bea much of anything, not even where Walt might be located. Bea hung up the phone and started to cry. She called his Detroit apartment, but the line was disconnected. She even called information in Akron, where he had told her his parents lived. She dialed every Adler in the whole city until she hit the right one, and by then she was tight with hysteria.

"I don't know where he is," said Walt's mother.

"But we were going to be married!" cried Bea.

"Married!" said Walt's mother. She immediately began peppering Bea with questions, inviting her out to Ohio right that very week, asking her what kinds of gifts she might like, what kind of wedding. Bea couldn't speak. She begged Walt's mother to call her if there was word from Walt and then she clicked down the receiver.

Bea waited out the week. She felt as if everyone around her were sleepwalking and she was the only one awake. The air was thick and sludgy around her. She couldn't seem to breathe, couldn't keep enough air inside of her to live. At work she hunched over the books and silently wept, keeping one hand over her face, sluicing away the tears. Mel knew something was wrong. He put his arms about her. "You want a vacation, honey? You just say when."

"I'll be fine," said Bea. He looked at her curiously,

fatherly, but she couldn't tell him. Saying the words might finalize it, and she was afraid.

Bea found a doctor who would give her Valium and she gulped them down like hard candies. She went to work in a hazy shock. She came home and wrote WALT CALL BEA in large red letters on sheets of watercolor paper, and she masking-taped them all over town, at their favorite haunts, at Frenchie's. She called his office over and over and over again, demanding information. Why wouldn't they tell her where he was? Why didn't they know? She sometimes had a sickening premonition that he *was* there, listening on an extension, his arm thrown carelessly around a pregnant blond. She could see the two of them, laughing at her. When Bea came home, she stayed in front of the radio, listening to the voices flowing into one another. She kept the phone at her feet, and when it rang, it was like an electric current.

She fed her fantasies. She lost weight, and then she binged on potato chips and superstitions. If I sleep four hours, she thought, Walt will call. If I eat this soup, Walt will show up in front of me. Mel finally took Bea into his office and ordered her to take a vacation or lose her job. "You're scaring the customers away," he told her, "and I like you better than I like them, so the only solution is for you to take a paid vacation and then come back to work when you feel good again."

So Bea bought a ticket for the Caribbean. She had hired an answering service for any calls she might receive, and had left her hotel address with the post office. She was airsick on the plane. She grabbed the greasy white vomit bag from the seat pocket and fled to the bathroom. She was in there for so long that the stewardess rapped on the door.

Bea purged herself. For the first time she felt something besides the raw weaving ache Walt had left her. She felt anger. She straightened up and stared at herself in the filmy mirror. She was still beautiful. She fluffed out her hair.

There was a gray strand and she violently plucked it out, letting it drift onto the floor and die. She checked her eyes for wrinkles, and then she stumbled back to her seat, a faint brown vomit stain on her lapel, marking her.

Bea hated the Caribbean. She liked the cold, the indoors, and here everyone was grilling themselves up like minute steaks. But she pushed herself into a new red bathing suit and let her hair skid down her back. She had a hotel room on the beach and everyone watched her behind their sunglasses when she gingerly padded onto the white sands, dragging a black velour towel behind her. No one had black towels, and no one looked like Bea. She squinted around her. Everyone reminded her of Walt, and she made a silent vow that she would never let the next man in her life go anywhere without her, not even to the drugstore for aspirin and a newspaper. She fished around in her beachbag and gulped a Valium. That little yellow sun warmed her more than any burning orb in the sky. She supposed that she ought to go swimming. It was quite hot, but she was afraid of the ocean. There were all sorts of animals that made it their home; crabs with pincers, jellyfish, huge prowling sharks. She had an impulse to call her answering service, but a dizzying flood of anger stopped her. She'd cancel that service. But not just yet.

Enter Ben Nelson, my father. He was a real athlete back then, a runner. It wouldn't be until much later that he would take on layers of fat, insulating himself. He was a Boston lawyer on vacation, running up and down the beach like a crazy person, tearing up the sand along the water's edge and skimming his feet in the froth.

"He surprised me," Bea said. "He didn't run in the morning when the beach was deserted. It would be cooler then, easier to run than in the sticky heat. He was always up by six anyway. Sometimes I'd see him in the coffee shop, making some waitress squeeze him fresh orange juice and boil him an egg. He'd read while he ate, usually some ponderous-looking law book, or philosophy. He started his running at eleven, when the heat had peaked, the beach had become carpeted with flesh, with tones of pink and white and brown. He wove in and out of the blankets, carrying himself above the ground like a ballet dancer. He never slowed his pace; he kicked up the sand and he sweated."

Ben had not always been in such good shape. That story was one he himself loved to tell, over and over again, savoring the outcome, proud of it. Even now, it is the only part of the past he will talk about.

He had nearly died at fifteen, of some rare respiratory disease. His parents kept telling him he had inherited it, that there was a legacy of illness in the family line, but he never saw anyone else who had what he had. He hated the whole business. They gave him three different medicines and he had to carry them with him wherever he went. He had two bottles of green and white pills and a small inhaler that spritzed a whitish mist down his throat and into his laboring lungs. He took to wearing blazers in the summer, shirts with pockets, pants with large kangaroo pockets. But even so, his pockets bulged with the shape of the inhaler. One day he went out and bought some surgical tape and taped the inhaler to his thigh, under the baggy fabric of his pants. He worried all day that the tape would fail him, that it would unstick and his inhaler would clack down to the floor, branding him, mocking him. When his air choked itself off and he needed that inhaler, he ripped off the tape in the men's room, in a stall. He felt as if he was defoliating a jungle. The hair ripped from his legs. The tape immediately lost its stick; he couldn't retape the inhaler, and he ended up with the same loathsome bulge in his pockets. No one knew he was sick. His friends kidded him about wearing his pants so baggy. He wished he could carry a purse like women did. He had nightmares that one day he would be caught without his medication and he would strangle in front of enormous crowds of people, all of them gawking at him, so he went out and got triple refills of his medication, stockpiling them in his room.

Her parents were no help. They were devout Catholics and instructed him to pray to God for a healing. At first, when he was still going to church, he did. But when he continued to be sick, he soured on religion and announced that he didn't believe in anything. *"That's* why you're ill," his mother said angrily.

His parents helped to smother him; he felt that they were prodding his lungs to malfunction, that they used his coughing as proof that he needed the church.

It wasn't until Ben was in college that he started to change. There was a tiny diner near the campus. It wasn't very clean, but Ben liked to wander in and buy endless cups of hot tea. He'd lean into one of the blue booths and watch the old European owner make the tea. She made tea like no one else, sifting out the leaves from heavy glass jars, steeping them in a copper bowl, and he struck up a conversation with her. It was she (he still remembered her name years later—Emily Breuger) who told him about folk medicine, about herbs, about vitamins in foods. She didn't talk to many people about her knowledge because they never believed her, they thought she was a quack. Back then, no one cared about herbs or vitamins, or brewed up teas that could whisk away a cold or cure an upset stomach. Everyone wanted wonder drugs, wanted clean hospitals and candy bars. Emily was so delighted by Ben's interest that she let him prowl among her books; she was free with her herbs and recipes and with her advice on how he might get well. You couldn't really get good vitamin supplements back then, but Emily made up a list of foods that Ben should eat, and she told him to run.

He trusted her. He could run only a tenth of a mile at

first before his lungs protested. It took him months, but he got better, stronger, he needed less and less of Emily's herbs. He stopped going home. As soon as he stepped into that house, his mother would ask how his health was, and his lungs, obligingly, would fold up on him. He hated her a little, the way she twitched toward him whenever he coughed, the way she rubbed his chest. "You see?" she'd say. "You're hardly better. You come and live here with us again, and we'll soon set you right." He couldn't stand it. He began harboring a theory that *she* was responsible, that she hadn't eaten correctly when she was carrying him. When he accused her, she took to her room, weeping; and in disgust, he decided to cut himself off from his parents, to start a new generation of Nelsons.

The doctors he saw were not as amazed by his progress as he would have liked them to be. One even told him that it was fairly common for a childhood illness to be outgrown, and that Ben might as well have swallowed sugar pills as herbs. It was then he lost all his respect for doctors. He continued his herb and exercise regime, and three months later he was cured. He never cared that people called him a health nut, a fool, that he was the only one running on the Boston streets on his way to work, the only one on that hot tropical beach who really moved.

It amused Bea to watch him. She told me she could tell he had noticed her. Every morning he ran around her, dipping down to catch the title of whatever book she was reading. The jackets attracted him like bright bits of metal. Eventually, he stopped running dead in front of her. She was reading Proust, and she glanced up at him, shielding her eyes from the sun with the flat of her hand.

"You read a lot of books," he said.

She smiled. "It comes from working in a bookstore."

He sat down beside her. It became a habit. At first they didn't really talk much. She didn't like being interrupted when she read, and he was content to be beside her and tan. She opened up to him very slowly, speaking in that husky voice of hers, blinding him with her wit, her intelligence. They began going out to lunch together, stretching that into dinner. And he persuaded her to run.

Bea always thought he would get bored with running, that with her there, he'd be willing to sit more and run less. But one day he presented her with a gift, all wrapped up in silver paper and silver ribbons, and she ripped it gracelessly apart. She lifted out a pair of screaming yellow running shoes and started to weep. "What's the matter?" he said, baffled. "Is it the color?"

"Oh," she said, wiping away the tears with the side of her hand. "It's nothing."

She never got used to running, to having to use her body, but she liked the companionship, the way Ben was always a few steady beats ahead of her. He decided she should learn tennis. "He was a foul teacher," she told me. "He'd try to be patient, but he kept pursing up his mouth just like a dried fruit. I couldn't handle that look so I began waking up an hour early to take lessons from the local pro. Ben never found out."

They were there for over a month. For Bea, it was a totally different kind of life than the one she had shared so blissfully with Walt. There were no evenings in, certainly no dreamy long afternoons. Instead Ben made her attempt waterskiing, and had her riding horses. Riding was the worst. He was always prying her hands off the saddle horn. "You'll never learn to ride that way," he told her crossly. She meekly held the reins, but as soon as he cantered ahead, she grabbed for that leathery knob as if it were a lifeline. She was leary of her horse, a small dappled mare. It looked as if it might like to bite her.

Ben was different from Walt. He remembered everything, even what someone had said to someone else years ago, things that she didn't think mattered. There was a preciseness about him. He was clean of Walt's giddy recklessness. At dinner one night she carried on with a man sitting across the way. She smiled and blushed and tipped her drink at him, all the time glancing at Ben, gauging his reaction. Ben got up, and something twisted within her. She stopped flirting and looked down into her drink. But when Ben reappeared a few moments later, he handed her one perfect red-black rose. She dipped her nose into the petals and smiled.

They began to tell each other everything. She knew he was an only child, that he didn't like to talk about his parents, that he was as intelligent as he was impatient. He thought he knew everything about her, even about Walt, but she didn't tell him that she was still trapped by memory, that she still wondered and worried over her answering service back in Detroit. Ben told her he loved her. It was a relief to listen to him making rules, talking about relationships as if they had edges and boundaries to bounce against. When he asked her to marry him, she bit back on a hasty answer. They hadn't known each other that long, and besides that, Walt was still coursing through her blood, she couldn't forget him.

She panicked. She saw the long lonely weeks spreading out ahead of her, the silent apartment, the routine of her job. She liked Ben, but she wasn't sure. He had told her there had been other women in his life, that women really liked him, but that no one had captured him as Bea had. If she said no, he could easily find someone to say yes.

She didn't want to have to make the decision at all. She called her mother long distance. Bea's mother was practical. "Is he kind? Is he generous? Forget all that romantic garbage, that stuff bleeds right out of a marriage fast enough. If he's those things, then marry him."

So Bea said yes. The hotel told them where to get blood

tests and the license, and even produced a local official who could marry them. They were married in the hotel dining room, right away, the two of them standing in that big room, listening to the ceremony in broken English. Bea couldn't help thinking that if she were meant to be with Walt, then he would somehow find her in the next few minutes. She would know. She told me she imagined him calling her service and getting her number; she saw him distraught, trying to phone her and then abruptly, impetuously, hopping a small plane. The plane bobbed and weaved in her mind while she tottered on satiny white pumps. She had on a new short white linen suit with cap sleeves and she was clutching a rose. She heard the engine in the plane failing, and she held out her hand for Ben to claim, holding her breath until his flesh touched hers and dragged her back into reality. She thought of Walt for another second, and then she relinquished everything to become Ben's wife, to blot out her past with a new name, a new identity.

They stopped in Detroit for two days so Bea could pack up what few things she owned. She took him to meet her parents, who ignored Ben's stiff politeness and told Bea they thought he was wonderful. She had to prod him into phoning his parents, into letting her speak to them. When they kept asking her if she would convert to Catholicism, she looked helplessly at Ben, who grinned.

Bea didn't bother contacting her answering service, but mailed them a check, with no forwarding address. The last night in Detroit, she walked around with Ben, linking arms, holding her head very high. She took him with her to say good-bye to Mel, and she even brought him into Frenchie's for a red cream soda. She laughed when he complained that the carbonation would ruin their stomachs. And when they left for Boston, riding high up in a plane, she didn't look out of the tiny window down at the city she was leaving, and she kept her hand clasped firmly in Ben's.

CHAPTER TWO

Bea loved being married. Everywhere she went, she held out her hand so her diamond could catch at the light and hold it, could warm her with its flaming beauty. She liked to call the local store and mention things her husband might want, mention her name. And she found more and more to love in Ben because he was her husband. She ran with him mornings before he went to work, still loathing the jumpy pace, but loving the image of husband and wife doing something together. She imagined the neighbors sneaking furtive peeks at them from behind the lace curtains, envious of the bond she and Ben had.

She began to cook again. Every Thursday she took the subway to the North End to Haymarket Square and picked out fresh fruits and vegetables, screaming at the merchants when they tried to pack up some of the bruised produce for her, hiding it with their large beefy hands. Let them leave that spoiled stuff for the beggars who were always scrounging around the bins after everyone else had left, bagging up the brown bananas, greedily lunging for the blackening broccoli. She bought only what she needed and began cooking at three. She surprised Ben. It took her a while to figure out what he would eat and what he wouldn't. He hated tomatoes. She used imported oils and real butter and she grew her own spices in the windowbox of their apartment.

Every morning they both drank special herb tea. She packed him lunches with imported cheese and Bing cherries, with bread she baked herself and juice drinks she made in her blender.

When Ben came home from work, they ate and then went out walking or out to the courts for a quick splashy game of tennis. She waited for the nights. She was most happy just lying beside him, the two of them half asleep, bodies fitted against each other like old friends. Life breathed around her, drawing her in and pushing her out.

"Let's have a kid," Ben said one day. Bea smiled blankly. "Don't you like kids?" said Ben, surprised. "Kids are a delight."

"Oh, I guess," said Bea. "Let's make popcorn, with melted cheese dribbling all over it, OK?"

She learned early about her husband's sulks. They sometimes went out to dinner with his clients. She was always bored, barely listening to the conversation, smiling when she could remember. Sometimes they brought their wives, and then she had a better time; she could talk about food and housecleaning, they could chat about husbands. She would listen to them babble on about their kids, bobbing her head at them, glad the children were someone else's and not hers.

One evening, though, she and Ben and a middle-aged man were eating at the Ritz when, abruptly, Ben stopped talking. It was awkward. The client continued to speak, but then he foundered. Bea had to make small talk for the rest of dinner, talking about books and art, and then helplessly realizing she was running out of topics. She was delighted when the man said he had a tight headache and left to call a cab, extending his hand to Ben, who politely glanced at it, and then returned to his dinner.

Bea confronted Ben as soon as she saw the client was out

of the building. "What kind of a way is that to act? That's your client, for God's sake, what did the poor man do?"

"He knows what he did," said Ben mildly, the angry sulkiness drained from him.

They didn't discuss it further. Ben simply refused. But she saw him put on these sulks with others, and at first it frightened her. She began to spot a pattern. He could be silent with someone who had forgotten his name, silent about a missed appointment. With her, though, his anger took shape and then dissipated. His dour face would quickly fade.

They had been married nearly a year when Walt showed up. Bea was fiddling around in the kitchen, caught between several red plastic mixing bowls of yeasty dough and a whirring blender of egg whites. She had on a blue apron and her hair was carelessly knotted up on her head. She had several dots of brownish flour speckling her nose like freckles. When the bell rang, she cursed, then she went to push open the heavy wood door, all the time brushing off her hands against her apron and worrying about the bread she wanted to make. It was a new recipe and it required careful braiding, and she was a little nervous about it. But maybe the bell was the Avon lady. She collected the pretty imitation gold lipsticks they gave out, kissing her wrists to examine the shades.

Bea told me she didn't recognize him at first. He was in a dark suit, his hair roughly cut, and holding on to his left arm was a thin pale redhead. Bea stiffened, suddenly flooded with memory. She fluttered her hands to her hair.

"Can I come in?" He had forgotten the woman at his side, thought Bea, or maybe he just took her for granted. Bea stepped back, untugging her hair, ruffling it down her back.

"What a dandy home," said the woman, looking up at

the ceiling. "We have just a tiny place in Kansas. Are all the apartments here this nice?"

Bea followed the woman's glance to her ceiling. She stood there stupidly, trying to remember just what it was that a hostess did and how she could possibly speak without stuttering. "Coffee," she blurted. "We can have coffee in the kitchen."

They sat around the white Formica table while Bea cleared away some of the clutter and made coffee. Nobody spoke during her preparations and Bea was acutely aware of every sound in the room. She poured out the coffee and Walt took a deep happy breath and blew on his, spilling a few drops onto the table. He wiped them away with his sleeve and then looked brightly from one woman to the other. "Oh God, what a moron," he said. "Bea, I can't believe I forgot to introduce you. What a jerk. This is Jess, my wife." Jess jabbed out her hand. "I've heard all sorts of nice things about you," she said.

Bea gulped her coffee, burning her tongue. "When did you get married?" she said, staring into her cup, sightless.

Walt reached over and tugged at Bea's hand. "Sit," he ordered. "Oh, come on, don't look like that. Jess knows everything. You think I wouldn't tell her?"

"Of course not," said Bea dully.

Walt grinned sheepishly. "I'm sorry. You can't know how sorry. Tell her, Jess, tell her how you've been screaming at me to make my amends."

"I thought it was just plain awful," said Jess.

"I got fired," said Walt. "I was really all set to come and get you, but then they called me into the office and said I wasn't selling enough, that I wasn't worth their time. *Damn* them. I was so ashamed. I holed up at a Howard Johnson's in Bridgeport, wondering what in hell I could possibly do with myself. Every night I thought about calling you. I'd sit and stare at that phone, I'd will myself to get up and dial, but I couldn't. I don't know. I called home and my mother started asking me all kinds of things about you, saying you had called and how sweet you sounded, and what was the matter with me not telling her anything about you? I couldn't speak to anyone, not to her. I gave her some lame answers. I went out to Kansas. I heard there were jobs opening up like cans. Maybe for some people, but not for me. I went to this bar to get drunk and I met Jess. She's a dentist, can you beat that?"

Bea looked helplessly at Jess's smooth, even face, her white teeth, hard as bone.

"She kept talking to me. I stopped drinking to listen. She got me a job through her father, who owns a whole chain of those paperback places I kept jawing off about. Remember that was what I always said I wanted? I love my job," he said proudly. "What else can I say? I was happy. I should have called you, but it was an easy thing to put off, and I was scared the job might fall through. I wanted to give you something secure, not just a promise. I kept thinking, one more month, just one more. And then I was seeing more and more of Jess and—well, look, Bea, you were so beautiful, so worth having, I was sure someone else had snapped you up, someone better." He glanced around the kitchen. "And someone did, didn't they, Bea?"

"That's right," she said.

Jess politely excused herself, asking Bea where the powder room was. Walt watched her leave and then he leaned closer to Bea. "It was hell to find you," he said. His voice changed; it took on twists and shadows. "I even got dramatic about it and hired myself a detective to boot. Took him four weeks to find you. I felt sick when I thought about it, about losing you, messing everything up. Don't get me wrong. I love Jess. I truly do. But sometimes in the morning when I wake up, I think the woman next to me is you and—"

"Stop—" cried Bea, getting up. He reached for her

hand, but she jerked it back and held it protectively against her.

"We're on vacation," Walt said. "Jess doesn't know about the detective. Lucky for me that Boston's a good place for a vacation. How would I ever explain Akron?" He whispered to Bea. They should meet later, the two of them.

"What for?" said Bea.

"I love you."

"Are you mad? I'm married. You're married. What are you trying to do to me?"

"Bea, would you just listen?" He held up his palm. "Remember? Look. Two lifelines. Two chances, Bea."

"*Stop*," said Bea.

Jess reappeared, her cheeks freshly splotched with red, her hair puffing on her neck. Bea idly wondered if Jess had sampled some of the perfumes she left in the bathroom. She gave an experimental sniff, and then saw Walt watching her, and her heart withered inside of her. She fumbled with the coffeepot. She herded them both out. She couldn't breathe with them in her house. "We're at the Plaza," said Walt. "Room 222, easy to remember. Give us a call and the four of us can do the town."

Jess clasped Bea's hand. "We could all have a nice dinner. I'd love to meet your husband."

"Me, too," said Walt.

When Bea went back to the kitchen, her baking fever had burned itself out. She gathered up the yeasty mound of dough and the egg whites and dumped them out. She couldn't be in this kitchen, not with Walt's scent in here. She went to the bedroom and stretched out across the double bed, staring at the ceiling and trying to piece things out, to find her center again. She saw the number 222 in her mind, the numbers waving and dancing. She stretched again, reaching for the phone, and called Ben. He was short with her. "Christ, Bea, I've got two clients in here. What is it? What's the matter?" he said.

She hated him. "Nothing," she said, and hung up. She began dialing Walt's number, but then she caught the glittering of her diamond and she slammed the receiver down.

It was always hard for Bea to make a decision. She liked having fate stage events for her, order things out. She didn't mention Walt's visit to Ben; she didn't want to have the wound opened to his soft probe, and she certainly didn't want to go out with Walt and his wife. She stopped answering the phone, the sounds stinging her. She tried to keep herself busy, to bake elaborate pastries and make fancy aspics. But there were always spaces of time left over when, despite herself, she went digging through her old photo albums, finding the four framed Woolworth shots she and Walt had taken for a quarter. She fingered the grainy surface, looking for life.

Bea showered and put on a lacy nightgown and got into bed. When Ben came home that night, she was drowsing. He sat beside her, resting his hand on her forehead. "Sick?" he said.

"Let's start a family," said Bea. "Make us permanent. Right now." She pulled him toward her, biting him, tasting the salt on his skin.

She never did call Walt and she got used to the bruising ring of the telephone, the whine of the doorbell. She was hot and jittery the whole week until she was sure Walt had left, that he was out of her state and back in Kansas. Whenever she got a twinge of memory, she placed her hands on her belly. "Bastard," she said, over and over, out loud, branding the words into her life. Her anger soothed her.

Every morning she woke up anxious, waiting for a familiar nausea, some secret prickling within her that would tell her she was carrying life. The closer she got to her period, the more nervous she became, examining her panties for the faintest smear of blood, taking cold baths in hopes of stopping any flow. She took long walks, wondering what it would be like to have a child, making herself queasy with fear, but she didn't see any other way to keep her life intact and ordered.

Two weeks later, the phone caught her by surprise. It was Walt and he was frantic. "I'm going to have a baby," she said defiantly, shutting his flow of words before they could claim her and make her his again.

"What?" said Walt. "What are you talking about? We talked about that, don't you remember?"

"You heard me," said Bea, "and it has nothing to do with you. It was planned, too." She hung up, staying by the phone, tensed against it, but it was silent. Good, she thought, stroking her belly, her fingers like dowsers searching for water. She had said the words and now Walt would never want her.

She was silent when Ben came home and she couldn't eat any of her dinner. "You feeling blue?" said Ben, and Bea burst into tears. He came around the table and put his arms about her, kissing her neck, cooing pet names at her, but her grief made her deaf.

Bea found out that she was pregnant on a Monday. There *was* life, a life that would become Rozzy. Even then, that far back, Rozzy was affecting people, was sealing up fates as tightly as any surprise package.

Ben immediately began planning. He became really interested in prenatal care. He went out to the bookshop and came back with two red crinkly bags full of baby books.

Every evening, he and Bea would read aloud, discussing passages.

"I'm really pregnant," said Bea, wistfully.

"Isn't it terrific?"

In the morning, Ben made her up a sticky health drink, an old recipe of Emily's. It was a sludgy orange mixture of apple juice, raw eggs, oil, and oats. It was thick, viscous, with a faint chocolate odor, and Bea puckered up her mouth with nausea. "It gives me gas," she complained.

"That only shows how much you need it," he said.

"You drink it then."

He shrugged and made himself up a drink. He poured it into a glass, tipped the glass at Bea, and drank. "It's not exactly champagne, is it?" he said, making a face. "Never mind, drink it anyway."

Ben enthusiastically began to subscribe to a new health magazine, *Prevention*. You couldn't get it on any of the stands, and it was looked upon as an oddity. He studied each issue religiously, and then he spent one weekend cleaning Bea's kitchen, ridding it of food with high fat content, of spices she didn't need, of sweets. "But how will I cook?" she wailed. "Simply," he said. He went through her cosmetics, tossing out her lipsticks and perfumes, even her scented soaps from Avon. "Oh, don't!" she cried, clutching at him as he calmly tossed a handful of bright bottles into the trash. He ordered her special "natural" cosmetics from *Prevention*'s mail order service, but when the lipsticks came, they were waxen and oddly colored, the toothpaste was grainy. Still, she obeyed Ben, she let him take charge.

"He loved my being pregnant," Bea told me. "He loved it when I started to swell up. He couldn't keep his hands away. At night he traced outlines on my stomach, ignoring my pleas to stop or I would wet my pants. Sometimes I did, but he didn't care about that." He wanted her all the time. She said she couldn't even cook dinner without his sneaking up behind her, pushing his rough hands down into her shirt, cupping her breasts, which were tender and sore. When she bent to pick up some spilled salt, she would find his hands groping about her, insistently rubbing. He surprised her in the shower, pulling her down on the wet bottom of the tub; he made love to her on the kitchen floor, in the living room. She protested that the shades weren't drawn, that it was daylight, but his hands kept reading her flesh, kept refusing to hear. She finally lay, detached, and let Ben kiss and touch her and push her into orgasm after restless orgasm. How could anyone make love to a pregnant woman?—Walt had said that.

"What are you feeling? Is sex different for you now?" Ben was always asking her questions like that, demanding that she tell him her dreams. He would pull himself down and rest his head on her belly, and he began to whisper to the fetus, telling it how brilliant it would be, how perfect. "You talk to it," he urged. She felt foolish gibbering on to something she couldn't even see, but Ben's hopeful face made her speak.

She showed up one day at Ben's office wearing a bright yellow maternity dress, feeling pretty for the first time in a long while. Ben was sullen. "What?" she demanded, as they clacked down the sidewalk on their way to lunch. He stopped and faced her. "Are you ashamed of being pregnant?" he said. Bea stared.

"Listen. Pregnancy is beautiful and you go and hide it under all that damned yellow cloth. You look just like a sailboat."

Bea cried, but then he told her she was lovely, mesmerizingly so, and that he simply ached to show her off. He wouldn't let her buy any more maternity clothes, but insisted that she wear pants with elastic waists and tuck-in tops. She felt like some enormous blow-up clown that could be bobbed back and forth. As soon as he left for work, she shucked off the clothes and slipped into the big comfortable muumuus she kept hidden in the closet.

She was huge with Rozzy. For a while the doctor even thought she might be carrying twins. "Oh Lord," she said, sighing. She took to standing in front of her mirror, mourning for the old Bea who had died, that slim supple girl who was now being usurped by this bloated cow. She had bluish veins crisscrossing her legs and stretch marks rippling across her belly and thighs. That baby was robbing her teeth of calcium (why did that make her mind flicker on Jess?), stealing the shine from her hair. "You look wonderful," Ben said, nuzzling her belly, snapping picture after picture, and Bea wept silently because she had never felt herself uglier or more ruined.

"He was ahead of his time," Bea said, "and I suffered for it. No one was having natural childbirth that I knew, not back then. But your father found a doctor who knew the breathing exercises, who was willing to teach them to both of us. *Both of us.* Ben wanted to be there when the baby was being born; he wanted to help. Everyone gave me advice, told me I was crazy, but it didn't matter." Evenings, Ben made her get down on the rug and practice her breathing. On weekends they went house hunting, in the suburbs where it would be good for children.

The last month of her pregnancy, Bea began spotting deformities around town. She couldn't get on the subway without being pushed up against someone who was spastic. The loose, drooling mouth, the jittering limbs, made her clutch her belly convulsively. People hobbling on canes terrified her; she kept imagining them as babies, their toes looking innocent and pink and healthy. She emptied her purse into the tin cans of every beggar on the street, running through her house money in days instead of weeks. She thought of it as an ancient ritual to appease the gods, a sacrifice of sorts, guaranteeing her a healthy baby. When she told Ben how frightened she was, he laughed at her. "Come on," he said, "you eat right, you exercise, neither of us has any disease, what could go wrong?" He cuddled her until she gave him a tearful grin.

Rozzy gave Bea twelve hours of labor. Bea screamed and writhed while Ben held her hand and talked to her throughout the breathing. "I'm here," he said, clutching her hand, but when Rozzy's head crowned, already dusted with downy black hair, Ben fainted and had to be dragged out by the orderlies, leaving Bea weeping, grabbing at the air until she made contact, until she found a nurse's hand. Bea strained to see the baby, to check its limbs, its face. "She's perfect," said the doctor, and Bea relaxed, closing her eyes, suddenly not caring about anything or anyone, save sleep.

They brought the baby home, to a new house in the suburbs of Belmont. Bea looked at that little foreign thing in her arms and ached with sudden possessiveness. She was surprised and delighted with her child. Her stomach was down again, but it had lost its tone, and Bea felt as if she, too, had lost something, had lost her past and Walt completely. She nuzzled the baby.

They named her Rosalind, no middle name, and right from the start she was Rozzy. She had soft black hair and large black eyes and everything interested her. She rarely slept, and she almost never cried. She would spend hours looking at her colored bird mobiles, touching her toes and gurgling. Bea completely forgot her obsession with cripples and her house money was now eaten away by things for Rozzy, by toys and frilly dresses.

Ben centered his life around his daughter. He called Bea from work at least six times a day. Was Rozzy eating? Was she doing anything new? He sprinted home from work to see her. He could spend hours just watching her sleep, marveling at her toes, her fingers, her hair. He diapered her and sang opera to her and carried her about the house. "I love you. I love the baby. I feel complete," Ben told Bea.

Bea began to get out. She found a reliable high school girl to sit for a few hours (Ben had insisted on interviewing the parade of giggling young girls himself; he looked so stern that he made one little blond cry) and she began taking afternoon exercise classes. It felt good to be off by herself, but there was something curiously touching about coming back home to her baby, too.

They made all of Rozzy's food in the blender, whirring down the same meats and fruits and vegetables that they ate. They played Mozart and Bach all day and Bea hung different bright pictures from the magazines on Rozzy's ceiling for her to look up at. She'd lift Rozzy up so the child could slap her small hand against the glossy images.

"Do you have your old baby pictures?" Ben asked Bea.

"Oh, somewhere, I suppose."

"Here, give me Rozzy. Go get them, would you?" He hoisted Rozzy up, swooping her into his lap.

Bea went and fished around in the back of her closet until she found the gray album, the pages tearing. She plunked it beside Ben and riffled the pages. The pictures weren't really in focus, and a few had yellowed, but there was Bea, sitting on a blanket, staring into the camera.

"I knew it," said Ben.

"Knew what?"

"Rozzy is your image. It's like getting you all over again."

"She's part you, too, you know."

Bea was always surprised at the flood of feelings Rozzy inspired in her. Just seeing that downy black head lifting up, the tiny hands sifting through the air for her, made Bea's heart weak inside. Sometimes she felt the urge to find Walt, to show Rozzy off to him. He'd change his mind about kids when he saw that one. Every reason she ever had for not having children diminished with Rozzy; Rozzy became every reason to bear kids. Even Ben became more attractive to her because of Rozzy. She'd stand in the other room and watch the two of them at play. He got down on all fours to pat a ball back and forth to her, his face shining. When she cried, his face contorted, taking on the pain.

She got a card and stuck a birth announcement and a small photo inside of it, and thought about finding Walt's address somehow, about mailing the card to him. Somehow though, she never got around to it.

The three of them went everywhere. There was no place Ben wouldn't take Rozzy, restaurants, the zoo, an outdoor art fair. She never cried. Sometimes Ben took her by himself, staying out the whole day. He never told Bea what they did, and she never asked, but when they came bouncing back into the house, both of them would be grinning, pleased with themselves and with each other.

They never discussed having a second child. "I wouldn't want the next one to look like me," Ben said. But as Rozzy started growing, she would allow people to touch her less and less, and it made Bea yearn to hold a newborn baby again. Rozzy was independent. She weaned herself, bracing her feet against Bea's breast and pushing herself away. She wiped kisses from her face, and she wouldn't hold anyone's hand when she crossed the street. Affection was on her terms. She taught herself to dial Ben's office, and she would call him, clamoring for him to bring her home a book. Bea, watching these phone calls, decided to begin going to bed without birth control, to leave it all up for grabs.

Three months later, she was pregnant again. "Great," said Ben. "Rozzy's old enough to learn the facts of life." He showed Rozzy Bea's stomach and told her something was growing in there, but Rozzy was uninterested.

It was nobody's fault. The first birth had been a miracle, but the second—my own—was routine. Ben was so wrapped up in Rozzy that he really didn't have room for anyone else. He still did the same things, had Bea drink the sticky drinks, but the fever wasn't there, and he couldn't supervise Bea as closely as before because of Rozzy.

When Bea was really big, he had Rozzy feel the belly. He wouldn't mince words. He wanted her always to know the truth, so he told her about the penis and the vagina and birth, and she sat quietly, playing with her thumbs.

The day of my birth, he and Rozzy were working on some simple Chopin études at the piano. She was two. I was a breech birth, and at last Bea got the gas she wanted. I was born as drugged as Bea, and for the first two weeks of my life I closed my eyes and slept. I didn't cry; I almost didn't exist. Ben looked into the crib and dandled a finger at me. When I didn't respond, he said that I was certainly bald and went to find Rozzy.

Rozzy and I were linked even then. She would rip herself free of Ben's arms and toddle over to where Bea was nursing me. She'd stroke my face, or finger the material of my dress. If she thought I was sleeping too long, she would wake me up. She seemed to like me best when I was in my playpen, contained. She showed none of the sibling rivalry kids are supposed to have. Not then, anyway. She didn't need to. She was the focus and the center of Ben's world and she could afford to be generous.

That would all change.

CHAPTER THREE

We were always a pretty isolated family. Ben had purposely set up his law practice in Boston to put as much distance as possible between him and his family; and he never would have stayed in the area even had he married someone with family there. It wasn't that he hated his parents or disliked his relations so much. It was simply that he found something unnatural and smothering about all these people laying claim to him just because of a biological quirk. He resented the advice they gave him, the way his parents told the stories about his sickly youth, the patient way they kept pushing him back toward the church. But even so, once a year, until they died, he and Bea would fly out and visit both sets of parents in Detroit and St. Louis. He was on his best behavior, polite and distant, but as soon as they reboarded the plane, he fussed.

It was worse when Rozzy and I were born. Everyone wanted to see "the children," wanted to buy us stuffed toys and take us for the weekend. It was hard for Ben, especially with Rozzy. He was so proud of her, but his wanting to show her off would have been a rotten trade. He would have to deal with his relations, with Bea's. "You can't hide kids from their grandparents," Bea scolded. "It just isn't right. And I want to see my parents, even if you don't."

So Ben put up with it. He'd walk into the house and find it cramped with relations. He'd see people sitting on his couch where he sat, dandling Rozzy on their knees, stroking my flaming hair. There wasn't room for his topcoat because of the suitcases; he kept suggesting hotels but Bea wouldn't hear of it, she brought up the army cot from the basement, she pulled out the sofa bed. Ben sat down and said nothing, lifting his head when a question was asked him. Bea smoothed over his sullenness with the cakes and pastries she had spent hours baking, with her smile and with her beauty.

Everyone thought they had the right to give advice. Our aunt Judith said we didn't look healthy; she thought we should be sent to summer camp. An uncle said Rozzy was ruining her fingers playing the piano at such a young age. Religion was always a sticky issue. Although Ben and Bea never went to church, they both believed in knowledge, in options. We were told about God, and told that when we were older we could decide for ourselves whether we wanted to go to church—or to temple—or whether we wanted to believe in anything at all. We never cared. It was more fun to stay in bed Sundays, to color in our coloring books, and to eat cookies, littering the bed with crumbs. We had gifts at Christmas, we had eggs covered with chocolate at Easter, and we had Ben's parents' angry disapproval. Ben's mother was always asking us to come to church with her, and shaking her head at our supposed ruin. "Leave them alone," Ben said. "They're not yours." Bea would smile and offer more cakes, more tea, anything to change the mood.

We were always fussed over, especially Rozzy. My aunt Judith would stand our cousin Trina up against Rozzy, back to back. "Look at the little gypsies," she said, "little angels." Rozzy would sit and play a few rough tunes on the piano, looking over her shoulder at Ben, enchanting him as she enchanted everyone else. When she was finished playing, she got up and made a delicate bow and everyone clapped. I stood against the wall, dreaming.

They all said the same things. They could see where Rozzy got her beauty, her black hair already halfway down her back was clearly Bea's, her grace, her style. And they all squinted over at me, wondering aloud where on earth I got that hair, hair that looked as if my head were on fire. Aunts and uncles gave us toys and warned us to share, our grandparents gave us candy and told us not to spoil our dinner.

When both sets of grandparents died, Ben put an abrupt end to the socializing. "No more interference," he said. "No one's going to raise these kids but us." The relatives didn't understand, of course. They kept phoning long distance, sending invitations, urging Bea to come and visit. She didn't know how to explain about Ben, so instead she lied, making up business meetings and illnesses until the invitations gradually faded from our lives.

Even in our own family, we were never really like family. It was never "Mummy" or "Daddy," but always Bea or Ben. I never thought to call them anything else, and for a while I didn't understand about parental pet names. I thought that Mummy and Daddy were names the same as Dick and Harry and Shelly, names people were labeled with at birth, the same way I was Bess.

Things jumbled. I had one friend besides Rozzy, a girl named Hilly Winston, who lived up the block. Hilly and I had roller skates, and we spent hours practicing at the playground, pretending we were skating stars, until, exhausted, our knees sore and dirty, we would head for her house for cookies and milk. I once called her mother Mum, the way Hilly did. Her mother gave me a peculiar smile. "Call me Mrs. Winston, dear," she said, filling up my glass with more milk.

"Yeah," said Hilly, "I don't go around calling *your* mother Mum."

"Of course you don't. Her name is Bea."

"You call your mother Bea?" Hilly was fascinated. She stopped eating her cookie and left it suspended in her hand.

"And my father is Ben. That's their *names*."

"Can *anyone* call them that?"

I told her she was welcome to call them Bea and Ben the same way I did. Instantly, she clamored to visit, and we decided on the next day. When she came over, she trailed rapturously after Bea, asking, "Bea, could I have a drink of water?" or "Bea, I like that dress you have on." Bea found it all very amusing and encouraged Hilly to visit.

As Rozzy and I got older, we began to have little unhealed jealousies that scarred us both. I began to notice how it was, how Ben would bundle Rozzy up and take her places, leaving me alone to play with my plastic zoo or tag after Bea. "Take both kids," Bea would insist. "We're a family." Ben would reluctantly take both of us, trying to talk Bea into coming along. But Bea knew better, she knew who would be paired off with whom, so she made excuses about books she had to finish, pies she had to bake. Ben never enjoyed these jaunts. Rozzy and I would race ahead of him, lost in our own secret world, but then Ben would take her hand and I would be straggling behind, a lonely caboose.

There were physical exchanges, too. Rozzy wanted curls like mine in her sheet of inky hair, and she whined until Bea gave her a supermarket home perm. Rozzy's hair frizzled and broke for six weeks until it grew out. Later on, it would be my turn to try to iron out my curls, to bend my head over the ironing board and let Rozzy iron and smooth the hair as carelessly as she would a blouse. Even when we were both adults, I would sometimes feel stings of jealousy; I would have to stop and remind myself: it's *Rozzy* and jealousy is out of place.

Rozzy's accomplishments were always held out to me like a carrot I had to nip at, hungry or not. At seven, she was playing Bach, and so I had to have piano lessons, too, immediately after Rozzy's. Bea set up a special time for us to practice, in the evenings when Ben could listen. Neither of us really practiced. Rozzy had an ear for music and could instantly play any piece she chose, and as far as she was concerned, playing the same thing over and over again was a waste of time when there were so many other pieces to master. I always hated practicing. I would feel a dime-sized headache curling up inside my head, waiting to spring. I could never manage to match the sounds I heard in my head and I would punish the piano for my failure, banging on the keys until I was sure they would break.

When it came time for our lessons, I straggled home from school. Rozzy was always first, but I had to sit in the living room and listen, my legs skittering under me, wanting to run and jump, to do anything save sit, anything more active than pressing down a piano pedal. But our teacher, Mrs. Pearson, insisted that you could learn a great deal from another person, and every once in a while she would savagely twist around on the piano bench to make sure I was being attentive. She would ask me questions: had I noticed how Rozzy phrased the last bars, had I noticed how she corrected her errors without being told? I got very good at pretending, at keeping an alert look drifting across my face while I dreamed about fields and beaches and teeming cities full of light and life.

Mrs. Pearson was a small woman with a mouth full of teeth. I don't know why Ben even bothered to pay her to teach us. She didn't do any teaching that I could see. Oh, she praised Rozzy's technique, her control, but these were all things that Rozzy had excelled in long before Mrs. Pearson came. Rozzy's pieces were penciled off as quickly as she could learn them. But Ben had checked the teacher's credentials. She was supposed to be the best music teacher in Boston and had turned out concert pianists like pretzels.

Ben even kept a list of these famous students in his desk.

When it was my turn for my lesson, Mrs. Pearson attempted more strenuous kinds of teaching, more discipline. She jabbed at my knuckles with her pencil point. "Curve those fingers," she shouted. The only time she ever checked off one of my pieces was when she was simply too exasperated to hear me butcher the music once again. I couldn't concentrate with her sitting so close to me on the piano bench, crowding me to the edges, poising that needle-headed pencil over my thin fingers. I was aware, too, of Rozzy, sitting quietly on the couch, her eyes shut.

When lessons were over, Bea would come out and pay the teacher and chat with her about us. I sat and played with my hands, listening to Mrs. Pearson urging Bea to buy a better piano because Rozzy was "beyond" our small spinet. Rozzy sat beside me and whispered a rude commentary about Mrs. Pearson's horse teeth. "Look," Rozzy hissed, baring her own teeth, showing as much gum as she could. She didn't stop until I was giggling, until Bea glared, shaming us into innocent expressions.

Rozzy was always moving from one thing to another, and it took her a short time to be bored with the piano. "I hate it," she told Ben, her mouth setting stubbornly. He tried to get her to continue. He even went out and bought a baby grand, so large that it dominated the whole room, but Rozzy wouldn't go near it, she acted as if she didn't even see it. Ben would fumble out some Bach, hoping to shame or inspire her, but Rozzy simply shut him out. Her lessons stopped, and because she was no longer playing, I was allowed to quit as well. Neither of us ever touched a musical instrument again.

Rozzy's inventiveness was always noticeable. I was in the first grade and she in the third when she began her famous Museum of Self. She took up four of the six shelves of our bookcase for her museum, making me double-pile my books under my bed. She borrowed some pretty glass pastry dishes from Bea and positioned them carefully on the shelves. She filled them up with what she called "artifacts of her existence," with nail clippings and red scabs she purposefully picked from her knees with a pocketknife, and even with her baby teeth (she ignored the tooth fairy, although I never ceased to be amazed and delighted with the shiny new quarters I always found tucked under my pillow in exchange for my tooth). Rozzy was always picking at herself. She bit her nails and chewed the chapped pale skin from her lips. She pulled out her eyelashes and peeled the hard skin from the soles of her feet. She even started to chew her hair, collecting some of the ends she bit off, ingesting the rest. Bea looked askance. "Rozzy," she said, "don't you know about the poor little girl down the block?"

"What little girl?" said Rozzy suspiciously.

"The little girl who had to be rushed to the hospital because she was always eating her hair. They had to cut her right open, and do you know what they found?"

Rozzy looked at Bea. "Disease?" she said.

"Unhunh." Bea looked triumphant. "A hair ball," she said. "A hair ball that stayed inside her stomach because she couldn't digest it, and it tangled up her insides but good."

Rozzy continued to be doubtful though. Whenever we saw cats outside, Bea would watch for one that was coughing, and then she would prod Rozzy. "That poor kitty has hair balls in its tummy. It ingests its own fur when it cleans itself. Do you want to go through life hacking like a cat? Someone might just keep you as a pet, make you eat smelly tuna and liver mixtures, put you out at night." But Rozzy took to the idea of being a cat. She experimentally tried licking herself clean, ignoring her bath full of bubbles and hot water and waiting to see if Bea would notice the difference. She even tried to lick a large gray tomcat that wandered into our backyard, before Bea caught her and whisked her away into the house, where Rozzy was made to gargle with Listerine. When Bea told Ben, he laughed and said Rozzy was developing a fine sense of logic.

Ben encouraged her museum. One evening he came home with a large brown box housing a microscope, and he spent days teaching her how to prepare slides of her cheek cells, how to look at her hair and her nails. They poked at the insides of their mouths with yellow toothpicks, arranging the cells on the slides. I sat and watched. Once I saw Rozzy stop fooling with a slide to lick at her hands. She had bitten her nails until her fingers were bleeding, and she secretively wiped them on her skirt, staining it.

Her museum was never finished. Every dish was labeled and she gave tours to Bea and Ben on Sundays. She was always adding new things, insisting that a museum, like a person, had to grow, had to have a sense of history and of change. She dated her artifacts. There were two kinds of teeth—baby teeth and the adult teeth that were pulled for her braces—and she took new hair and nail samples every month. She was as precise and meticulous as any scientist.

If Rozzy was so much Ben's child, you would think that I was Bea's. That wasn't exactly true. Bea did give me attention. She twisted my red hair into curls and spirals after my bath, and she gave me large yellow sheets of paper to scribble on. She hugged me and took me places, but she didn't give me the same kind of devotion that Ben gave Rozzy. She just couldn't. She would play Clue or Scrabble with me evenings before Ben came home, and I would deliberately misspell a word so she would reach across the board and affectionately ruffle my hair, teasing me into the proper spelling. But as soon as she heard Ben's key jiggling in the lock, she would leap up to wrap her arms about him and lead him into the kitchen to talk to her while she fixed the salad. I finished the game by myself, playing both parts, letting myself win. It never felt like any sort of victory.

I began to draw, to paint. It was a thing that Rozzy couldn't do, a thing that left her tense and frustrated. At night, I carried my sketch pad under the sheets with me and propped up a small flashlight. I drew in school, and at the supper table until Ben reminded me that there was a place for everything. Bea took the best drawings and framed them and hung them about the house. I decided that I was going to be famous, that I would lead an artist's life, and I clamored for art classes at one of the museums. "When you're older," Bea said, and to pacify me, she bought me a set of pastels that I soon smudged over paper, on my clothing, on the walls.

Neither Rozzy nor I really made friends in the neighborhood. I had Hilly, but Rozzy had only me. Rozzy and I made our toys challenges. We cut the strings on our puppets in hopes they might come to life like the Pinocchio we had seen on television the night before. We shaved the hair on our dolls so that we might watch it grow back in. When one of my dolls died (a casualty from a toss into the air and onto the cement) we staged an elaborate funeral, gathering all of our dolls. I wept copiously and choked out a few words over the broken doll. We carted the dead out to the backyard, to the garden for burial, pushing her in my red wagon. I wailed, clutching at Rozzy, begging her to bring the doll back to life. Rozzy handed me a blue beach shovel. "Dig," she said. I was crying so hard that Bea came out and took me into her lap, soothing me, stroking my hair. "No more of this game," Bea said, but later, in the evening, Rozzy and I crept outside and finished burying the doll, putting a small red stone over the grave to mark it.

Rozzy and I liked to roam in the wood beyond our house and capture insects in glass jars. We tormented butterflies by plucking off their wings; we let scores of grasshoppers loose in the house.

We were noisy, raucous; we misbehaved. Bea always smacked us and sent us to our rooms to think. But Ben never punished us so clearly. Instead he simply acted as if we weren't there. He sat. He became silent. I would stand flush against him, waiting for him to glance up and see me. He took his time. He rustled his paper, he hummed, he checked the laces on his shoes, and if he did look up, it was always at a point directly over my head, it was never at me. Sometimes we didn't even know what it was that we had done to make him ignore us. We'd run to Bea, who didn't know either. She'd confront Ben, exasperated, but he said that we *were* aware of our bad conduct. It was one of the few things Ben did that enraged Bea, and they fought about it.

Rozzy was as stubborn as Ben. She played his game right back to him, talking animatedly to Bea and to me at dinner, pointedly ignoring Ben. But I never could stand the silence, the refusal. I apologized for everything I could think of, standing in front of Ben, muttering that I was sorry I had eaten all the candy that Bea had been saving, that I was sorry I had shouted that I hated him, I was sorry I hadn't cleaned up my paints. Sometimes I hit it right, and then Ben would soften and hold out his arms.

"Why do you do that?" Rozzy would growl. "How can you grovel around like that?"

Ben's silences always stopped eventually, often as suddenly as they had started. We never asked him what he had forgiven us for, or why. It was enough to be free of the quiet.

When we walked to school together, I had Rozzy all to myself. She always had interesting things to say and she treated me as her equal. She told me how hard it was becoming to control her body, that it threatened to get up and walk away from her unless she watched it every second as if it were a naughty child. I thought she was teasing.

We were in different grades, but we went to the same school, and we kept our link by dressing alike. Bea would take the subway to Filene's basement and come back with matching outfits for us. She laid them out across our twin beds. Rozzy and I would race home from school to examine our booty. Sometimes we didn't like the dresses and Bea would get angry. "Good, wear ratty old T-shirts and jeans, then," she said, scooping up the dresses and rebagging them before we could reconsider. But usually the clothes were wonderful. We had green plaid Scottish togs just like Shirley Temple wore in that movie where she played a Highlands girl. We had pink skirts with white poodles stitched across the hem and white eyelet blouses and Poll Parrot red patent leather shoes with T straps. I always felt shy and happy when I spotted my own dress flouncing down the hall on Rozzy, when I saw how she looked in it; and looking down at my own dress, not seeing my own face, I could imagine my body to be Rozzy's—my face, hers.

I liked school. I drew on everything, on my arithmetic papers, on covers for book reports, and I told anyone who would listen that I was destined to be famous. We had to learn how to swim for gym class, and it was then that I discovered my second passion—the water. At home, I would fill up the tub with cold water and put on my stretchy black tank suit and climb in. Once I broke a piece of my front tooth when I slipped against the edge of the tub. I told Bea it happened at school, in the playground.

The first incident happened when Rozzy was in the fifth grade. She abruptly got up from a test, complaining that the numbers were scooting off the page. The teacher, fresh out of college, told Rozzy to go to the girls room and splash a little cool water on her face, she would feel better. "There's nothing to be nervous about, honey," said the teacher, smiling. "It's only a test." Rozzy went into the bathroom and sat down on the smeary gray tiles and let her body do whatever it wanted. A sixth-grade girl, sneaking into the bathroom for a quick smoke, found Rozzy sitting dumbly in her own urine.

Bea had to come to school to fetch Rozzy, and she slapped her right in front of the nurse. I sat up with Rozzy that night. "I didn't cry," said Rozzy, and because I didn't make fun of her, she told me I could wear her string of red glass beads the next day.

Ben refused to believe it had happened. He called Rozzy over to him and had a long talk with her and gave her a silver dollar. "She's not eating right," he said, and drove out to Haymarket Square by himself, coming home with forty dollars' worth of grapes and dark green peppers, which Rozzy loved and ate like apples.

I thought about what had happened to Rozzy. I began to practice. We had two school bathroom breaks, one at ten, and one right after lunch, around one. There were only four stalls for three classes of thirty girls, but everyone lined up. If you really had a stomachache, you could ask the teacher for special permission, but then she would write your name on the blackboard and everyone would know you had an upset stomach. It was just the same as if the whole class was standing there in the bathroom watching. I never worried about wetting my pants until Rozzy had her incident.

I began to prepare myself. I tried holding in my urine for as long as I could, until I thought my bladder would burst. At first I could only last until lunch. While everyone pushed to the bathrooms at ten, I stayed in the room and did my before-school work or dallied at the drinking fountain, afraid to actually imbibe any liquid, but moistening my lips. When lunch came, I rushed for the bathroom, my bladder aching. I found that if I concentrated on something else, if I dug my nails into my thighs, I could hold it even longer. Gradually, I worked up to an entire day. I was really proud of myself. I was quite careful about the whole matter. I didn't laugh much in school or jounce around with the other kids; I kept myself erect and still and serious. I remember much later, with my first lover, Jay, that I would spend entire days at his house without using his bathroom. I held it in, even during our lovemaking, wincing when his penis jabbed at my bladder. He thought I was having an orgasm. One day, though, he looked at me in exasperation. "What's the matter with you?" he demanded. "Don't you have normal body functions? All I do is pee and you never go at all." I blushed and hotly denied being abnormal, but I couldn't break the habit I had nurtured in grade school, I held it in until I got home.

There was suddenly more to worry about with Rozzy than her having wet her pants. She began talking out of turn in class, disrupting lessons by suddenly singing or asking questions that had nothing to do with anything and asking them so seriously that the entire class stared at her instead of tittering. At first, because Rozzy was so smart, the teacher ignored it. She thought Rozzy was simply bored with the work, that it was too easy, so she gave Rozzy special sixth-grade readers and workbooks. It didn't matter. Rozzy was being Rozzy. She turned the pages and talked to herself, slapping at imaginary birds flying around her, pecking in her hair for bread crumbs. When it began happening more and more, the principal was called, then Bea and Ben, and Rozzy began seeing a doctor, a child psychologist.

Ben cried. He slumped in his favorite brown chair, his head dipping into his hands. Bea soothed him.

"Ben," I said, tapping on his knee until he looked at me.

"Leave Ben alone right now," said Bea wearily.

Ben drove Rozzy to the doctor. Every Thursday at two, he stopped work for the day and picked Rozzy up at school. He was convinced his baby would soon be well and brilliant once again. She was only ten; everything was ahead of her, waiting for her. The doctor was a woman, Emma Zondike, and Ben had thoroughly checked her credentials. She wouldn't let him sit in on the sessions, and because Rozzy asked her not to, she wouldn't tell Ben what went on in the sessions. I thought he would be miffed that Rozzy didn't offer him the information herself, but instead, he seemed almost relieved not to have that knowledge, that burden.

Ben and Rozzy got home around dinner time. I would help Bea set the table, listening for the car, peering out the window for the first shiny glimpse of fender. Rozzy was sullen and angry when she came in. She kept her lips tightly pressed together, opening them only as much as she needed to fork food in.

Rozzy wouldn't talk to anyone about her doctor. Ben would try to joke her out of her black mood, but as the sessions stretched across the months, pulling time tight like stitches on a knitting needle, Ben became as tense as Rozzy. The two of them crept silently into the house, faces glum and stormy. He arranged to talk to the doctor. She told him she thought Rozzy was somewhat psychotic, that she might get better, she might get worse, no one really knew about these things. She wasn't sure of the cause, and there was no definitive treatment. Rozzy was still very young. For now, there were the weekly sessions and Rozzy could start on Valium to calm her down.

Ben stopped driving Rozzy to the doctor, leaving it up to Bea. He stopped bringing home books and records for Rozzy and he never asked to see an exam of hers anymore. It hurt Rozzy a great deal. She tried to crawl into his lap, but he pushed her away. "You're too big a girl for that," he told her.

"I'm four foot two," said Rozzy. "That's not so big."

I watched Rozzy listlessly go outside, saw her sit on the front porch and hunch over her knees. Sometimes I'd go and sit beside her, not talking, but placing one hand

on her back just to let her know I was there. I didn't understand what was happening to her, but I kept wondering
how we were still alike, how we differed, all the time hun-
gering to crawl up inside her skin and *know*.

"Do you love me?" I asked Ben.

"That's a very stupid question. You know the answer
to that."

"I need to go to the doctor's, too," I said abruptly, watching his face, and he slapped me.

"That's not funny," he said, and my cheek smarted for
days afterward.

Bea had a conference with the doctor, too. I wouldn't
find out until much later just how upset she really was,
how she had numbly walked up and down Newbury Street
for a full hour before coming home. There was a metallic
stickiness riding on her tongue. She flagged down a cab
and rode home, one hand over the other.

When she got home and into the house, Rozzy glared at
her. "Where *were* you?" she sulked. Bea touched Rozzy.
"I'm sorry, honey," she said, shucking off her coat, going
in to pay the sitter.

I saw how Bea began studying Rozzy, how she kept
looking for problems that she could catch and stop. She
worried about everything, talking out loud to herself. Why
did Rozzy hole up in her room like that? Why was she now
tearing so frantically up and down the hill?

"Rozz-zee—" she cried, holding open the back screen
door, letting in the buzzing flies. That small girl, only ten,
raced over to her, crunching red sneakers down on the
small stones on the patio. Bea put her hand on her daughter's
forehead. "What were you doing, baby? You looked
pretty busy."

"I'm a horse today," said Rozzy. "I have to gallop."

"Oh, a horse," said Bea, "but you're still Rozzy, aren't
you, still my girl?"

"Not right now," said Rozzy, sprinting ahead, flashing up along the swelling grassy hill, her hair flying out behind her, a horse's mane. Bea shut the door, then put her hands to her temples, rubbing. "Don't you feel good?" I asked, looking up from my drawings scattered across the kitchen table. Bea smiled weakly and sat down beside me, leafing through my pictures. "This one's nice," she said.

"Bess," she said, "does Rozzy ever play, oh, mermaid when we go to the beach, or do you kids ever go in the woods, pretend there's a gingerbread house?"

I poked around my crayon box for a purple crayon. "Gee, I don't think so."

She paused. "It's fun to pretend, isn't it? But you know, don't you, that you can't really breathe underwater, that you can get lost in the woods." Her voice trailed off. "Never mind, baby," she said. "Go and color some more."

Bea began changing when she was around Rozzy. She tried to forge bonds of sameness, as if that would tie Rozzy safely to herself. "We're both dark," she told Rozzy, making the child stand by her, both of them facing their mirror images. "I looked exactly like you when I was your age." Rozzy pulled away.

"We're alike, don't you think?" Bea persisted.

"No," said Rozzy calmly, "no, we're not."

"We both have stubby fingers," said Bea sharply. She saw Rozzy's stubborn face suddenly darken, saw the way Rozzy surreptitiously studied her hands, and saw that for a whole week, Rozzy was ashamed to hold a fork, to take a glass of water from anyone. But Bea couldn't stop herself. "Look," she'd say, "isn't it funny how you're developing the same pot belly I have? There's nothing you can do about it. You think those pullover tops you wear hide it?" Later, when Rozzy was in her teens, I would see Bea do it without even thinking, automatically. When Rozzy began pushing out of that prison of a house, Bea would stop her, edging her way into Rozzy's consciousness, reminding Rozzy to keep her skirt over her knees so she wouldn't show the same blue veins Bea had, the same knobby structure.

Bea worried that Rozzy had no friends. "There are plenty of kids your age kicking about. You should be out with them."

"They don't play the games I like," said Rozzy.

"What games?"

"Just games. No one plays them any good except for Bess."

Bea started. She began a new watch. In the middle of the week, she phoned my third-grade teacher and asked to see her. My teacher had had Rozzy, had fallen in love with that bright darkness. She didn't know much about me, about my quiet dreaminess. I did the work, she told Bea, I got A's, and I was a talented artist. Bea told me the teacher started laughing about a class project I had handed in, a carefully detailed set of paper dolls with the genitals inked in.

Bea went home, took off her coat, and told me she had seen my teacher. "Why? How come?" I demanded. Conferences were always for Rozzy, not me.

"Oh, I just wanted to see how you were doing."

"That's not why," I said angrily. "You could have just asked *me* if that was why."

"It *is* why," said Bea, stroking my hair. When I pulled away, she went into the bedroom and shut the door. I could hear her dialing the phone, speaking in a low voice, but I didn't want to hear, I didn't want to know who was on the other end, so I went to find my paints.

One day after school, Bea hired a sitter for Rozzy, a high school girl with a Beatle haircut. "The Beatles are the newest thing," the girl told me, "the face of the sixties."

I struggled out of my dress, but Bea stopped me. "Don't change," she said. Rozzy was reading, curled up on the sofa. "It's just the two of us today," Bea said to me. "There's a friend of mine who wants to meet you. Hurry up now."

"Who? Who wants to meet me?"

"A lady. Her name is Ellen Goodman. Now come *on*."

We took the subway into Brookline, crowded in among the people. I couldn't see Bea, but I kept a damp hand clasped about the silver pole. It was only a ten-minute ride and then Bea's voice wound its way through the people and caught me. "This stop, Bess. Out."

We didn't have far to walk. Bea took me to a brick building.

"Hey, this is a *doctor's* office," I accused.

"She's a doctor, so what. Everyone has jobs. She's busy, so we came during her working hours."

"I don't believe you. Why do you want me to see a doctor?" I felt the tears trembling behind my lids.

"Bess, please." She pushed open a door and led me into a waiting room. "Sit," she ordered.

"Is she a doctor like Rozzy's?"

"She just wants to talk to you."

"Is she Rozzy's doctor?"

"No, honey, she isn't."

We weren't sitting out there very long. A woman with white hair came out and smiled at me, and Bea motioned me to follow. "I'll be in in a minute," Bea said. "I want to finish this magazine."

I was prepared to hate Ellen Goodman, but she gave me paper and asked me to draw three different pictures with different members of my family, and then one whole picture of all four of us together. I didn't want to stop drawing. I forgot everything, I relaxed, and I was annoyed when she took the drawings away. While she studied them, she asked me to talk about Rozzy. I answered in vague half-sentences, and then she said I could go out and tell Bea to come in.

It was my turn to wait outside. Bea wasn't in there for very long and when she came out, I stood up, dragging my coat on, ready to get out of there. "How come I had to talk about Rozzy?" I demanded. Bea fiddled in her purse. "How come, how come?"

"Why, that lady is just a friend of mine," said Bea. "She wanted to know all about you."

I stared at Bea. Even then, I could always pick out the lies associated with Rozzy. I could see them before they even left anyone's lips. I hadn't said anything to the doctor that I knew Rozzy wouldn't want anyone to know. I had kept all our secrets. "Do I go back?" I asked.

Bea shook her head.

"Good. I wouldn't go back anyhow."

We didn't catch the subway back. Bea swiveled around and led me to a Brigham's, where we sat at the counter and she ordered two dripping hot fudge sundaes. I had never eaten one before. Ben thought sugar was poison. I didn't even want to eat it at first. I just hunched protectively over it and breathed in the chocolatey steam that rippled up over the ice cream. I bent down so low that I got a spot of ice cream on my nose. The waitress, a bored young girl, kept frisking by, dropping fresh glasses of water before us. Bea sipped each glass as if it were wine.

"My God," said the waitress, when I started spooning down the sundae. "Look at that child eat."

"I've never had one of these before," I said, looking up at her.

"Oh, now, go on," she said, grinning.

When I lifted myself off the red whirling stool, my face smeared with chocolate, Bea bent and kissed me.

"You have chocolate on your face," I told her, pointing out the spot.

She took a clean white paper napkin and dipped the edge in her water, dabbing her cheek clean. "Thank you, angel," she said.

"Where did you go?" asked Rozzy when we came back. Bea looked carefully at me.

"Oh, nowhere," I said, thinking only of the sundae.

Bea cooked a special dinner for Ben that night, a stuffed fish, marinated vegetables, a mustard salad, and mousse for dessert. She shuffled us off to bed. I got up an hour or so later and wandered into the kitchen for some water. I drank half of it and then I poured the other half over my hands, enjoying the sensation. On my way back to bed, I passed my parents' bedroom and paused at the door, pressing my ear against it and listening.

"You think I cooked a good dinner?"

"I told you that you did."

"One more question and then I'll shut up, OK?"

"Shoot."

"Do you still think I'm beautiful, that I look like an angel?"

He laughed and then she told him that she had seen Rozzy's doctor, that Rozzy's problem couldn't be labeled, but that it might disappear, or it might stretch across their lives like a silky spider web.

"She was such a beautiful baby, wasn't she?" Ben said quietly. "No one was formed the way she was, skin all the same even shade, like she was cut from one single piece. So gorgeous, so smart, speaking, walking, doing everything so quickly, so soon, so perfectly."

"She may grow out of this," Bea said.

"She was so smart."

"She's still smart."

"She was so—" he fumbled. "She was miraculous."

"I had Bess tested," said Bea, her voice gone hard. I stiffened against the door. "Rozzy's doctor wouldn't see another member of the family, but she gave me the name of this other doctor. She's normal."

"Normal," said Ben.

"Just like any kid on the block."

I heard Ben's heavy steps, heard the bathroom door opening and shutting, the shower hissing on, and then Bea weeping. I stood outside the door for a long time, and when I left, the shower was still running, was still gently stinging the air with sound, branding it.

CHAPTER FOUR

Ben never blamed Bea, no more than he blamed himself. It was always something in Rozzy, in her metabolism, her diet, things that could be controlled. He and Bea had done everything, he said. When Rozzy wandered over to him, whining that she didn't feel right, that the Valium she took mornings made her groggy, he would snap at her to behave. When she brought home her test papers, decorated with odd squiggles, the big shaming F waiting for his signature, he would refuse to sign them unless she admitted that she hadn't tried, that she could have received an A. Rozzy's face would contort bitterly, but she would never say what he wanted to hear, and Bea always ended up signing the test the next morning before Rozzy dashed off to school.

Bea would get depressed, would have terrifying headaches attacking her all day. Ben catered to her. Rozzy and I watched huge baskets of fruit appearing at our door, bunches of flowers tied with ribbon. I saw the look on Rozzy's face, and I took a few of the flowers and spread them out on Rozzy's dresser, on my dresser, too, where everyone could see. When Bea took them and put them in the vase with the others, I pulled some of the petals off, I left a defiant trail on the rug. I wanted Ben to find the petals that way, but Bea always quietly swept them up, without comment.

Rozzy sensed things were changing. She was home alone more and more often. When Rozzy ran into kids she knew on the street, they would suddenly remember dentist's appointments. Rozzy would stand stolidly and watch them make their way into the distance. She stood there until they became pinpoints. When Rozzy decided she wanted an eleventh birthday party, Bea was enthusiastic. They spent a whole afternoon buying paper plates, matching cups, name tags. Rozzy licked all the stamps for the invitations and put them in the mail. She had invited everyone she knew; some of them had never said more than a few words to her, but she didn't mind. "Everyone's coming," she said emphatically. Bea made a cake with burned chocolate frosting. The day of the party Rozzy remembered she had forgotten potato chips and made Bea drive her to the Thrift-T-Mart, leaving me to watch the Saturday morning cartoons. They were only gone for half an hour, but by the time they bumped up the hill, four of the seven girls Rozzy had invited had called to cancel. They were sick, relatives were visiting, they had to go to the doctor's. When I told Rozzy, she went to the phone and immediately called the others. "There's no party," she said. "It was a mistake." She hung up after the last call and sat down at the kitchen table.

"Let's all go to a movie," said Bea brightly, watching Rozzy.

"No, thank you," said Rozzy politely. "I'll be fine here. I'd rather watch TV all day anyway." She carefully carried her cake and two bottles of cherry soda into the den. She didn't come out until dinner.

I bounded out of the house, looking for those girls. I wanted them to say something to me so I could coldly and deliberately turn my back. But there was no one outside other than a few of the rougher neighborhood dogs, and I slowly went back home.

That summer Bea made us climb the hill to the school playground, where they had hired two college kids to teach us punchball and the art of making gimp lariats which we could hang uselessly about our necks. We never went. Rozzy would shoot up the hill and then lead me back down around the outskirts of our neighborhood. We were on the prowl. We sang tunes from the hit parade, rang doorbells and ran before people could jerk their doors open and catch us, and played stealing games at the Thrift-T-Mart. Rozzy liked to steal small things like soap or wrapping paper, but she never kept anything; the fun of it was putting it back. She always had the store detective completely baffled. He'd follow us as soon as we took a step into the store; he'd watch Rozzy as she fingered the tissue paper, the magazines, as she stuck a wad of envelopes into her pockets. But always, just as he seemed ready to pounce, Rozzy would calmly replace every single object she had taken. We stayed at the Thrift-T-Mart until it became dusky and cool, and then walked home, making up stories about what we had done at the playground to satisfy Bea.

I was nine that summer, and for the first time Rozzy was my babysitter on the humid evenings that Bea and Ben went out. We would make phone calls. We sent fifteen taxis to the lady across the street. We dispatched cesspool cleaners and diaper services to the old people. We'd pretend we were giving away thousands of dollars if people could just answer one simple question: what did "Zabadaba" mean? No matter what people said, even if it was "I don't know," Rozzy would scream into the phone that oh, my dear God, they had *won*.

I adored her. On Halloween we stuffed empty candy wrappers with tissue paper and ate the candy ourselves, our fingers sticky with chocolate and greed. Rozzy spooned dollops of chocolate pudding into paper towels and hand-tied the whole sloppy mess with blue satin ribbon. She grandly handed these out to each trick-or-treater as if they were money.

We both worried about the same things: remembering when to blink, how often to breathe. I was convinced that if I didn't consciously push air in and push it out again, I would end up gasping like a fish on land. I couldn't concentrate on what people said to me, my schoolwork suffered. I was panicking, juggling breathing and blinking until every breath, every blink, became a droplet in a Chinese water torture. When I stopped worrying about that, as abruptly as I had started and with as much reason, Rozzy and I began experimenting with our hands, wondering and worrying about how far we could stretch our fingers apart before they ripped.

I gradually stopped these habits. They got in the way. But Rozzy continued. We were in the movies one day, waiting for the lights to dim, when abruptly Rozzy turned around in her seat. She jerked her head as far around as she could, straining, until a small throbbing blue vein pulsated on her forehead. "Rozzy, cut it out," I said, and she turned around again. "What were you doing?" I hissed. "I don't know," she said, staring down at her hands. "I couldn't help it." She began doing it at school, she later told me. Once I had to deliver a note to her teacher. I saw Rozzy slumped in the back of the room, dreaming, but beside her, a boy was mimicking her, twisting around fiercely in his seat, making faces. When he saw me staring at him, he scowled.

Ben would yell at her when he saw her twisting around in a chair at home, when the vein popped out. I heard him talking to Bea about what they should do, and he began locking himself away in his study, poring over medical journals. He stopped Rozzy on her way to the kitchen. "Stick out that tongue," he ordered. He traced a B-vitamin deficiency sprouting along the grooves and buds of her tongue, making the surface textured, the color more raw than normal. "Maybe your whole problem is vitamins," he said. He was suddenly excited, and so cheerful that Rozzy kept quiet. There were more health publications around, and Ben began ordering them, letting them slap through our mail slot and pile up on the floor until he could study them. He kept them filed away in his study, and before long, he was sure he had the answer.

Once he ordered vitamins from the back of the magazines, and he made up special supplements for all of us, tying them up in Baggies and leaving them on our breakfast plates. Rozzy had more vitamins than anyone, twenty-three different pills of different shapes and sizes. He watched Rozzy swallow every single pill. "It's all chemical," he said. But a half-hour later, Rozzy threw up all of the pills onto her bedspread.

It depressed Ben, but he didn't give up. He pored over his health magazines, he bought books on hypnosis. "We'll let you heal yourself," he told her. "I'll just give you a suggestion." He made her sit in his brown chair with her back very stiff and straight. I crouched by the window, watching. Rozzy was very strong-willed though. She couldn't let go enough to be put into a trance. "Rozzy," Ben snapped. "I'm not doing this for me, you know. Now relax." He tried all sorts of little tricks to relax her, making her think her hand was made of feathers so it would float on the air, telling her she was out in the blistering heat so she would take on more color. But when it came to the crucial point, she would blink and jerk herself awake. He was furious, so annoyed that he didn't see how my own lids were dropping, heavy as iron.

"Well, then let's just forget it," he told Rozzy in disgust.

Rozzy foundered. "Maybe you could try again," she offered, but he turned away from her and she left the room with her head down, quivering.

I was in a hazy half-dream. I was weightless, weaving in and out of the air. Ben said something, moving his face so close to me that I could see the places where he had nicked himself shaving. He snapped his fingers, a sudden violent clicking that hurt deep inside of me. I started, and woke. "You feel all right now?" he said. He gave me an odd smile and cupped my face in his hands. I nodded at him. "Go and play," he said. All that day, I felt his hands on my face. I kept reaching up to touch my skin.

When Rozzy was fourteen, she insisted on going to the doctor by herself. She let me come with her only once. I sat in the waiting room, fiddling with the magazines, and when the nurse got up to check something outside, I went to the door and listened. Rozzy was shouting something. I couldn't make out the words exactly, something about witch doctors and no one knowing anything, but the tone of her voice caught at me. It got tangled up inside, making me feel giddy with illness. I had never seen the doctor, but I heard her voice, raspy, as if she smoked too much. I didn't want to be in the office anymore, so I went outside and into the street, waiting.

Rozzy came out in about ten minutes. "I thought you had gone home," she said. She hunched into her black fake-fur coat. "Let's go to the movies," she said. "I can't go home yet."

We saw two sets of movies that day, one right after the other. We ate candy bars until the heady shock of all that sugar gave me a headache. By the time we got home, Rozzy was laughing and forgetful.

It was the mid-sixties. Rozzy was fifteen, I was thirteen, and we still dressed alike, in flowery tank tops, our hair braided. Every Sunday we took two buses to Harvard

Square. There were free concerts in the summer in the park, and everyone came dressed in costume, in velvet and fur, carrying kittens on their shoulders, waggling silver goblets for spare change. Rozzy climbed right into the crowd, making up stories to anyone who would listen. She was a painter from California, I was a dancer, we both worked as camel trainers. Sometimes people believed us, their eyes glassy with drugs, with LSD fog spiriting their reason away. Anything became possible. We stayed in the park until the sun started cooling, then we wandered over to Holyoke Center and sat down against the hot buildings and waited for someone interesting to come by and try to pick us up. Someone always smiled at Rozzy.

Rozzy suddenly became moody and silent. She ignored me, accusing me of copying her. She wouldn't go into Harvard Square with me anymore, saying she was too old to toy around with babies like me. "So who needs you?" I said. One Sunday I put on an old red silk dress I had bought for a dollar in a thrift shop and cajoled Hilly to come with me. "This is dumb," Hilly said. She didn't like the people milling around Cambridge, and the smell of the dope made her nose pucker and itch. We left early. No one interesting had said anything to us, and I had the wilting suspicion that they were all with Rozzy, who was somewhere in the crowd.

So Hilly and I began spending our weekends sitting on her porch, pricking the names of boys that we liked into our skin with rose thorns, waiting for the names to scar. We'd try on makeup at the stores; we would draw, Hilly leaning over my sketches, telling me how famous an artist I would be one day. Evenings, Hilly's father would sometimes drive us to the club where he had a membership and we would swim. When I came back home, the lulling rhythm of the water a memory, my hair smelling of chlorine, I would want nothing more than sleep. I didn't need Rozzy.

Something else began happening, something scary. I heard things about Rozzy in school, about how strange she was, how she could disrupt a class just by humming loudly. Whenever I saw a group of people giggling, I tensed, afraid they were mocking Rozzy. And deep within me, I was fearful that the ridicule was catching.

"Why don't you act right?" I screamed at her. "No one will come to the house because of you, no one will be my friend."

Rozzy turned away, her face burning, talking to herself in a low reassuring voice.

"I hate my house," I told Hilly. "Let's go someplace else." Hilly, who was not big on her home either, was indifferent. But we were planning on a movie and I hadn't any money with me. "We can stop at your house. It's on the way," said Hilly.

"Can't you give me a loan? God, it's only afternoon price."

Hilly dug into her jeans and shrugged. "I have bus money and candy money and movie money and that's it."

No one was home and the house was silent and clean and smelled of lemons. "Wait," I said, but Hilly trailed me into the room I shared with Rozzy. I grabbed some bills crumpled on my dresser, but Hilly was peering at Rozzy's museum. Rozzy hadn't touched her museum in a few years, but she still liked having it in the room and she refused to consider dismantling it. "Jesus," said Hilly, whistling through her teeth, "these things aren't what I think they are, are they?"

"Come on, let's go." I tugged at her sleeve.

Hilly held up one of Rozzy's baby teeth and then let it drop to the floor, as if it had been a spider crawling along her leg. "It *is* a tooth," she accused.

I picked it up and put it back in the dish. "You've been

here before," I said. "You've seen this. It's Rozzy's."

"I never noticed it before," said Hilly.

I couldn't concentrate on the movie we saw.

"You have to be patient," Bea kept telling me, stroking my hair. "Rozzy isn't like most people, and after all, she *is* your sister." Patient. When Hilly called, Rozzy sometimes got on the extension and made strange throaty noises, and for the first time in my life I hated Rozzy, I wished her out of my existence.

Rozzy was probably the first hippie. She wore her hair in two thick black braids and draped herself with wooden beads and feathers, with leathers and laces. She could sing every single song Joan Baez ever recorded, but when I bought a Baez record for myself, she grabbed it and snapped it to pieces. "I discovered Baez," she said calmly. "Find someone else to listen to. Baez is taken."

Nothing was fair. Rozzy went to the doctor every week and came home sulky. She wouldn't tell anyone what the doctor said, and the doctor wouldn't say anything either, because Rozzy was her patient and Rozzy had asked her not to.

"Talk to me," I said to Rozzy. "You used to tell me everything."

Rozzy snorted in derision. "Come *on*," she said, shaking her head. She left her appointment cards, her Valiums, right there on the kitchen counter where everyone could see. I kept putting the cards in her purse, tucking the medication in the bathroom, hiding it behind the aspirin and the cold tablets.

There were reprieves in her behavior toward me though. When her life was going well, she wouldn't stiffen against me. She would become generous with herself, and all my hostility would melt.

Ben remarked one day that Rozzy was beginning to look

very much like Bea had when he first met her. As soon as he finished speaking, he ignored her, but Rozzy squirmed and looked pleased.

"She looks like herself," I said, but Bea, peering into that closed pale face, nodded. "You're a regular time machine, Rozzy," she said.

Rozzy went and pulled out the old albums, leafing through the yellowing snapshots, doubtfully fingering each picture. "You think I look like that?" she said, pointing one bitten nail at a small picture of Bea in a short white dress. "Really? You do?" She shook her head. "I don't know." She let the album flop onto the floor and went into our room and sprawled on the bed, staring at the ceiling. I sat Indian-style on the floor, glancing at the dust balls drifting under the bed. "We should maybe buy some of those little gold stars and stick them right up on the ceiling just like a constellation," she said. "When one unsticks and flutters down, it could be a shooting star and we could make wishes on it." Rozzy stretched languidly. "I'm tired. I want to just sleep," she said, "maybe even forever."

The next morning was a Saturday and Rozzy jiggled me awake. "I just remembered it's almost Bea's birthday, and if we chip in we can get her something halfway decent." I hated shopping, but it had been a long time since Rozzy had asked me to do anything with her, and I had endless strings of sentences to say to her.

Once in Boston, though, she was preoccupied. She was dreamy, distant. She kept stopping in front of the shop windows. She never went into any of the stores. She never even asked if I thought Bea might like any of the things she was so fervently staring at. She stopped in front of a toy store. "Oh, come *on*," I said. Rozzy was still, and then she stood a bit taller and spread her hair across her back, tied her scarf tighter about her throat, and then leaned forward toward the window. When I finally got her inside the stores, she would dally in front of the mirrors positioned on the counters, turning her face this way and that, studying it. Rozzy even grabbed some poor young kid who was wearing mirrored sunglasses and asked him where the shoe department was, all the while scrunching herself down an inch or two so she could see herself in his frames.

We didn't buy a gift for Bea that day. "We can order roses," said Rozzy. "Let's go home. It's dark now." As we walked across town to the subway, Rozzy's eyes kept flickering from window to window, but everything was now badly angled against the street lights, and the glass had become blank and innocent.

Rozzy began spending hours in front of the full-length mirror in our room, changing poses as carefully as a model. She trailed Bea, muttering phrases Bea was fond of, and she began borrowing Bea's clothes. Rozzy slid the expensive silk shirts off the hangers and onto her smooth back. She pulled on the velvet jeans and the leather boots, and then she would sit in the living room and wait. Ben came in at seven, a newspaper tucked under his arm. "Vulture," he said, when I rushed for the paper. He looked at Rozzy. "Well, don't you look nice," he said.

Every evening Rozzy would wait for him, a bait. Bea, eyes bright, would remind Rozzy of how the daughter had balked at being anything like the mother. "This is different," said Rozzy. Ben was not always in a pleasant mood when he came home. Sometimes it seemed as if he didn't even see Rozzy; he was busy yelling at Bea for taking up too much space in the drive.

Rozzy was careless. At dinner one night, she dribbled red wine onto a white silk shirt. "God *damn*," said Bea, hopping up, dipping her cloth napkin into the water glass. She daubed at Rozzy's chest. "I can do it," said Rozzy, taking the napkin from her. "A ninety-dollar shirt," said Bea. "That's just wonderful. I think I liked you better when you dressed like something out of Harvard Square. Go change. The cleaner will take care of it." Rozzy got up from the table uncertainly, but when she came back, she was wearing Bea's white linen skirt and a black silk shirt.

"I give up," said Bea. "You know you could buy yourself some clothes. And you—" she looked over at me. "Now you really look like a little ragamuffin. Black is much too hard a color for redheads, you need a color that *sings*— blue or maybe a nice bright green. And God, look at that hair. People with curly hair should clip it short. Look at— oh, what's her name, the one you like—Joan Baez—she had long curly hair and she cut it." She shook her head. "*Do* something with yourself. Look in those fashion magazines you buy. No one I've ever seen looks the way you do."

"I hate Joan Baez," I said.

"Oh, you do not."

"Rozzy likes her, not me."

"You smell of chlorine. And half your clothes have paint smeared on them."

"I'm going to be famous," I said.

"Fine, but be famous in your old clothes, can't you?"

Bea never told Rozzy not to wear her clothing though. She did criticize. "You going to the ballet?" she'd ask Rozzy, as Rozzy swished past her in a chiffon skirt, in pearls. I never tried to copy Rozzy's style of dress. I had one pair of ripped bell-bottom blue jeans that I wore every day. When they ripped out their knees completely, I sewed on different bird patches from an old Indian purse I had. I owned five different black T-shirts, a black sweater, and six bathing suits. I thought it was a good, workable wardrobe.

That night at dinner Ben asked Bea if she would like to go rock climbing in Colorado.

"Rock climbing," she said, teasing her peas with the prongs of her fork. "Didn't we try that once already?"

"You were just a little unsure, that's all," he said, reaching for the wine. "Come on, this time you'll love it. We could go now or in the spring. It's beautiful out there."

"Colorado," said Rozzy. She had on Bea's peach-colored robe, her hair was coiled on top of her head.

"What do you say?" said Ben.

"You really want to go?"

"Sure."

I brightened a little. I was fourteen, halfway through my freshman year of high school; Rozzy was sixteen, a junior. We wouldn't need a sitter. We could take care of each other. I glanced over at Rozzy, but she was frowning.

"Why can't we go on any of the trips you take?" she said. "Why can't we be like other families? We're your kids, for God's sake."

"That's precisely why," said Ben.

"Oh Ben—" said Bea, but Rozzy was up. I followed her, and she was already in our room, scrounging through the closet, dropping all of Bea's clothing into a messy pile, separating out the few things that were hers. Her arms were filled with a slithery rustling, with colors and sounds, and she carried all of it back to Bea's closet and just jammed it all in there. Some of the shirts slipped off the hangers, a few hems caught. Rozzy went back to our room and put on some old jeans and a peasant blouse.

Bea never said anything about her clothing being smothered back into her closet like that, and Rozzy went back to dressing in the cottony kinds of things you could pick up at the Harvard Coop for ten dollars. Whenever she was with Bea, she was careful to spread her hair across her back, fanning it outward like a veil, the way Bea hated.

Bea and Ben left for vacation the next week. Rozzy barely said good-bye to them, and she wasn't really speaking to me either. Being in the same room with her was suffocating. We always ended up listening to her records, and she even went out and bought a cheap set of headphones, shutting out the sound to me. When I got to the stereo before she did, she wouldn't let me use the headphones, but would make faces at my music, grimacing. "How can you listen to the Beatles?" She'd mimic them, singing along in a gritty kind of voice, slurring the sounds. If I was studying, she would be noisy, and if I was nosing around the room, she would sigh. We lived on TV dinners, but we never ate together. At night, I sometimes went over to Hilly's, slapping out the door, not telling Rozzy where I was going. If Rozzy wanted to be alone, if she wanted to shut me out, I could shut her out as well.

Bea and Ben came home six days later, and I immediately approached Bea. She had huge purple bruises traveling along her legs, and when she fixed dinner that night, she tottered. I made a face at the braised lamb and she swiped at me with the towel. I could hear the small TV in the den playing *Dennis the Menace*. Lately, when Rozzy came back from the doctor's, she would sit and watch TV for hours, never bothering to change the channel. I sat on the kitchen stool and watched Bea. She was humming, her black hair tumbling to her waist.

"Why couldn't I move into the den?" I said. "No one uses it much except for Rozzy, and then only when she watches TV." I sucked in a breath and held it. "If I had my own room, she could take the TV into her room and then everyone would be happy."

Bea smeared some sauce from her hands onto a blue towel that said "Kiss the Cook." "The den?" she said. "I guess it would be OK. I don't see why not. You're certainly old enough to have a room of your own, and maybe it would be good for Rozzy, too."

I jumped up, itchy to move, but Bea pushed me right back

down again, slapping my bottom onto the chair. "After dinner, please," she said. "How about shelling these peas for me?"

Rozzy never said anything about the move. I did all the moving, pushing my twin bed into the den, dragging the TV into Rozzy's room. I gathered up my clothes and books, took down posters, ripping them off the wall, not caring when strips of blue paint came away with the tape. Rozzy sat reading on her bed, not looking up, not moving. Every once in a while, a page would deliberately turn.

I spent weeks fixing up my room. Ben bought me a reading lamp so I could read in bed and told me that having a room of my own meant more responsibility—whether the room was clean or dirty, livable or unlivable was totally up to me. Bea let me paint the room. It took me a few days. I sang as I painted, slipping on the newspapers I had lined the floor with, dribbling paint on my hands and in my hair. The fumes annoyed Ben, and as soon as he set foot in the house, he clicked on the air conditioner. I waxed the wood floor and bought a new Indian print bedspread and red curtains. I framed a poster of the Beatles and hung it over the bed until I began worrying that the nail might not hold and the poster might fall onto my head at night and kill me. I took it down and hung it on a far wall. I had some money saved up and I bought a tinny-sounding portable record player. It had no speakers and sometimes it ran backward, but I didn't care. I raced home from school to be in that room. I could bring Hilly home with me, and the two of us could shut ourselves off, could close the door and prop up books against it. I could paint, and listen to the Beatles, I could dream.

Rozzy kept her door shut. She liked slamming it. When she and Ben fought at dinner, she would dash down her napkin and rush to her room, banging the door as loudly as she could. "That girl," Ben would mutter, getting up to yank her door open again. "It isn't your room," he would shout at her, "not when you bang doors like that. Have some respect for property."

The school year was ending, and the summer started to yawn out ahead of me. Without Rozzy's friendship, without school to fill the time, I had nothing to look forward to. I began moping until Ben suggested I look for a job. "Now's the time," he said, "right now while you still have an allowance. Your money stops the same day school does, you know."

I made a few phone calls, half hoping no one would want me, and I ended up with a job as a junior counselor at Blue Skies Day Camp, which was ten minutes away. I had no desire to work away my summer, but I had even less desire to stay at home with Rozzy in a silence that would only be punctuated with the slam of her door.

CHAPTER FIVE

The day before I was to start work, the last day of school when no one did anything, when everyone came dressed in blue jeans and faded T-shirts, Jay Keller asked me out. Jay was infamous, every parent's nightmare, every girl's twitching daydream. He was a transfer student from Cambridge, a loner with few friends and a few enemies. He took every drug there was to take: acid, speed, diet pills, cold capsules, mixing over-the-counter drugs with prescriptions and creating effects he claimed no one else had experienced. He supplied half the school, staggering belligerently in the halls, jittering through his classes. He had very long brown hair that he kept slicked back with oil during school so they wouldn't throw him out. When it was washed, it touched his shoulders, it frisked along the top of his back. He always wore blue jeans and the same blue denim workshirt that he washed out every evening.

He was bright, but he was always being thrown out of class for saying things about God being dead and the war being wrong and how he would just as soon go to Canada as fight. Belmont High School had a small pack of hoods, and one day they grabbed Jay in the parking lot and beat him up. "Get a haircut, faggot," they screamed at him, kicking him with their heavy boots, in his face, his stomach, wherever they could make contact. Jay wouldn't fight. He crouched down and tried to shield himself with his arms, but it only enraged them. They left Jay bleeding and torn in the lot for Mr. Ames, the driver education teacher, to find. Mr. Ames took Jay to the hospital and waited in the emergency room. He called Jay's parents and took Jay home. After that, Jay came to school with a bodyguard, and he wouldn't leave the building until the guard, a big stupid-looking blond, showed. He kept the guard for over a month. Jay and Mr. Ames became friends. No one knew what they talked about, but you could always see the two of them drinking coffee in the cafeteria. It was funny to see a teacher and a kid like that.

I had no classes with Jay. He really didn't know me. After he was beaten up, he became a sort of celebrity. Girls flocked around him, and there were stories that he used them up and discarded them as easily as he would Kleenex. Someone said he had a woman in Maine who had borne his child; someone else said he had a twelve-year-old girl friend in Texas. He slept with all kinds of women—and, it was hinted, with men, too.

I was talking with Hilly outside the school, swinging my legs against the high stone ledge we were perched on. Jay walked by. "Boy, he's gorgeous," said Hilly. "He gives me wet dreams." She looked at me and giggled.

"Shut up. He'll hear you," I hissed.

Jay suddenly pivoted, freezing me into position. "Hi, Jay," said Hilly, blushing.

"Your name is Bess, isn't it?" he said, studying me, unsmiling. I couldn't trust myself to open my mouth, so I nodded, feeling like a fool. "You work after school?" he said. "You want to meet me at Ralph's, you know where that is, by the market? We can have coffee, I can be there in an hour. I have to clean up some things first." He suddenly grinned at me, his face changed. "It'll be OK. Can you make it? An hour?"

I swallowed and moved my head up and down, a yes. "Good," he said, "I'll see you then." I didn't speak until he was further down the road, away from us.

"Oh my *God*," I said.

"Everyone in the school will know in five minutes and you'll be famous," said Hilly. "Jay Keller. Can you believe it? I'm so jealous I could puke."

"I'm terrified. He doesn't even know me."

"Well, anyway, even if he ever asked me, I wouldn't be able to date him. My parents would have a fit, the drugs and all."

"Parents," I said, feeling suddenly queasy. I could see Bea zeroing in on Jay, demanding information from him as if it were her right. She'd want to know where we were going, what we were planning to do there, and how serious we were going to become. And Ben—oh God, Ben—would judge, would want to check Jay's family, his past, and then there would be no relationship, there would be no Jay in my life. And of course there was Rozzy to think about. I could just see it—a cozy little dinner with Rozzy making strange noises at the table.

"I'm not telling my parents about Jay," I said.

"You're not going to tell them anything? You could lie and say it was another boy."

"No, they'd want to meet him."

"Well," said Hilly, "you can use me as an alibi anytime you need, but you have to promise to tell me all the details."

"OK."

Hilly walked me to Ralph's and then we parted. Jay was already there, pushed into a red plastic booth in the back, smiling. I was nervous, but Jay turned out to be funny and smart, in perfect control. I couldn't think of things to say, and sometimes I would be so busy trying to phrase a sentence that I would lose track of Jay's words. I babbled a lot. I spilled my coffee on the table, making the waitress irritable with me. She wiped up the liquid with a damp blue checkered cloth.

"I want to see you tomorrow," said Jay. "Is that OK?"

When I didn't say anything, he said, "Look, I *like* you. I've been watching you in school, how you move, what books you read during lunch while everyone else fucks around and acts like a cretin. But you—there's something different about you, something special."

I blushed.

"You seeing someone else, is that it?"

"No, I do want to see you, really. It's just that there's something I have to tell you about, something we'll have to work out. My parents—"

Jay held up his hand, amused. "Aha, parents," he said. "How well I know that routine." He was used to parents not liking him. He had been hidden in closets by girls, threatened with the police by fathers, screamed at by mothers. It didn't bother him. He had devised elaborate systems to avoid detection, codes and signals. "Who wants to have to get dressed up and eat some crummy dinner at some parental table, all the time having to answer nosy questions. Every adult thinks they have the right to be your parent." He reached across the table and touched my hand. "Look, when you want to talk to me, you do the calling. If I call and you don't answer, I'll hang up. Is there anyone that might sound like you at home?"

"Rozzy—my sister," I said. "You better not call."

"Fine. And you don't have to worry about my folks. They're almost never home and my sister is so dim I could feed her any line and she'd believe me." He stretched. "We'll spend a secret summer together."

When I got home, heady with Jay, Bea called out to me that I was late. Rozzy was in the kitchen, eating brownies from the pan, digging them out with a knife. She had just washed her hair and it was all silky and wet and she looked lovely. I had promised to call Hilly, but I didn't want to talk about anything. I didn't want to share.

"You missed hot brownies," said Rozzy.

"Who cares about that?" I said, smiling. "I have better things to think about than brownies."

"Suit yourself," she shrugged.

"I do," I said and went to wash for dinner.

I had never had a summer quite like that one. Every morning, I said good-bye to Bea and walked to the corner bus stop for camp, avoiding the few young kids straggling around, punching one another and snickering. I waited for them to hop onto the Blue Skies bus, and then I caught a downtown express. I called the camp from a pay phone and told them I was sick. They didn't seem to care. There were three people assigned to a unit, and they were probably delighted to pocket the extra money.

I walked to Jay's house from downtown. Jay didn't work. He never left his house all day, but stayed home smoking dope and playing his flute, having the whole empty place to himself. "I can't meet you," he said. "You have to get here by yourself. You can come upstairs and wake me. I'll make sure the front door is open for you." I didn't mind. I didn't see it as unfair because he was creating a special secret environment for us.

All that sleepy summer, we never saw another person aside from each other in that house. I never met his mother or father; I never even bothered to ask what they did, and his sister was away at camp. Inside that house, neither of us had a family. We sprawled on his small blue bed upstairs and let the shrill whining fan blow hot dusty air over us. He played me moody pieces on his flute and liked to watch me sketch and I made pocket-sized pictures of him that I carried in my wallet like snapshots. Evenings were terrible. I was wrenched back into the world. I escaped with swimming. Bea would drive me to the Y and arrange to pick me up, and sometimes Jay would show up. He didn't swim, but he would walk around in the shallow part or flick water at me.

Jay gave me my first kiss. It surprised me. His kiss felt sharp, uncomfortable, his hands moved inside my blouse. He wanted me so much that I couldn't imagine not letting him have me. He tried to build me up to it. We'd lie on his bed, in our underwear, beneath his printed sheet. I was shy about my body, thinking it was too thin, too uncurved, but Jay was rapturous. He wouldn't let me touch him at first, but spent hours rubbing and stroking my body, taking his finger and gently sliding it in and out of me. I didn't know what I was supposed to feel, most of the time I simply watched his face, the way his eyes flickered under the closed lids. When I thought he was getting tired, I sighed, signaling a finish. I rolled over onto my stomach. Then he would stretch out and place my hand on his penis and guide me in stroking him until he shuddered in orgasm. He'd doze, one arm thrown carelessly onto my belly, and I would watch him and wonder just what it was that made his face take on that expression, that feeling.

When we finally made love, I wasn't quite aware of what was happening. He was on top of me and the whole side of my body was falling asleep, tingling into pins and needles. We were doing the same sorts of things we always did, and then, abruptly, something was pushing inside me. When I opened my mouth to cry, to wonder, Jay closed it with a kiss. I watched his face, his eyes shut, his mouth open and wet. When he sat up, panting, he looked very pleased.

"Well, well, looks like little Bess had her first big O," he said, brushing back my hair with the flat of his hand, swooping to claim a quick kiss. I grinned like a fool, wondering what he was talking about. "You did, didn't you?" he frowned. "Everything tingles," I said, rubbing circulation into my legs and feet. Something wet was dripping and oozing out of me and I worried about staining the sheets. "Good, you had one then," said Jay.

No one knew I was making love, not then, not unless they had heard that Jay and I were going together. And no one I knew was making love. The pill had just come out, and girls that took it were considered ruined before they had even started. Bea had warned me about girls like that. "This isn't wrong, is it?" I said, taking Jay's hand, stroking each finger.

"What's not wrong?" said Jay, lifting up the sheet to look at me.

"Oh, nothing," I said, and lifted up my face to be kissed.

Jay never took me home, but he did call me cabs. I went home that day bleeding into my underwear. I had the cab leave me off two blocks away from the house, and after I checked to make sure no one was looking, I slipped off my panties and balled them up and dumped them into the nearest trash can. It would be easier to wash the blood from my legs than to rid my panties of that red. I didn't want that part of my life to be a part of the household washing.

"What do you do all day?" Hilly demanded on the phone that night.

"We talk, we listen to records, you know." I saw us cuddling on his sofa in the game room, a soap opera spinning its web on TV, while we kissed and touched each other, our jeans unzipped. "And kiss?" said Hilly.

"Yeah. That, too."

The sex had begun to surprise me. I felt as if my body were separate from me, that it knew what it wanted and needed from Jay, but couldn't relate that information to my brain. "Stop making those moans," Jay said. "It doesn't hurt anymore." We used no birth control. "Rubbers are sick," said Jay, "and anyhow, I know this herbal remedy if you get knocked up." He tried to pull out of me in time, spilling his seed on the sheet, on my stomach, my back, my legs; but as soon as he was out of me, I felt deserted, fearful, and I wrapped my legs about him, pulling him close.

Toward the middle of the summer, we began to venture outside for quick trips to the ice cream stand, for walks along the deserted ski slope behind his house. We even sometimes built fires up there. "We should spend a night," said Jay.

"I have overnights at camp," I said. "I could lie."

"Why don't you just quit that job? You never go anyway. What if your parents had to reach you and called the camp?"

"I'd lie," I said. "I'd say I was there but they were too stupid to find me."

"Quit," said Jay.

I picked at a nail. "I can't," I said.

When I told Hilly I was spending a night with Jay, she gave me a quick curious stare. "There's nothing wrong with it," I said defiantly.

"I didn't say there was, did I?" said Hilly.

"We'll probably get married."

"That would be great."

"You won't tell anyone, will you, about the overnight?"

"Why would I?"

I looked at my hands, the nails bitten. "You think I'm trash?"

"No," she said, "but can we not talk about it anymore?"

I wore my heavy white sweater to the market where I was meeting Jay. I had no idea how cold it might get up there. And I didn't really know how much more warmth

Jay might be willing to share. The market was in an odd part of Belmont, but there was no real reason to be afraid. Bea would never shop at a fast-food place like this, no one she knew would. Even so, I felt watched. My skin prickled. Jay had a dentist's appointment and was going to meet me there by five. I had wanted to go to the dentist with him, to sit in the leathery chairs and read all the junky magazines that always catch my eye in the supermarket but make me too ashamed to buy them, but Jay was adamant. "It will give us time to think about each other," he said.

I wandered into the market. They had two dirty aisles filled with food and toys and kitchen goods, in no order whatsoever. I picked my way up and down the aisles, checking prices, fingering the rubber toys, anything to eat away the minutes. The market had a small ladies room in the far corner and I thought about hiding out in there, but I was worried about the closed door, about not being able to face whoever might be on the other side of it. Thinking about the ladies room made me have to go, and I dug my fingers into my thighs, killing the urge.

Jay was ten minutes late. I was hovering by the bathroom, annoying one of the young salesgirls by asking her the time every few minutes. Jay tapped me. His cheeks were puffy from Novocain. He was in his blue workshirt, jeans, and had on gray cowboy boots. His hair was shiny down his back and he looked wonderful. "Come on," he said, talking thickly, "let's blow this hole."

We walked uphill to the slope, holding hands, talking about the movies we wanted to see, the books we liked, nothing at all, really, and I wanted everyone in the strange brick houses lining the streets to disappear, to stop being a boundary for us as we passed. It took us about fifteen minutes to make the top. Jay had gone up there earlier in the day to leave off a sleeping bag, blankets, matches, and a few cans of soup. He knew no one would steal any of it—the bag was musty-smelling and torn, the blankets tattered, and the soups indifferent. Up there on that hill, we had a fire and insects and I felt the love moving within me like breath, expanding, threatening to split my very skin apart with its force. Jay made some canned soup, but we didn't have spoons or bowls so we waited for it to cool and then took turns sipping it from the can, mouths against the raw edge of tin.

We didn't sleep that night. Jay wanted us to shuck off our clothing and walk around in the woods, but the dark made me timid, I saw monsters in the shadows. We lay in the sleeping bag, holding each other, twining arms and legs, making love. When the wood noises made me start, Jay took my hand. "I'm here," he said. "I'll always be here."

In the morning, we each had about forty insect bites scattered on our arms. My face was smudged with dirt, imprinted with pine needles. Jay was still half asleep, drifting in and out of some dream. He squinted at me and then burst out, "Bill, I thought you had left."

"I'm not Bill," I said, reaching for him, but he roughly twisted from my grasp, his eyes accusing. He never really came out of that dream, but began rolling up the sleeping bag, gathering the cans of soup and stuffing them into the pockets of his folded blanket. We stumbled downhill. Jay kept tripping over the small stones seeding the mountain, ignoring the path, flashing stormy looks at me.

"You're dreaming," I said, cheerful and friendly.

At the bottom of the hill, Jay pivoted. "I'm going," he said. "Don't you come."

I didn't care. I was energetic with love. I walked to the camp, singing to give my steps beat, ignoring the rude beeping of the cars, the smart stinging remarks of boys hanging out of car windows. The camp was very surprised to see me; everyone asked how I was feeling. I went to one of the bathrooms and tried to wash off some of the dirt, tried to get some of the needles out of my hair. I kept wishing I could keep everything close to my skin, have it be a part of me.

I called Jay around lunch time. He was baffled about the morning. "You were still dreaming," I said. "Don't worry about it. What are you going to do today without me?"

"Oh, nothing," said Jay. "I might go into Cambridge."

"Oh, *Jay*."

"Look, I don't involve you in it. I'm careful."

"Yeah, sure," I said, hanging up, suddenly depressed.

Going into Cambridge was Jay's synonym for dealing drugs. He'd hang out around Holyoke Center, casing faces, never making an approach, letting others approach him. He'd never let me go with him. "Your face is too open. Any cop on the street could instantly tell what we were doing." He never pushed drugs on me, although they were always available to me. In hopes I'd smoke dope with him, he went out and bought chocolate-flavored papers; he bought blotter acid on pictures of cats or hedgehogs, but I never tried anything, I never had the interest.

Jay had a *Physician's Desk Reference*, a big red book that had pictures of different kinds of pills and told what they did. When Jay walked around on the streets, he always kept his eyes down, searching for pills people might have dropped. "Drugstores are really the best places to look," he told me. "People always open their stupid bottles to check and make sure they got the right medication, and usually they drop a few." When he spotted a tiny circle of color, he'd pounce. He'd take it home and match it up against his book. Even if he didn't know what it was, he would take it, reveling in its effects.

"You know," he once told me, snickering, bumpy on speed, "people will never believe you don't do drugs, being with me and all." He patted my thigh. "It's OK, though. You do whatever you like."

A large part of the money Jay earned from selling drugs

went into gifts. He was always presenting me with leather-bound books of poetry and fiction, with blocks of expensive paper and watercolors in tubes. He'd wrap everything up in Museum of Art wrapping paper, with bows and tags and considerable élan. Sometimes he surprised me with a handful of poppies or a recording of Bach. I was afraid to take these gifts home with me. They all seemed alive with Jay, and I couldn't risk detection. I kept everything at Jay's, in his little room, which that summer had really become mine as well. He even cleared a space on his shelf for me, an area in his closet.

"It won't always be like this," he said apologetically.

I looked at him in surprise. "I like it like this. It's secluded, no one has any piece of it except for us."

It was when the summer began cooling that I told Jay about Rozzy. It was hard for me to talk about her being sick like that; I didn't like hearing the words and I stammered a lot. "She slams her door against me," I said. "It's horrible, for everyone, not just Rozzy."

"God," he said, "she sounds like she's tripping, but without the acid. I can kind of relate to that, I think. I always feel like my body's getting away from me, that I can't control it, when I trip." He gave a short laugh. "It might be nice to feel that without having to take LSD."

"That's a stupid thing to say."

"You just don't know how to deal with it," he said.

I thrashed away the sheets and stood up, pulling on my jeans, my rumpled T-shirt.

"Oh-oh, someone's mad," he said, grinning.

I tugged at my zipper.

"Be mad then."

"I will." I slammed out of his house, knowing I would be back the next morning, and hating him for knowing it, too.

The days weren't peaceful anymore. Jay suddenly became irritable, changed. "Why do I have to change my whole lifestyle for you?" he said. "And even if I don't, what fun is it for me to trip with you sitting there straight as my mother?"

"I love you," I said, standing quietly against his door, feeling the knob pressing into my back.

"Oh, yeah, love," he snorted. "I've heard that baloney so many times from all kinds of girls."

"We'll go out," I said. "You just feel closed in."

"Yeah, and what if we run into your parents?"

"I'll risk it."

"Forget it. That's not the problem."

"What is?"

"We'll talk about it later," he said. "Let's go make cheese sandwiches."

Later never came, though; he never wanted to talk. One morning I came by to find his front door locked. I walked up and down his street, then I made my way to a pay phone and dialed his number, letting it ring and ring, the noise jangling in my ear. I finally went back to his house, panic growing within me. An hour later, he rambled toward me, carrying his flute, whistling. I stood up. "Where were you?"

"Out," he said, easily, reaching for his key.

"Out."

"Do you want to come in or do you want to stay outside and sulk?"

I followed him up to his small blue bed.

It began happening more and more. If I caught him on his way out, he would hunch into his jean jacket and ignore me, snap at me, make me uncomfortable enough to leave. I called Hilly and begged her to be my friend and to trail him, just for one day. In exchange, I would give her my new black silk shirt. Hilly came over a day later for the shirt. "He didn't go out at all," she said. "No one came in. I sat in front of his house the whole day. I don't know what I would have done if he had seen me. Probably lied, said I had a crush on him."

I slumped on the couch, punching the pillows down and fluffing them up again. "You should have rung his bell and asked him out. He would have gone."

Hilly sighed. "School's starting up soon. We should go into town and shop."

I picked at the pillow fringe. "Yeah. I guess."

"Maybe there'll be some cute guys this year."

"Maybe."

Hilly didn't stay long, and Jay didn't call me that night. I didn't go to his house the next day or the next, waiting for him to panic and call me. I was at camp working for the whole last week. None of the little kids in my unit knew who I was. They wouldn't listen to me; they clamored for the other counselors, straying from my touch, my unsteady voice.

I didn't have to think at camp. Everything was organized for the kids. They were shuttled from art to swimming to the pony rides, and I trailed listlessly after them, thinking about Jay. Every once in a while, someone would ask if I was feeling all right, would say that I still looked a little peaked.

The day after camp ended, I called Jay from a pay phone, my throat closing. I started crying on the phone, pleading with him to tell me what was wrong, why he suddenly hated me.

"I don't hate you, Bess," he said. He was calm, rational, and it made me weep even harder. "Are you going to speak,

Bess, or are you just going to cry on the phone? I can't just sit here and listen to you crying."

"You didn't call," I said, my nose running.

"So I didn't call. Do I have to report in every single day? Do we have to be together every single minute? Look, there isn't anyone else; I'm not interested in another girl. I just need time to be by myself again."

"You can do that with me," I sobbed.

"Bess, I *can't*," he said.

I hung up. I leaned against the glass of the booth, not wanting anything, wanting everything, weeping until I had to catch my breath. I dug out more dimes from my jeans and began calling him. When his voice sounded, I told him I loved him, I pleaded to see him, but it only made him angry, he told me to stop.

"I don't know how I feel about anything," he said. "I just want to be by myself now."

I hung up the phone again. I didn't know where to go, so I walked until my legs started hurting, then I turned around and walked home. Camp was over and school would be starting in a week. Each day I got up, dressed, and walked into town and back, six miles each day, not thinking, just moving, just getting from one place to another. I couldn't draw and I didn't swim. Hilly came over every evening and the two of us would shut ourselves up in my room and talk.

Bea knew something was wrong. She tried to get me to talk, but I froze her out. It was Rozzy who heard me sobbing one night. She came into my room and wrapped me up in her arms and let me cry. She wouldn't let me say anything, and she didn't ask questions. She simply rocked me until I fell asleep. When I woke up, she was gone.

I was glad for school, for something to fill up the hollow spaces in my day. I didn't see much of Jay and I was careful to avoid the routes I thought he might take. It was difficult, hellish. Sometimes in class I'd hear his name, and I'd have to get up and go to the girls room. I'd pass the insolent stares of the girls who were teasing their hair in front of the mirror, applying eye liner, smoking. I'd go into one of the gray stalls and flush the toilet over and over, the sound masking my weeping. When I came out, my eyes raw, I ignored them.

I wanted people to ask what was wrong, though; I wanted people to know that Jay had been in love with me once. A few people knew, Hilly told me, but a few didn't believe it. She promised to spread the story. "Be sure to say I won't talk about it," I warned Hilly. "I want them to know, but I don't want to have to think about it anymore."

Evenings I did my homework or talked to Hilly on the phone. Rozzy wandered in and out of the house, sometimes staying out late at night, cabbing home. I'd hear Bea yell at her, ground her, but the next evening Rozzy was off again. I wondered about Rozzy. She would never understand Jay. She had never had anything like that. At least I didn't think she had.

It wasn't that boys weren't attracted to Rozzy. She could have had anyone. When she walked down the street I could hear the hearts fluttering from sheer wanting. Men would always twist their mouths into smiles for her. When she fumbled with her change, spilling pennies and dimes in a shiny confusion of coins, there would always be some man stooping gallantly to retrieve her money. At the movies she could always find a palm with that extra quarter she was missing. Waiters always gave her extra whipped cream, another splash of sherry. Even our paper boy, a pimpled fleshy blond, had a crush on her and he would sometimes leave us three papers in his baffled lust for her.

She *was* beautiful. There wasn't a moment that I didn't bleed to look like her. But she was different, too, and there was something a little unsettling and ominous about that, something no boy wanted to risk taking on. They couldn't feel comfortable around her. But they could dream. Jay had told me he saw Rozzy's name on the bathroom wall on a list of girls that "we'd most like to fuck." "What number was she?" I asked. "One," said Jay. I asked Jay to erase it, but he gave me a hard look.

"It's kind of an honor for her," he said. "You don't want to totally isolate her, do you?"

"Was my name on the list?" I said.

Jay had rolled me over on the bed, one hand unzipping my jeans. "No one's going to know about you but me."

When Rozzy was out at night, I sometimes prowled in her room, careful that Bea didn't catch me. I snooped, sliding open drawers, peeking into the closet. I found her diary in her top desk drawer. It was unlocked. I kept thinking that if I didn't move it much, she would never know I had been dipping into it. Besides that, I reasoned, she usually hid it quite well. If it was this easy to find, she probably *wanted* me to read it.

A lot of her diary was garbled comments, things that never jelled into any sort of sense. A few times she mentioned things about me, ordinary things—how I had looked at dinner, a new dress I had that she liked. There was no mention of the night I was sobbing and she had comforted me.

But then she began writing about men. Men on the fringes, in their fifties, married. She was answering ads in the personal section of *Boston After Dark*, letting these men buy her dinner and wine her and sometimes seduce her. "I don't see what the fuss is about," she wrote, "but at least I have the experience now." I shut the book. I could see those men in my mind, all lined up in their plaid jackets, balding, paunchy, and there was Rozzy with a gun, aiming, shooting them down, one by one, a clean shot every time.

I waited up for Rozzy that night, until Bea was through

scolding, and then I went into Rozzy's room. "You OK?" I asked.

"Sure," she said, pulling her dress over her head.

"Rozzy," I said, biting my lips where they were chapped. "I don't think you should go out nights anymore."

"You, too," she sighed. "Isn't Bea bad enough?"

"I read your diary."

Rozzy stiffened, and then she sat on her bed and faced me, resigned.

"It was unlocked," she said.

"There's a difference between fucking and making love," I said.

Rozzy laughed. "Listen to the expert. How the hell would *you* know? I know, and there's no damned difference at all."

"I've made love," I said abruptly, "with Jay Keller."

Rozzy's face changed. "You have not," she said uncertainly.

"I have. All summer. No one knew. I didn't have to advertise it the way you do. It was different than what you do. Better." I was boiling over with anger. "We *loved* each other."

"I don't believe you," said Rozzy. "I want to go to sleep. Get out of my room."

We were angry with each other for days. She would avert her face at the dinner table. I was worried she might tell Bea about Jay, but it wouldn't have mattered. Jay was over now. And then Rozzy's anger twitched into depression. She couldn't sleep and she had to have special pills that made her groggy in the morning.

She didn't go out evenings anymore, and her diary disappeared. I thought she had stopped writing in it, but she wore a tiny gold key around her neck on a piece of yarn. Knowing Rozzy, though, maybe it didn't unlock one damned thing at all. Maybe she just wore it.

I really didn't see much of Rozzy at school. She didn't take the bus the way I did. Instead, she rode her white ten-speed to school every day, even in the winter when the streets were cracked blue ice. A few times her bike was stolen from the school parking lot, cleanly lifted off the tree she chained it to, but she always managed to find it again, usually tossed on its side in the neighboring woods. I stared out the smeary bus window mornings, spotting Rozzy's flash of hair, a blot of ink against the sky.

I had my first-period study hall in the old boys' gym. It wasn't a bad place for a study hall. No one studied; no one even expected that you would. Everyone sprawled along the wood bleachers, scattering themselves across the rows. I liked to sit way up high, in the very top row where no one else was behind me, where I could see everyone. Kids passed out sticks of gum, scenting the air with sweet fruit, or Lifesavers. They would poke the tips of their tongues through the holes, forcing the candy open, making sexual jokes. A few kids tried to sneak a smoke or two before the study hall teacher would yell and flash her pad of pink detention slips.

The boys' gym was partitioned off from the girls' gym by a large gray flexicurtain. Sometimes the curtain wasn't drawn, whether in carelessness or by intention was never clear. The gym teachers never made any move to close it. You could watch the gym class that was going on. I always hated that; in fact, I dreaded gym days, fearing that yawning open space, those spectators snickering from the bleachers. I was terrible in gym. The one activity I could do was swim, and that had stopped in junior high school. I would have been more than willing to swim away my gym class at the Y, to earn my credits with side strokes and frog kicks, but the school would have none of it. I had to play different kinds of ball games and climb ropes and march along with everyone else. The uniform, with its long white bloomers and tank top, humiliated me. Without pockets, I never knew what to do with my dangling hands.

The curtain was gone today, and I stiffened in surprise. Rozzy's class was slowly filing in, talking among themselves, shuffling their sneakers along the polished wood floor. Rozzy stood out because she was so pretty. She had one long braid snaking across her uniform. She had rolled the bottoms of her bloomers up to her thighs, and she was the only one wearing bright red sneakers. Her feet flashed red against all that white. All the girls were lagging behind, poking at one another and whispering, glancing at the study hall. Rozzy stood very straight and apart from everyone.

"OK, girls, let's go," shouted the teacher. Miss Yin was a small Chinese woman in her thirties, and she loved anyone who tried. I never got along with her. When we had to play softball, outside in the green spongy grass, I hid behind an oak tree. My team wanted to win, so they pretended I didn't exist; they helped shield me. Miss Yin wasn't fooled. The last day of class she made me stand up alone in front of everyone while she tossed hard white balls for me to bat at. All the time she was smiling, her eyes hard and shiny. There were rumors about her, too; when we had to take showers after class, she would stand on a box and look in on us. "Just making sure you get wet," she told us, but there was no way you couldn't get wet in those cramped little cubicles, with the water pressure so tight and hard it felt like gunshot.

Miss Yin slapped her hands together. "Well, come *on*," she urged, leading the class over to two flat gray mats. Suspended over the mats were two limp-looking ropes. "One at a time. You've had climbing before." One girl after another gave a silly grin and then clutched at a single rope, flailing her white legs uselessly. The boys in my study hall hooted and jeered until the study teacher hauled them off the bleachers and made them sit by her on the floor. The boys sulked and punched one another in the ribs.

Miss Yin patted each girl on the back as the girl approached the rope, and frowned in disgust when the girl, failing, slunk back into line. Rozzy kept lagging at the back, hands playing deep in her braid, not looking at anything. When it was her turn, she walked to the rope and leaped up, catching it, wrapping her legs around it. She climbed effortlessly.

"Good girl! That's the way!" cried Miss Yin, giving a little jump up. "Try for the top!" Rozzy continued to climb. There was a real grace to her movements, a stride. She moved up on the rope, controlling it, making it support her. She was almost to the top when she stopped and remained motionless. "Look up, honey," called Miss Yin. "It's not really that high up, and you won't fall." Rozzy glanced down at her and then reached across for the other rope. "Rozzy, don't make it harder," called Miss Yin. "You haven't learned how to work two ropes yet." Rozzy repositioned her grip; for a moment it looked as if she were going to drop the second rope, but then she executed an awkward somersault, struggling to retain her balance. Everyone in the gym and the study hall quieted. I could hear my own breathing. Around me, conversation began to slither and hiss.

"OK, Rozzy, come down now," said Miss Yin quietly. "We're all very impressed by your showing off." Rozzy didn't move. "That's an F in gym then." Rozzy climbed a little higher, making herself more secure on the ropes.

"Fine," said Miss Yin. "I'm coming up to get you. You'll be very sorry, young lady." Miss Yin rubbed her hands together. She jumped up and began climbing the ropes, her mouth set. The other girls in the class craned their necks, watching in silence. Miss Yin was halfway up when Rozzy lost her balance for a second. She kicked out her leg to resettle herself. It was just a kick, but it startled Miss Yin enough to make her lose her grip, and she made a soft smacking sound when she landed.

She didn't get up.

Rozzy looked down, released her hold, and fell, crumbling. "Holy shit," said a girl next to me. I was suddenly up, clamoring toward my sister, feeling something snaking inside of me.

Later, when it was all over, I was glad and grateful that it happened on a Friday. It gave everyone a wide weekend of things to blur the memory, to wedge the whole incident away from the present. No one was really hurt. Miss Yin was simply bruised and furious, her pride banged up a bit. But Rozzy had fallen at a funny angle and had broken her ankle. The doctor said it was lucky; the principal said it was a disgrace and he suspended Rozzy for three weeks. Even then he said he wouldn't allow her back into school until he had had a conference with Bea and Ben and with Rozzy's psychiatrist. "Something has to be done about that girl," said Ben, "and soon."

Rozzy had a tutor, a college kid who came on Tuesdays for an hour, and who seemed bored and made restless by the whole business. He never said anything to any of us, but went right into Rozzy's room and shut the door, emerging an hour later. When Bea prodded him for information, he simply shrugged and said that Rozzy was doing fine. I had to go around to each of Rozzy's teachers and get her schoolwork. I always put it off until Friday, when everyone was hustling to leave, racing off the school scent. Rozzy's teachers were always very polite to me, very curious. They hoped Rozzy would be back, they said; she was a senior and couldn't afford to miss much school if she wanted to graduate. They all asked what grade I was in, if I liked being a sophomore, if I was as bright and quick as Rozzy. I wanted to ask them if Rozzy had ever sung in class, if she had ever answered questions aloud that they hadn't even asked, but the words dammed up within me.

I felt eyes following me. I was afraid to go to gym class, afraid to face those twin brown ropes. But when the time came, the same polite curiosity had taken hold of everyone. No one snapped a towel at me, no one punched me on the arm, and the gym flexicurtain was firmly shut. I climbed the rope easily and when I came down, Miss Yin hugged me, renouncing my blame. I felt as if I were ruining Rozzy right then.

Ben was furious with Rozzy, and she was sullen. She stayed in bed, averting her face when I brought her dinner. She had a small cast and she had scribbled things all over it, names and dates, drawings of spaniels with the words "oh, those eyes" inked in underneath, and "Best wishes and love, Mark" when she didn't even know a Mark. She spent days decorating her cast, experimenting with different kinds of handwriting, with words written in clumsy Spanish or French. She wouldn't let me sign her cast, and when I saw her probing into it with one of my knitting needles, I grabbed it from her hand.

I began having dreams about her. I'd watch her drowning, or falling off some huge ragged cliff. I couldn't help her because there were silken ties holding me against a silver pole, but I didn't want to. I was content to stand very still. The moment Rozzy disappeared under the water, the second she hit the bottom of the cliff, my bonds loosened; I was free, buoyant.

It took a while, but the meetings at school about Rozzy were finally set up. Everyone spoke with everyone—the doctor, the principal, Bea and Ben. Only I was left out. I wasn't sure what was going to happen. Rozzy's cast was coming off any day now, and she was getting restless.

Ben didn't say anything to Rozzy until after her cast was removed. He waited until Bea and Rozzy came home from the doctor, Rozzy carrying the cast in her arms, touching all of those names—none of them ours.

We were at dinner when Ben said, "Rozzy, you know, your doctor thinks you might do better at another school."

"Anything's better than that rat hole," said Rozzy.

"Good," said Ben, turning to Bea. "No problem."

Bea toyed with her salad. "We're supposed to discuss. This is hardly a discussion." Nobody discussed anything, nobody said anything except for Ben, and he was perfectly rational. The doctor had suggested a special, experimental school, kind of a halfway house for people who didn't really need to be "committed" (I flinched when I heard the quotation marks Ben put around the word committed), but who did need some sort of controlled environment, with doctors. "You'll go to school, but at your own pace. You can finish your senior year in two years if you like, or three. The important thing is you'll see a doctor, every day," said Ben.

"I saw a brochure," said Bea, trying to smile. "It's way on the tip of the Cape, in Truro. You aren't a prisoner; you can go to the ocean."

"You're sending me away," said Rozzy flatly.

"You can't go back to high school here. You can see that, can't you? Not after all the trouble you caused," said Ben.

"May I be excused," said Rozzy, pushing violently up from the table. "I think I'd like to throw up."

"Oh, Ben," said Bea, "couldn't you have been a bit more tactful? How can we put her away like that? She's our daughter, our baby."

"She's *psychotic*," said Ben, "and don't you listen? She's hardly being put away."

"What do you think, baby?" said Bea, turning toward me.

You never think about betrayal while you're doing it. Your mind is always filled up with your own pain and with the incessant hammering need to rid yourself of it so you can just stop a moment and breathe. Anyway, I betrayed Rozzy at the dinner table that night. I should have stood up for her, should have argued that she belonged at home, that she was fine a lot of the time and didn't need a school like that. I felt something folding up inside of me, and I was suddenly crying, sobbing, making each sound a rip from the soul. "She should *go*," I spat out.

Bea scooted over and tried to cradle me in her arms, but I wrenched back. I was nobody's baby.

"There, you see," said Ben. "It's really for the best. For everyone, including Rozzy. You'll see." He wolfed down a small white potato. "Eat your dinner, Bess," he said, and I fled the table, hating him, hating Rozzy, hating myself.

Only Rozzy didn't see the logic. She ranted and threw things and destroyed her Museum of Self with one sweep of her hand.

"You're making your sister ill," Ben shouted at her, and she stopped, paralyzed.

"You're in on this, too?" she said. "You were never anything to me, do you hear that? *Never.*"

All that week Bea took Rozzy on shopping trips, to the movies, to restaurants. Rozzy pretended that I didn't exist, and I was miserable. I stayed home on the day Ben and Bea drove Rozzy to school. The school was called Parkburst and it was five hours away. Rozzy's doctor had promised to meet Rozzy there to get her settled, as a special favor. Rozzy had dressed in white and had tied a blue silk scarf about her head, pulling it down low over her eyes, which were focusless and glassy. I wasn't going. I didn't need to see Parkburst. I watched the car from the front window, my nose pressed against the glass, and when the car was out of view, I went to Rozzy's old room and wheeled out the TV and watched it until my eyes were unfocused and useless in my head. I wouldn't go near Rozzy's room again. Ever. I wanted to board it all up, to seal it up hermetically, along with all the feelings storming inside of me. I heard Bea and Ben coming back, their voices pressing against the door. I rushed to my room, shutting the door. I had nothing to say.

Bea felt guilty and she tried to be a good mother, a friend. She cooked me hamburgers glistening with grease, making me promise not to tell Ben, she took me shopping for bell-bottom blue jeans, which she swore were going out of style within the next month, and she even tried to engage me in earnest little conversations about my life. But I was uneasy around Bea's friendliness. I wasn't used to it. Finally Bea heaved a sigh and said, "I give up. You never did cooperate."

I had never been close to Ben, but now I pulled away even more. I would bolt down my dinner before he got home, timing it so that when he entered the dining room, I could stalk silently past him, pressing my body against the wall, making sure he saw that I was letting no part of it touch him. I blamed him more than I blamed Bea, or myself. When he didn't react, when even Bea said nothing, I went into my room and closed the door, bracing a chair against the knob, hoping they would try the door and find themselves shut out.

Kids at school were impressed by the news. I kept trying to explain that my sister Rozzy had *had* to go to a special school or I might go mad, too. No one wanted to hear any of it; even Hilly changed the subject. They all had their own noises to listen to, to try and drown out. In fact, the only person who seemed to understand was Jay. He grabbed me one day as I was trailing to class. I tried to jerk free. I couldn't breathe when he was around me anymore. Even the gossip about him that slid around school made my stomach twist. "Bess, please, look at me," he said. "You don't have to tell me anything, but I just want you to know that if you ever need to just *scream*, well then, you call me." He touched my chin, making me flinch. "Look, I know, I know, but I'm around for you. I wanted you to know that."

"Yeah. Sure," I said, stumbling blindly away from him. I wondered if he was following me, but I was afraid to turn around. I didn't stop walking until I reached the ladies room, and then I went into one of the gray stalls and leaned against it and angrily cried.

The teachers were sympathetic. When I skipped class, when I began hanging around the art room, no one said anything. I began spending my lunches, my study halls, in that room, painting, getting lost in color and form, in lines that had no beginning, no end. It was kind of funny, I guess, but I was good. Two of my watercolors were put into the art show, and I won first prize—fifty dollars and free Saturday art classes at Massachusetts College of Art downtown. Those classes turned out to be the one thing in my life that gave it shape, and Bea now complained that I smelled not only of chlorine but of turpentine as well.

Rozzy was in Parkburst for two and a half years. She wouldn't see Ben or Bea or me, and at first I was glad. The doctors there said she was better, that they were controlling the psychosis with drugs and that Rozzy seemed completely in touch with reality. She was finishing her senior year very slowly, credit by credit, and was talking about college.

I got through my junior year and began my senior. I was no longer a celebrity at school. I knew I'd be leaving home for college soon, severing the ties, and I began missing Rozzy. In the winter, I began sending her letters, apologies, snapshots. I waited for the mail every day. There was no letter from Rozzy, but there was an acceptance from Boston University.

Two weeks before I was due to leave for school, Rozzy phoned. She was going to a small college in Baltimore and she wanted to see me. "Just you," she said, "I'm not quite up to the folks, yet."

I didn't tell Bea or Ben that I was meeting Rozzy. She had a ride into Cambridge, and we met at a small café, the Blue Parrot. Rozzy wouldn't touch me at first, but sat apart, very formal. Her hair was wound into a huge knot at the back of her head and she was dressed in navy velvet and high brown boots. I felt stubborn. I was angry with her for not writing. I didn't want to talk about guilt and forgiveness and the past. I guess that sometimes there are just no reasons for anything, no explanations, especially for things that have to do with love. It was a funny kind of a reunion. We made small talk—all in the present tense. We ordered minted chocolates and Rozzy licked the whipped cream from her spoon, making small darting motions with the tip of her tongue.

"Bea wants to see you," I said.

"I'll just bet." Rozzy lighted a cigarette. "I smoke too much."

She was going off to school on a special scholarship. "Would you ever come out to Baltimore to see me? Or meet me someplace? Halfway?"

"You know I would."

Rozzy never did see Bea or Ben before she left, but she sent them a card with her address on it. "She's an adult, let her be on her own," said Ben, but Bea fretted.

I moved into a single room at BU while Hilly flew off to Stanford, reminding me to write. I liked my classes; I dated a little. I called home every Sunday and I swam. For some part of every day, I was wet. I'd rush to an art class, my dripping hair making dark pinpoints on my shirt, my skin scented with chlorine. My dorm room smelled of the wet leotards I swam in. People sometimes told me to try out for the swim team, but that had nothing to do with why I swam, with why I loved the lapping rhythm of the water.

Rozzy and I were linked by the phone, feeding it dimes so we could talk on into the night. She didn't much like Baltimore, and the old problems were edging their way into her life again. The depressions, the erratic behavior, were driving her from school. She saw a doctor through the student health service, but she couldn't read or concentrate with the medications he was making her take, and soon she dropped out of school. It wasn't really official. She didn't inform anyone. She continued to live in the dorm, to eat in the snack bar, poised for flight as soon as she had someplace to flee to.

She was often hysterical on the phone. "Everyone here *knows*," she said.

"Rozzy, forty thousand people can't *all* know."

"Why can't they?" she said, suddenly bitter. "How come you're always around when I get the boot from society?"

She called me every day that week. She was tying up the loose ends, packing, unsure where to go. "There are other schools, you know," I told her. "Go to the library and look at the catalogs. You got one scholarship, you can get another." So Rozzy dragged herself to the library every morning when most of the other students were in class. She plowed through the catalogs, going through every state.

A month before Christmas, she called. She was fixated on a school in Texas, on Rice. "You should see the picture of the place. Everything looks tropical. Steamy. I can't wait. I sent in my grades and everything." She paused. "Bess, I need to see you. When can I?"

I thought. The holidays were coming up, and Bea and Ben were planning to go skiing. The whole house would be empty. "Come home," I said. "No one will be in the house except for us."

She wasn't quite sure about it. She was afraid of stepping into that house and having her past tangle about her knees, ready to trip her, to pull her down and smother her. "You're sure no one else will be there?" she demanded.

"Positive."

It was easy enough to clear with Bea. "This *is* her home," she said when I called, a bit huffy. "But do you think I should stay home for her? She can't really expect us to be at her beck and call, though, can she? I wrote her all those weeks, and she won't even answer, not even a ten-cent postcard. What can I do?"

"How should I know?"

"Don't you be so snippy, miss," Bea said. "You tell that sister of yours that we'll call her, we'll try to get in early to see her." Bea stopped. I could hear her breathing over the phone, the hiss of air traveling through the wires that joined us. "Will she see us?"

"Call."

"There's time," said Bea, easily thrown off the subject. "Want to have lunch in town with me next week? My treat?"

CHAPTER SIX

I thought the month would solidify, would pass uneventfully until I saw Rozzy, but it was in that month that I met David. I had never thought much about dating. My mind always flickered to Rozzy, like a moth drawn to the flame, and if I ever thought about love, it was always with a wistful, dreamy sort of quality, it was always about Jay. That was a love I didn't think I could ever repeat, and I was not quite sure I wanted to anyway. Jay, in any case, was gone. Someone told me he took off for California the day of graduation with his flute and his stash of dope, trying to make his fortune among the blonds and the beaches.

A few times the dorm phone jangled for me, but it was always a setup of Bea's, sons of friends, all of them earnest students in the Boston area, well on their way to becoming doctors or lawyers or whatever it was that Bea found to be a financially promising profession. I was polite at first. I lied. I said I was already involved, but they never gave up. Enraged, I called Bea and told her to stop trying to fix me up, but she was undisturbed. "Oh, for heaven's sake," she said, "that's the last time I try to do you a favor."

I think I was first attracted to David because he loved monkeys. He was obsessed with them; they always came first. Even when he first approached me, it was because of a chimp. I was leaning against a tree waiting for a friend when he came and stood by me. He was wearing those cheap rainbow suspenders, and blue jeans, and he had clean brown hair that shagged down into his face. "Would you move for ten seconds, do you think?" he said.

I shielded my eyes. "What?"

"I need to take a photograph with a tree with low branches and this one's perfect. Please. It will just take a minute. I'm a rotten photographer, I don't take my time." He smiled a little.

"Hell," I said, but I got up, dusting off my jeans, sulkily standing away from the tree, waiting to reclaim it. He remained cheerful. He bent over a green knapsack and dug out a child's toy, one of those huge cloth chimpanzees with red stitching all over it. He perched it up in one of the branches.

"You have to be kidding, don't you?"

He looked sheepish. "It's a kind of joke," he said, crouching down, fiddling with his camera. "Christmas cards. I make my own. I'm a primatologist, or I will be when I get out of here and into grad school someplace. The West Coast has the best grad schools." He looked at me over his camera to see if I understood. "Apes," he said.

He took four different shots. "This will make a super card," he said.

"If you like monkeys."

He stood up, retrieving the cloth chimp, and laughed. "I love them. I have a whole collection of them. You don't believe me, do you?"

"Would you?"

"I'll bet you," he said; "nothing dramatic—an ice cream cone." He stashed the chimp in his bag. "Come on, just think how you can make fun of me afterward to all of your friends."

We walked to his apartment. He had a fairly old place

and you had to walk up five flights of dirty brown stairs to get there. "One more sec," he said, jiggling his key in the lock, and then he opened the door.

His place was painted dark green and there were plants growing lushly out of every surface, out of the fireplace, suspended from the ceiling, around the chairs. "Wait, wait," he said, snapping on the lights. Rubber apes dangled from lamps and plant pots, cloth monkeys sat in the chairs, and there were two wind-up chimps ready to clang metal cymbals together. An entire wall was covered with framed color photographs of baboons in the wild, their mouths exposing jagged yellow teeth. "I didn't take those," he said. "I told you I was a rotten photographer. I could never get shots like those."

"Look at this," he said. He pulled back a brown corduroy spread on the bed that doubled as a couch. The sheets were printed with gorillas and bananas. "Aren't they super?"

I stood there, feeling foolish. "Yeah," I said, "I guess they are."

I began seeing David, maybe because he startled me. We'd take the subway out to the zoo and then he would refuse to see any of the animals, not even the huge brown bears that lolled lazily around waiting for people to throw them marshmallows. The bears wouldn't even make an effort for their food; they'd just wait until a careful aim hit their mouths. David didn't even glance at them, but rushed me past to the monkey house and to his apes.

He knew all about monkey facial expressions, the meanings in every hoot, the nuances in each grimace. "You never stare a monkey in the face," he said. "Watch this. I'll do it just once to show you why and then never again." He looked into the cage and then pointed out a dust brown spider monkey who was industriously picking fleas from his back fur. David stared. The monkey snapped his head forward, his mouth ovaled, and his head began bobbing. David kept staring until the monkey screeched, and then David averted his glance. "I gave in," he said. "Let's go see the gorilla."

David got me permission to come to one of his special ape classes at Boston University. I sat on the sidelines in his primatology lab, breathing in the queasy formaldehyde smell. There were three silvery trash cans and in each one was a chimpanzee as big as myself, and as heavy. It took two people to lift one of the plastic-wrapped apes up onto the smooth lab table. "Look at this, Bess," said David, his face shining. I stood unsteadily, leaning my palms on the table. The ape still had expression to its face, its fur seemed alive. I looked once at David and then I went outside and sat in the courtyard until David came bursting out an hour later, jittery with excitement, smelling of monkey death, of monkey life.

I liked David. He was shy, the only son of strict Mormon parents who, from the time he was twelve, had made him get up at five each morning to attend mandatory church school. "If I wasn't up with that alarm, I'd hear about it all day from my father," he said, "and from all the other Mormons in Ohio, too, it seemed. The pressure was far from subtle." He shook his head. "My folks refuse to believe that I'm going to study apes in Africa. They think evolution is part of the devil's plan to ruin everything. I was supposed to take a whole year off after high school to go on this special crusade converting people. Can't you just see me? Going from house to house, politely invading living room after living room, spouting off about how my religion was the only truth. My whole senior year, my parents tried to get me ready. My father censored things that came into the house. I remember being furious with him because he threw out a magazine that had a picture of a girl in a bathing suit in it."

"You didn't rebel?"

He looked sheepish. "What do you want from me? I was stuck in the middle of Ohio, there weren't exactly thousands of role models of rebellion for me to emulate, you know. I wasn't stupid. I knew my life didn't feel right, I just wasn't sure what was wrong. Not yet, anyway."

"What about your friends, what were they like?"

He shrugged. "I was ashamed to have them to the house. I don't suppose you've ever felt that way, but my house was so different, so crazy. In the basement we had a year's supply of canned goods. A whole fucking year. We had to. Mormon law, in case of famine. Every time someone came over, I could see him looking at all those cans, and I could tell what he was thinking. I could take that feeling right up inside of me, and it made me sick. I never had anyone over for dinner, especially not on Wednesdays. Family night. Oh God, *family* night. My father read from this special book, intoning on and on about morality and faith, and I couldn't even daydream because there would be questions afterward. Guys I went to school with would be out sloshing down beer, chasing girls, and there I was, sitting at the table, answering my father's questions. It was so terrible."

David stretched. "No soft drinks for me. No cigarettes. Mormon law. And dating was serious. Mormons marry young, in the temple at Utah, and both of you had better be virgins. I never liked the girls in my church. I had one Mormon girl friend who said out of the blue that she knew her breasts were small, but she didn't care. I sat there beside her, starting to move my hand toward her, then she said she didn't really care, though, because they were the breasts that would feed our children.

"I escaped. I came east, I worked, and then I applied to

schools. My parents were shocked. My mother thinks I'll grow out of it; she says she has visions from God that I'll return."

"Visions?" I said.

"A sign from God, she tells me. It's a sign that God knows she has faith when he gives her a vision. Lots of people believe that. She thinks I'll have my visions, too, one day. If you ask me, she should see a good shrink."

I pulled at a strand of hair, pulling, pulling, until it gave a little *szit* and came free from my scalp.

"Families," I said, a little weary.

"Yup," he agreed.

I never met his parents. But I could always tell when they called. He'd be itchy. He'd prowl through his rooms, touching his monkeys, walking back and forth. His phone had an extra long extension cord, green like a Tarzan vine, and as he talked, he wound it round his arm. He was silent when he hung up.

He had a picture of his parents in his desk. I found it one day when he was showering. His mother was very beautiful, very young and blond, laughing into the face of a tall blond man. Neither of them looked like David. When David came out, dripping, wearing a green towel about his waist, the photo gave him a start. "How young they are in that," he said, "My father, God. He was one of the original communist-haters. He even started to build a bomb shelter out of the land on the side of our house. He insisted on building it himself, not trusting anyone else, fearing that even the workmen he had known for years and years still might harbor some Red Russian blood and might make the shelter weak. He wanted his shelter big enough for the elders of the church, but it took so long. By the time it was only half finished, the Red scare had died out. So it became a driveway instead." He laughed.

David wrote his parents every week. "Do you mention me?" I kept asking.

"Are you crazy? Do you want five sets of Tupperware to appear on your doorstep, along with numerous books on becoming a Mormon?" He grinned. "And anyway, now it's your turn. Tell me about your folks, about your life."

Bea was always delighted to cook for someone, and so I brought David. Rozzy was still away and all David knew about her was that she was my sister. She would be the last secret I would share. As soon as David stepped into my house, Bea began fussing over him, taking his coat, ruffling his hair. Ben was aloof, suspicious. He treated dinner like any ordinary dinner. He got up from the table and came back without explanation or excuse. He used whatever fork he wanted, and he reached for the dishes of steaming food before David had his share. He didn't talk, and when he was finished bolting his food, he got up and left the table. "Nice to meet you," David called after him, and Ben's retreating back stopped long enough for Ben to say that he had work to do.

David couldn't get over all the food that Bea had prepared, the Greek wines, the sauces. "You eat like this all the time?" he wondered. "I grew up on canned stuff, canned vegetables, tinned meats, canned juices." He made a wry face.

"Have more," said Bea, pushing the dishes toward him. "Bess tells me you love monkeys."

"I can't wait to get to Africa."

"So go. You like all that heat?"

"To tell the truth, I don't sweat. I can't tolerate heat all that well."

I looked at him, grinning. Another surprise.

He was embarrassed and he fiddled with his fork. "Really. I have a problem cooling myself down. When I was in the sixth grade, I had this lung infection and they had to finally give me this test where they take samples of your sweat and test it for certain chemicals that are indicative of diseases like cystic fibrosis. I had to strip right down and hug myself so they could wrap me up in this Saran Wrap mummy suit. Hot towels, heavy blankets. I was flat on my back for an hour with no one to talk to. The nurse had left the TV on for me, but it was a game show and it really annoyed me. I would have given anything to be able to turn that thing off. I remember the cleaning man walked by me and said that wasn't I the lucky one, and he turned it off for me. I couldn't stretch, I couldn't scratch any of the places that itched me so terribly. After an hour, the nurse wandered back in and took the wrappings off and scraped me down with a slide. It felt funny. Raw. But she had this queer look on her face. 'Don't you sweat?' she asked. 'Don't you ever ruin a shirt?' They had to do the damned test all over again, for another hour. I didn't sweat during the next hour, either. But they didn't do it again."

"You don't have cystic fibrosis, do you?" said Bea.

"Nope. My mother thinks it's because she came to my bed and prayed. She felt guilty about my being sick, as if it were her fault."

"I don't ever feel guilty about anything," said Bea.

"Good for you, then," I said sharply, and she started, tipping over her glass.

We stayed until ten and then we left. Bea made David promise to come back for dinner.

That night, David and I became lovers. If I made any sound that seemed like a cry, he would lift himself up and ask if I wanted to stop, was he hurting me, moving too fast, too slow. He kept stopping periodically, anyway, breaking the rhythm to simply hold me as if he were about to drift into sleep, before picking up the pace and the passion once again.

When we were finished, lying lazily in a tangle of monkey sheets, I told him about Rozzy. He was very quiet the whole time, and he kept running his fingers along the length of my arm as I spoke. "Do you want me to disappear when she comes in?" he said. "I will, if you want."

"I don't know yet," I said, and I felt his hand stop moving. "Let's go to sleep."

I came home with David's phone number and the house key Bea had given me since she had changed the lock. Bea and Ben had left on vacation already, but Bea had frozen several dishes for Rozzy and me to eat, and had left numerous notes seeded around the house, motherly reminders mostly, about shutting off lights, taking our hair out of the bathtub drain, and an emergency number at the ski lodge.

I was watching TV when I heard Rozzy outside, shouting something to the cab driver. I was unprepared for her entrance. She immediately began talking, dominating the house. Then she fished out three bottles from her purse and slapped them on the table. "Lithium, Valium, aspirin," she grinned. "The Father, the Son, and the Holiest of Ghosts. Meet my religion."

We didn't unfreeze any of Bea's dinners, but instead called up a Chicken Delight and had a greasy bucket of chicken delivered along with several cans of root beer. The skin peeled away from the chicken like wallpaper and the root beer was flat, but we were ravenous, and it tasted delicious. We were finishing up when David called, and glancing at Rozzy, I told him I would see him if we could double-date. "She's devastating," I said, "so you should have no problems finding someone."

"I'll get Hank," he said. "Hank's good."

"Oh, fuck," said Rozzy, when I told her. "Why'd you do that for? They won't like me. It will be horrible."

"It will not. And if it is, you and I can just leave."

"Really?" She looked at me. "You mean just walk out, wherever we are?"

"Why not?"

So David showed up at our door, Hank in tow, both of them relaxed and laughing and in jeans, both with the same clean shaggy hair, the smell of soap. David had on a new pair of peacock blue suspenders and he clutched a single yellow daisy.

We went to a Woody Allen movie and Rozzy swung her thin booted legs up over the seat in front of her and sat silently through the movie, never changing position or laughing or anything. A few times I saw Hank whisper something to her, but she never answered. After the film, we all went to Zorba's, a Greek restaurant in Central Square. Rozzy ordered coffee and kept sipping it, never looking at anyone. Hank clearly liked her, and he kept grabbing at her sleeve to get her attention, kept winking at her, trying to get her to smile. When she got up to go to the bathroom, he grinned at David. "You were right, friend," he said, "she sure is gorgeous, but shy. Too shy."

"She'll melt," said David.

When Rozzy came back, her hair looked wet.

"Rozzy?" I said, but she ignored me.

Hank was talking about his studies, about art history. He teased Rozzy, comparing her to a Toulouse-Lautrec, but her face was blank.

As we were getting up, Hank tried to help Rozzy into her coat, but she tore away from him, her face flushed and damp. "What's this, do-Rozzy-a-favor week?" She twisted around to me. "You, too. What the hell do I need your favors for either? Haven't you done enough for me?" She spun around and stormed out, jumping into a yellow cab that was prowling around the street corner.

Hank was angry, the enchantment was gone. "What the fuck is *her* problem?"

"You shut your mouth," said David.

I reached over and shyly took David's hand. He looked friendly and cheerful, despite what had happened.

"Let's get you home," he said. "She'll want to talk to you."

"Look—" I started, but David stopped me, placing his fingers across my lips. "You don't have to explain anything," he said.

"*I'd* like an explanation," said Hank. "What am I, some kind of monster?"

I must have looked as if I were about to cry. "Later," David told him. We walked to the car, Hank following us, muttering to himself, kicking at the Pepsi cans rolling in the gutters.

When I came into the house, Rozzy was sitting at the window, staring into the night. She jumped up. "It's *OK*," I said.

"I'm so thick and stupid," she said, waving her hands, "I just felt kind of controlled, like a puppet."

"Rozzy," I said, and she managed a smile.

Rozzy stayed only three days. She said she felt itchy. We spent most of the time inside, watching TV and making fun of the game shows and the movies. Sometimes Rozzy could be coaxed out, to a movie usually, or a play, but she was uncomfortable around people; then she changed. She wouldn't talk and she'd bite her nails or fiddle with her hair.

Rozzy never answered the phone the entire time she was home with me. David kept calling, but he accepted not seeing me. "Tell Rozzy I liked her," he kept saying. He was a funny kind of person. I had never met anyone quite so accommodating, so kind.

"David liked you," I told Rozzy, but she wouldn't be serious. "Enough to marry me?" she said.

When Bea called, Rozzy got on the extension and listened. Bea was spending most of her time on the bunny slopes while Ben skied the top. They saw one another at night, but by then they were too exhausted to do anything save tumble into bed.

"Is Rozzy OK?" asked Bea.

"Rozzy is ducky," said Rozzy.

"Rozzy, I didn't know you were on the line."

"Ben there?" said Rozzy.

"No, darling, he's still at the lodge. Shall I tell him to call you?"

"I don't think so."

There was a sharp click as Rozzy hung up, but Bea continued to chatter. When I got off the phone, I found Rozzy in the living room, hunched over her knees, playing with one long thread of hair.

"They didn't care that I came home for the holidays either," I said.

Rozzy looked up at me. "It's not the same thing at all, Bess," she said, "you and me. It's just not the same thing. We're like Beauty and the Beast."

"I've felt that," I said. I crouched down beside her, resting my head on her shoulder. "I used to get so sick of always being the Beast. Rozzy—" I started stuttering, blurting out words like bullets. "Rozzy, I *wanted* you to go to that special school. I wanted them to lock you up and keep you away." I started crying, parting my tears with my fingertips. "I just wanted a chance to see what it felt like to be Beauty for a change."

Rozzy turned to face me, astounded. "But Bess," she said quietly, "*I'm* the Beast." She put both arms around my shoulders, trying to still them. "I've always been the Beast."

She stroked my face, the skin of her hands absorbing my tears. "Shush," she said. "Don't cry. I'm right here."

Rozzy and I both left before Bea and Ben returned, and it was March before we saw each other. Rozzy had supposedly gone to school, to Texas, with traveler's checks from Bea, but she wrote no one, she didn't phone. "She'll be in touch when she runs out of money," said Ben. "We'll hear from her soon enough."

Bea called me one day claiming Rozzy had sent her a postcard from New Orleans announcing she had married. "What's she doing there?" Bea cried. "Ben's washed his hands of her. He said if she wants to get married, fine, let someone else wear that albatross of a girl around his neck for a while, see how he likes it. Can you imagine?"

Ben was in a state, and Bea couldn't possibly leave him, but I had a break coming up; would I go and see Rozzy?

"I'll go."

"I knew you would. Wait. I have an address."

"She didn't send *me* anything."

"Well, I'm her mother, honey," said Bea.

"Someone's at my door. I have to go, I'll get the address later," I said, clicking down the receiver. I lay down across my bed and stroked away the headache that was steadily taking root.

I wrote Rozzy, but all she sent back was a sheet of directions and the word COME in big red letters.

David drove me to the bus station. We had planned on spending the break together somewhere, maybe up in the mountains, and his understanding nature was making me tense and irritable. "It's better for you to go alone," he said. "You'll talk with her."

"I didn't ask you to come with me," I said, ignoring the bitten look on his face.

The bus ride was forever. I slept, I read a few cheap paperback novels, I made small talk with the elderly woman sitting next to me who was on her way to visit her daughter. I had hoped to save money by taking the bus, but the tedium and the ceaseless hum of the wheels made me resolve to fly back to Boston when I was ready to leave.

Rozzy didn't live far from the bus station. I had the directions jammed into my jeans pockets along with fifty dollars for Rozzy and a candy bar for myself.

Rozzy's apartment was in the middle of a student slum. James Taylor was crooning from a window, and a few cars sunned themselves in the dirty street. Her place was brick and it had a porch, and Rozzy herself answered the door when I rang. She was thin and sleepy and she wore a large red glass necklace that caught at the light and held pinpoints of it. Behind her, a sheepish-looking man with brown hair in his eyes grinned at me. "Well, well, aren't you something to look at," he said, "wild red hair, all in a tangle. I like that."

Rozzy yawned, motioning me in. "I can't believe it. You really did come. Tony, this is Bess—*the* Bess." She gave me a sleepy smile.

Her apartment was small and cramped, painted bright white, clean of posters and pictures. "Sit," she ordered, waving lazily at a mattress on the floor. "No, wait, let me kiss you first, make sure you're really here. Damn, I wish we had some wine to give you."

"We drank the last of it yesterday," said Tony, sprawling on the floor against the wall.

"Oh God, I'm so terrible," said Rozzy. "Bess, this is Tony Mandrello."

"Pleased, I'm sure," said Tony, winking at me.

"We're not really married," said Rozzy apologetically. "We still have a few bugs to work out."

"Bed bugs," grinned Tony. "I'm what you call a sexual innocent."

"You bullshitter," said Rozzy fondly.

"I want Rozzy to teach me, but she claims she's just too

nervous." He squinted at me. "You any good at teaching?"

When I flinched, he laughed. "You sure do take things seriously," he said.

"You never wrote me," I said to Rozzy.

She lifted up her hands. "I know, I know. I can't explain it. It was so easy to send Bea that postcard. It didn't even matter, but I couldn't write you, I couldn't."

"I don't understand," I said.

"You think I do?" she said. She got up, disappearing into the kitchen, coming back with a clean blue bowl filled with sticky buns. She plunked it down on the floor by Tony. "Tony's a writer," she said proudly. "I met him on the bus to Texas. We sat up all night talking, and the next day I called the university out there and set the wheels in motion for a year's leave, and we came here."

"I love New Orleans," said Tony, "lots of good jazz, lots of things to do, a good hot sun that just about burns you alive."

There wasn't much work though. They subsisted on welfare and the few odd jobs Tony could get, usually as a cook in some greasy spoon, lying to welfare about it. They had almost immediately spent Rozzy's traveler's checks.

"Tony never lets me see anything that he writes," said Rozzy. "I bet he just writes the same sentence over and over again just to make me think he's being productive."

"Yeah, sure I do," said Tony, annoyed. He pulled apart a sticky bun and popped the pieces into his mouth. Rozzy rubbed his hair and said, "Oh, Tony," with an amused smile.

Tony spent a lot of time with Rozzy, so I didn't really have a chance to be alone with her much. I walked down to the corner store and called Bea collect to tell her Rozzy wasn't married, that she was fine and happy, and that she had a year's leave from school. "Thank God," said Bea. "You need any money?"

Tony and Rozzy didn't seem aware of anyone else. I

began to get the feeling that I didn't exist for them. The third day I was there, they fought. I was glad about that; I didn't want Rozzy liking him so much. Anyway, Rozzy found out that Tony had fished fifty dollars from her purse to buy a guitar that was missing half its strings.

"That was rent money," she screamed at him, throwing a book. He looked sheepish, but then he retorted, "Forty more and I could have it fixed up, get the bridge redone. Maybe I could play in clubs and make some money."

"You're something else," I said.

Tony looked at me curiously. "Beg pardon?" he said politely.

"I don't appreciate you living off my sister."

"Who said I was doing that?"

"Oh, Bess, hush up, please," said Rozzy.

"He's using you," I said, waves of anger washing through me.

Tony grinned and dug his hands into the back pockets of his jeans. He had a big rip in one of the pockets, and the tips of his fingers stuck out. "Hold on now," he said cheerfully.

"What do you need this for," I said to Rozzy.

Tears were squeezing from her eyes. "You don't understand," she said. Tony was still smiling, ignoring Rozzy.

"Maybe it's you who should go," she said to me. "In fact, I think I'll call you a cab. You can afford a cab to the bus station, can't you?"

"How could you even think of marrying him?" I said. "You don't need him."

"But I do," said Rozzy, "he's exactly what I do need."

"Why don't you just simmer down and behave yourself and we might even let you stay with us for a few more days," said Tony.

"You were the first hippie," I said to Rozzy, "and now look at you. You have on plaid pants."

Rozzy looked surprised, and then she laughed and said, "Let's all go down to Juke's and get some dinner cheap." She wound her arm about Tony, sluicing off her tears with her free hand. "You walk with us, Bess," she said, and Tony hooked his other arm about me. But I felt alone again, my existence sliding between the two of them and not affecting anything at all.

I left the next morning. "But why do you have to go?" said Rozzy. Her eyes started to tear. "You haven't even painted me, yet," she said. "You could stay. Do some sketches to work from in Boston."

She reluctantly went to the station with me, dragging Tony with her, the two of them sharing a Milky Way. While we waited for the bus, Rozzy sang a few old folk-songs and Tony beat out rhythms with the flat of his hand on her knees. "See, I could make it in clubs," he said.

When the bus finally came, I found a seat in the back and looked out the window. They were still sitting on the bench, smiling at each other, holding hands. I shut my eyes, waiting for the bus to start up, to take me to the airport so I could fly home.

Rozzy didn't marry Tony. I never could fathom what it was she needed from him, what kinds of gifts he could give her. I didn't hear from Rozzy much, and it irritated me, but Bea seemed content, even relieved, and that irritated me, too.

In April, Rozzy sent me a card saying she was finally leaving for Texas, to get settled before she even thought about starting school. Tony could get a job there. I re-sented Rozzy's being happy without me, and I took it out on David, but he never argued back. He went off and came back with brilliant red poppies, with a bottle of red wine.

But Rozzy's life was circular. She could be well and functioning for periods of time, but her illness, her psychosis, always came spiraling back to the surface. She called me one morning at two A.M. She was hearing voices. "I need someone to be with me!" she cried. "I'm all alone!"

"What about Tony?"

"He's gone. He wasn't any help. Every time I told him I heard voices, he went to the movies." She sucked in her breath. "Oh God. We were going to Texas in two more weeks, and then he left. He said he only liked me when I acted right. I don't know where he is."

I tried to clear a path for myself through her nervous crying. "I love you," I said. I felt light, buoyant.

"Come, please come," said Rozzy. "You have to. I need you to come. I feel up for grabs. I haven't slept for days," she insisted. "I'm afraid to be in this house with Tony gone. It's a different house now, it isn't friendly to me. I keep thinking that once I fall asleep, I'll never be able to wake myself up again, that anything could happen, could take control of me. I think about robbers, about the gas jetting on. I keep seeing the blue flame, smelling it, being smothered. Every time I manage to drift asleep, I sense someone standing over me, clutching something—a fork, the silver prongs pointing at me, accusing. I try to jerk awake, but I can't. Sometimes I jolt up, shivering, sweating. It's so awful." She heaved a tight dry sob. "I found some pills Tony left. Uppers. He took them a lot. I took some. They gave me energy so I'd get to dancing to the pop tunes jingling out of my little radio. I'd have too much energy, too much, so I'd start trying to wear myself down, scrubbing floors, getting a Brillo pad and scouring the tub, the corners where all the soap and grit congeal into stone. I was never tired until the pill wore off, and then I was overtired, too tired to sleep."

"Rozzy, you must be sleeping sometime, even a little," I said, curling the heavy phone cord around my hand, tightening it against my skin.

"I've been going to public places," she said. "I leave my keys and money at home so I won't worry about being robbed. I stick the key in the dirt and put a plant over it. I don't know anyone else here. I was always with Tony; even the people who live in the other apartment in this house are strangers. I couldn't trust anyone with my key. I slept for a while in the bus station, but then I started having these dreams, nightmares. I woke up screaming once. Everyone was looking at me. Once I even had my hands on someone. He plucked my hands away from him as if he hated me."

"What about a doctor, Rozzy, a doctor might help."

There was a cramped silence. "I saw a doctor," said Rozzy. "Some man. Dr. Berger. He yelled at me for not coming sooner. He gave me pills for the things moving in my head, pills to sleep, and he insisted that I come back to see him. I got the pills, Bess, and I'm going to take them, too, but once I got back into my place, it all came back, it all crowded me. I get so afraid. I'll take the pills. I will, but not alone like this. With you, Bess, with *you*."

So there it was. I said I'd go out there, but Rozzy was strangling in that town and insisted on meeting me somewhere else, some halfway point. I made reservations at a Holiday Inn in Ann Arbor, Michigan, so that no matter who got in first, there would be a clean silent bed to sprawl across, a door to shut. I checked back with Rozzy to make sure she had money, to make certain she had transportation and would be able to make the trip.

She said she had called the ride board at one of the radio stations and they had given her four different phone numbers. She was nervous about calling, about having to speak with people. It was difficult clearing a path through the sounds in her head. Most of the people she called expected her to share the driving as well as the expenses, and Rozzy couldn't drive. One woman heard the panic wavering in Rozzy's stutter, and told her to be ready, she would give Rozzy a ride.

I borrowed Bea's car and started driving. David wanted to drive me. We could take a real vacation, he said, go and see Rozzy and then the two of us could skip school and see the country. He was always trying to uncrease every wrinkle in my life, and that made me uneasy. How could I possibly tell him that I didn't want him coming with me because I couldn't stand another person crowding Rozzy and me?

Rozzy had said that she had cut off her hair when Tony left her, had taken the gardening shears and systematically whacked it off to her scalp. She still probably looked marvelous. I always thought it was too bad that someone couldn't make a composite out of the two of us, a woman with Rozzy's flame, with her black hair skidding down her shoulders, her pale skin and large black eyes, all this meshed in with my long fine hands and perfect teeth that didn't stain yellow from cigarettes the way Rozzy's did. Her energy and zest and creativity—and my sanity. Together, neither of us would ever have to be the Beast. We could be two halves making up a complete healthy whole.

The sun glared through the windshield of the car. If I had been in Boston, I would be having some sort of dinner with David, carrying on and giggling. He always cooked and he always did the dishes, resisting his Mormon training that these were women's jobs. What more could I want? Why wasn't it enough for me? I had a math exam in three days and I had left my text and my notes at David's. It didn't matter. I was on my way to see Rozzy with a check from Bea and fifty dollars of my own stuffed in the back pocket of my jeans.

We were all getting older, I thought. Ben and Bea, me—even Rozzy. And I knew Ben had no intention of leaving use because it was so thick and clumsy in her hand. She bought a card and signed both their names to it, and then she held it at arm's length and gave it careful study. Rozzy didn't have an address yet, so Bea wrapped the package up with the card and tucked it away into the closet.

"You know, Ben might have signed that card himself," I said. "Didn't you even ask him?"

"It's better to just leave these things alone," said Bea.

I moved back to school, to the same dorm room, the same sudden loneliness. My whole first year had been taken up with David, with Rozzy, and I hadn't made friends, the connections others seemed to have. I didn't really know how to go about making friends, I didn't understand. I dawdled in the bathroom with the other girls, trading lip glosses and gossip, I made study dates with people in my classes, but nothing took. I wanted a closeness immediately; I couldn't wade through the preliminaries.

The art classes I took were disastrous. Techniques were taught; you were supposed to paint a certain way, and because I balked, I was in danger of flunking. The art history courses were no better. I was called upon all the time in one class; the professor liked me—until the day he propositioned me and I refused, and then I became a nonentity, an invisible waving hand in class. I began to think of another career, another route to fame.

I called David. We piled into his car and drove out to the Cape to walk on the beach, and we swam. It was chilly and gray and the sand felt gritty under my feet. David leaned against me, pulling a bottle of wine out of his pocket and uncorking it. He spilled a little bit of it on the sand, staining it red. "For the gods," he said.

"Rozzy left," I said abruptly. "She and Stewey married, went to Madison. I don't even have an address."

David handed me the bottle of wine. "Have some," he said gently, "it's really very good wine."

I spent that night, and a few others, at David's, but it didn't make me feel less alone. I think he sensed it. I would jerk awake to find him sitting in a chair by the bed, just watching me, his eyes dull, and when I asked him what was wrong, he insisted everything was fine.

We did some of the things I had done with Rozzy and Stewey, even eating at the same restaurant where Stewey had fed me energy through his hand, but it wasn't the same. How could it be?

Finally I got a postcard from Rozzy. After that they began coming, one each day. She found a new favorite card, a colored picture of the college mascot, Bucky Badger, a human-looking badger wearing earmuffs and a sweater and a big ferocious grin. "They even name hamburgers out here after him," Rozzy wrote, "and Bucky Burgers taste just as greasy as other burgers do." She wrote that they had a clock in the shape of a badger, and there were badgers printed on the wax milk cartons. She and Stewey went to the zoo to see them, but Rozzy said they were so skinny and ferrety they looked evil, and she wanted to leave.

They had found a place to live on Mifflin Street, the hip student district, and Rozzy began settling in. They had the whole top floor of a house, with a private entrance, and although the wood floors were badly scuffed and the plaster had a few holes punched out, there were no bugs, and the sun came in the windows in the mornings. Rozzy celebrated her twenty-first birthday in that house, and Stewey teased her about being a baby because she was five years younger than he. Stewey had phoned his parents to tell them he was married. He had written them that summer about Rozzy, and his mother immediately wanted to have the two of them come and visit. "We're just three hours away," she said. Both of Stewey's parents wanted to talk to Rozzy, but she was flushed and embarrassed and made Stewey tell them she was in the shower.

Rozzy found a part-time job working at a student-run pharmacy. The pharmacist had just graduated himself. He allowed Rozzy to give out the prescriptions and ring them up. Madison had a law that said you couldn't dispense condoms to anyone who wasn't married, and so Rozzy learned to feed the appropriate response to the flushing faces in front of her.

She couldn't cook. She couldn't even shop without coming home with boxes of exotic Oriental dinners, with Spanish hot sauces and cookies, but never bread and salad greens. She didn't clean either, but the clutter never bothered Stewey. They ate pizza almost every night, and then walked up and down the streets, wandering in the tiny shops, parading with the other students.

An uncle of Stewey's died, leaving the two of them enough money for Rozzy to go to school. She couldn't decide what to study. Rozzy spent hours plumbing the catalogs, sitting in on classes. She read, she sat out in the sunny library mall and struck up friendships with a few drifters, giving them names like the Opium Eater, the Dog, Miss Messy Hair. She showed up outside Stewey's classes with ice cream cones for them to lick. She unwrapped her scarf and they both wore it. She never sat in on any of his classes, though, feeling too shy. On Thursdays, they went to a function called "Donuts with the Dean," and while Stewey bantered with the faculty, Rozzy sampled all the filled donuts and got tipsy on wine.

They waited awhile and then went to visit Stewey's parents. "What did you tell them about me?" said Rozzy.

"Oh, only that you're brilliant and beautiful."

"Is that enough?"

Rozzy wrote me a ten-page letter about that trip. They drove up to northern Wisconsin one weekend in Stewey's

battered Chevy. The whole ride up, Rozzy sang along with
the radio, beating out the time on Stewey's knee, her nails
bitten and ragged. He grinned at her, teasing her to take the
wheel, lifting up his hands so the car shimmied and swayed.
Rozzy, lips set, would grip the wheel with white knuckles,
making the car glide into a straight path again. They got to
the town, Adam's Friendship, around midnight, and Rozzy
insisted that she couldn't see anyone without a proper
shower and a night's sleep. She made Stewey prowl around
that sleepy town until he found a motel. The first place they
found seemed to be empty. There was a sign-up sheet posted
to some corkboard behind a desk, and a box of keys. Rozzy
fished around in the box for a key and they signed Harry
and Suzie Sussman on the sheet. There was no shower in
the room, but there was an old claw-footed tub streaked
with rust stains. Rozzy wouldn't sit in it, sure she would
contract VD, but she crouched in the tepid water. Stewey
came in and sat on the toilet and watched her, and when she
asked, he scrubbed her back for her with a soapy cloth.

The bed wasn't bad, although some of the springs had
worked themselves loose and poked up through the mattress.
In the middle of the night, someone started knocking, shaking their doorknob, and Rozzy bolted up, shivering, waiting
for something to happen. The knocking stopped, but neither
of them could get back to sleep. They shared a candy bar
Rozzy had in her purse, and then dressed, sneaking out of
the motel, leaving the key and a five-dollar bill. It was still
early morning and they found an all-night diner where
Rozzy slumped over a hot chocolate and played the Rolling
Stones on the jukebox.

"Adam's Friendship," Rozzy declared, "is a stomach
cramp of a town." She tensed up during the ride to the town
where Stewey's parents lived. Stewey was from a huge
family, five brothers, four sisters, a pack of mewing furry
cats, and two big dogs. His brothers were all younger than

he, and so different that Stewey's mother affectionately told Stewey that he must have been left on her doorstep instead of born.

Stewey told Rozzy that his brothers clamored around the TV set and yelled at the sports announcers. They went out for sports, worked on cars, and wondered about which girls would let you finger-fuck them and which wouldn't. "Lovely," said Rozzy, rolling up her window and then rolling it down again, coaxing an imitation of a breeze into the car. His sisters, he said, were scattered in age, and they either fussed over him or worshiped him. They were all really happy living in a big house, content with small-town life, with everyone knowing everyone else and no one dreaming of leaving. It was only Stewey who felt smothered, who ached for buildings more than a story high.

"There was nothing in my house that wasn't touched by someone else," he told Rozzy, "and everything was covered with dander, with dog hair, so that I sneezed my way to manhood." As soon as he could, he had gone off to college, to the city. The boy who was supposed to have been his roommate had had a heart atack, right in the room, before Stewey ever even met him. It was the dorm counselor who found the tall thin boy, lying half on the bed, half off, his skin glassy. So Stewey was left to himself, for the first time in his life, and he spent whole evenings in that boxy little room, breathing in the silence and grinning like a fool.

"We're here," Stewey said, and Rozzy began fishing in her purse for a lipstick, a comb, some Kleenex. It looked like any other small town, the small white houses, the messy lawns, the gravel and the gritty stones on the sidewalk.

"I'm scared," said Rozzy.

She was crazy to worry. Stewey later told me that she charmed everyone. His brothers all fell in love with her, and kept mooning around her, dogging her steps and making her blush. The youngest pulled up a clump of yellow flowers from the garden in the back and presented them to her, clumsily tied with a blue ribbon. His sisters decided to grow their hair and took turns brushing out that black sheet of hair of Rozzy's. Stewey's father, a doctor, coaxed her into playing Clue with him and was delighted when she let him win. "You've got yourself quite a girl," he told Stewey, who beamed.

They didn't do very much on that visit. Everyone sat outside in the leafy backyard while Stewey's father barbecued steaks on the grill and baked potatoes in shiny silver foil. They played football, and when Rozzy hesitated, Stewey grabbed her by the hand and had her play right beside him, the two of them kicking the ball toward a makeshift goal. Before they left, Stewey's mother, a faded blond, took Rozzy aside and handed her a thick heavy quilt that she had made. "Every marriage needs warmth," she said, and gave Rozzy a hug. Rozzy inhaled the washed scent of soap, and started crying. Stewey's mother patted her on the back. "Goodness, it's nothing," she said to Rozzy, "you're *family* now, like one of my own."

The whole family stood outside on the curb, waving at them when they left. "Come back," called Stewey's father. Rozzy twisted around and waved and waved until they were pinpoints.

But later, Rozzy said she would never go back there, would never repeat that visit.

"But why?" said Stewey, dumbfounded. "You had a great time, and they *loved* you."

"I was lucky that time," she said, "just lucky."

I wrote Rozzy voluminous letters, knowing full well that they were Stewey's letters as well. I never admitted the terrible loneliness, the feeling of being cut off, and I never mentioned David.

I would have moved in with David into his monkey

apartment if it wasn't for the phone calls. The first Madison purchase Rozzy and Stewey made was a phone extension, and every night at eight, the two of them would call, joining themselves to me by a phone wire, a black umbilical cord. I didn't want anyone sharing that with me. I had a single, my own phone, and for the first time I loved the sense of isolation. Always before, I would see all those rows of dorm doors as barriers, shutting me out, intensifying my separateness—but now, it was I who was doing the shutting out, the isolating. With my door shut, I was in a womb. At eight, no other world existed. If I saw David, it was always for a late movie or an early swim, and if he minded, he said nothing.

The phone calls were not profound. We never said all that much, but simply ate away at Stewey's money with aimless chatter, a rambling kind of phone play. We got drunk on opposite ends of the phone, we ate grilled cheese sandwiches together (I wrapped bread and swiss cheese in tin foil and then pressed the sandwich into completion with a contraband GE iron). We talked about all the usual day-to-day things people do, to make us feel as if we were still living our lives twined together. As soon as I hung up that phone, I had to leave that room, that dorm; I fled. It was at these times that I was most manic about David. I hung on his arm, I prodded him into bed with me.

Eventually, Rozzy and Stewey each called on their own. Rozzy would call for a ten-second talk on her way to meet Stewey; Stewey would call me just before jetting off to class. Rozzy was happy. Madison was still sultry and hot, alive with insects. It was warm enough to swim in one of the lakes bordering the campus, the water frothing with detergent suds and rotting grasses. Rozzy told me that there were bats by the capitol, that if you walked down there you could see them fluttering and dying in the street, their fur matted, their teeth yellow and pointy. Once a bat flew into their place.

"I made Stewey bash it with the broom," said Rozzy. "He stunned it and then took it outside. I made him throw out the broom, too." She said they had ants, too, scattered like ice cream jimmies on their sunny front porch, their private entrance. Rozzy couldn't bear to stamp them into oblivion, so she kept putting sugar out for them, each day moving it further and further away from the porch, until finally the sugar was on the dirt. The sugar drew all the ants in Madison, or so Rozzy thought, and seeing that heaving black mass wriggling and alive made her ill. She had to retch on the walk and gag up her breakfast. Then she went inside and put the copper kettle on to boil, and came out again to scald the ant mass, washing them into the dirt, kicking the earth over them. She never put sugar out again, and the ants never returned.

Stewey got her another doctor, for maintenance, this time a woman. The days started to chill and the winds began whipping around campus. Rozzy brought out her winter clothing, although everyone was still in cut-off jeans and brightly colored T-shirts. She hunted for clothing in the thrift shops, buying herself a mothy-looking fur coat that she liked to snuggle into at night while she read.

Rozzy never phoned Bea or Ben, and Stewey called only when he remembered, and only when Rozzy was out, so as not to upset her. Rozzy did send Bea postcards, which pleased Bea, and Bea inked in Ben's name in the address and showed off the cards to him. David and I started coming to dinner on Saturdays.

They had cleaned out Rozzy's room, boxing and labeling all her things and stashing them in the basement. Bea seemed a little edgy, but I didn't think anything was wrong. Not yet. That was a story Bea herself would have to tell me; I would have to live it through her, as I did so many other stories.

It was this way.

Rozzy's marriage, her leaving, her being so happy, set

something off in Bea. Bea would lie awake at night imagining their life, seeing how Stewey took care of Rozzy. She would remember the two of them, how they were together, the way Rozzy became brilliant and excited when she was with Stewey, dejected and sulky when she was alone.

And then, every once in a while, something would remind Bea of Walt. The sudden sharp tang of memory, the surprise of feelings she thought had long died, scared her. She'd be marking down dental appointments when she would forget what year it was, her stomach folded and twisted. Dates swam across her mind, numbers rising to the surface, smells erupting, sensations. Later, it grew even more subtly, even more confusing. She would be standing in the bakery, waiting for Ben, hanging on to the string-tied white box of whole wheat rolls, and then suddenly her head would be suffused with the smell of those apricot-filled cookies Walt used to love. She could taste them in her mouth, feel the buttery crumbs sticking on her tongue, and she would remember how she and Walt would get sluggish from the shock of all that sugar. She would touch Ben's sleeve, and the feel of the material, familiar and real, would catapult her back into the present. She began to be sick and dizzy with her past.

She began calling me more and more, pumping me for information about Rozzy. "You think they'll stay together?" she said. "Even with Rozzy sick like that?"

"She's not sick now, she hasn't been sick in a while."

"They seem like they're *meant* to be together, don't they?" she said. "You think passion like that can last?"

"I don't know. I have to go," I said.

Bea tried to get reoriented. If she was home, she called Ben, feeding on his voice. If she was with him, she pulled him toward her, making sure that some part of him was always in contact with her. She surprised him with roses, with cards that said she loved him. She did things she knew he liked. She baked bread, forgetting the dough sometimes so that it overrose and stuck in a yeasty mound to the stove, taking her all afternoon to scrape it off with a bread knife.

She would later tell me that it was at this point that she started sending cards to Walt. She didn't even know where he was anymore, but she sent everything to his old address. She never wrote a return address, so she never knew if he received her letters. When the mail came, she always felt tense and panicky, as if she might be forced to re-examine her life. Sometimes when she felt particularly blue and loathsome to herself, she would write him long and deeply felt letters. Walt became her priest, a man hidden from her and yet acutely there. She didn't want answers, at least she didn't think so.

The fall slid toward winter. I had an uneventful Christmas break, staying in the dorm and studying, seeing David. When classes started up again, I tried to concentrate, but I ended up writing letters to Rozzy, neglecting the notes scribbled on the board in front of me. When I was with David, all I wanted to do was see movies, double feature after double feature, and when the film was over, I didn't want to talk, I wanted to make love and fall asleep. I was barely passing my subjects, and my advisor gave me a frowning admonishment, which David seconded. One night I baited David until we argued and then I went home and called Rozzy.

Stewey answered, his voice tight.

"Something wrong?"

"Oh," he said, "it's just Rozzy. I can't find her. I don't know where she is." He sighed. "I guess it's nothing. It's pretty early still, sometimes she goes to classes, sits in. Look, I don't want to tie up the line, in case she's trying to get me or something. I'll call you back."

Stewey didn't call me back for another two weeks. I

tried calling but there was no answer, and then finally, he jerked me awake at three A.M. one morning. Drugged with sleep, I staggered to the phone.

"Something's wrong," he said. "I come home and Rozzy's not there, and when I find her, she's out at the bus stop with a suitcase, smiling at me, waiting for me to find her. Last night she stumbled in wearing someone else's filthy jean jacket over this lovely cashmere sweater, and when I asked her where she got the jacket, she yelled at me, said it was none of my damned business. When I asked her if she was still seeing the doctor, she just laughed and said, 'Poor Stewey, always hope, isn't there?'"

I held the phone close to my chest.

"Where is she?" he said. "A million times a day it's 'Do you love me? Do you love me?' She never believes that I do, that I'll stay with her."

"Stewey, is she on medication, is she hearing voices?"

"I don't know. I tried to check her pill stash and she got furious. She hides them now. Sometimes at dinner, she'll pretend to take them, and then when she sees me relax a little, she'll give me this triumphant look and show me her hand, uncurling the fingers so I can see the pills resting right there in her palm."

I flexed my feet until they cramped. I didn't have to think; all I had to do was move.

"I have no one to talk to. I won't call her doctor without her permission. Rozzy would never trust me again if I did. Oh, thank God for you, Bess." There was a silence and then he said, "Sometimes I think I married the wrong sister."

I stopped flexing my feet. "Rozzy will turn up, things will be all right," I said.

"Did you hear what I said?"

"Stewey, call me when Rozzy gets in."

Stewey began calling me more and more, always with some new horror story. I comforted him as best I could. I tried to call Rozzy myself, I sent her letters and cards, but there was never any response.

I hated not hearing from her. Every time Bea asked me, "What have you heard from the kids?" it enraged me to have to lie, to have to utter all sorts of platitudes about new places and busy schedules, to have to see the look washing across her face.

Stewey and I spent hours discussing Rozzy, picking apart the relationship. We worried about her together, we clung, we lifted each other's spirits. A few times Stewey would insist that we weren't going to talk about Rozzy at all, that we were just going to laugh and crack bad jokes and make fun of people. I'd hang up from those calls feeling all warm and good inside, and it wouldn't be until I was half dreamy under my sheets that I would realize where I was and what was happening.

In March Stewey called me, weeping into the phone, so incoherent that I had to ask him to repeat what he had said several times before I understood. Rozzy, he said, was pregnant, and she said the child wasn't his.

"But how do you know? How can she prove a thing like that? Is she even sure she's pregnant? Did she see a doctor?"

"She saw someone. She even called him to confirm it while I was there."

"But how do you *know* it isn't yours?"

"She said she had been sleeping with other men—" Here, Stewey's voice cracked and it took him a hairbreadth pause to continue. "I said I didn't believe her, that she was just saying that to torment me, but she said it was true, and that she knew the moment she conceived, she just had an intuitive knowledge of the event.

"But then she had to show me, she had to prove she wasn't lying. Last night I came home and Rozzy was in bed with this skinny kid with acne, and he was absolutely terrified when he saw me. He jumped out of bed, called me sir, and apologized. And Rozzy—she sat up and smiled. I let the kid rush past me, all the time still babbling some apology or another. I couldn't move. I just stood there and looked at Rozzy and then she started to cry. She said she felt so lonely she couldn't bear being inside her own skin. She said she knew the baby finished us. I told her I loved her. What else could I say? She said Bea had once sent her a ticket to Boston and she had never used it, but she was going to use it now, she was leaving."

"She *loves* you."

"What has that got to do with anything? She packed a knapsack and she left here an hour ago. Oh God, I wish you were here. I wish you could just be here and we could have things the way they were in Boston, at the beginning when it was so sweet and nice. I could help Rozzy then. She listened to me, she trusted me."

"I can take the next plane out there."

"Don't you understand? She's *gone*."

"What flight did she take?"

"Shit," said Stewey, "I don't know."

I spilled out promises. I would find her, I would get to the Boston airport and figure out flights. My sophomore year was over next week, but I'd be going to summer school to make up the courses I had failed, I'd have a dorm room to house Rozzy.

"You want me to call you when she gets in?"

"If," said Stewey dully, "*if* she gets in."

I dressed and took a cab to the airport. I had this queer panicky feeling that I was missing Rozzy even as the cab sped and dipped toward the planes. I might be two feet away from her, she could be in another cab traveling in the opposite direction.

It was late and the airport was nearly empty. I searched the monitors for clues. I remembered what David had told me once when he had to get home for his father's birthday and had no flight; no one would listen to him, they kept telling him to wait. He had slammed his suitcase down in the middle of the floor and had shouted that he was going mad, that he couldn't take it. At first he was ignored, but when he shouted even louder, three stewardesses rushed toward him, all of them taking his arm. They took care of everything. They put him on a flight (in the smoking section, which made his nose quiver with allergies, and his eyes leak) and a stewardess brought him two aspirins and a glass of water.

I couldn't do that. I stood in the middle of the lobby and wept. There were a few people straggling in, businessmen, college kids, and they lowered their heads when they passed. A young girl with a horse face and a thick tail of hair approached me, but she turned out to be with the Krishna people and she wanted to convince me the money I might give her would go to start a drug program. When I refused, she squinted darkly at me. "Something's wrong, isn't it?" she said. "Krishna knows. He knows everything." She reached out a hand and tried to touch me, but I stopped it in midair. "Look how nervous you are," she said. "It could all stop"—here she clumsily snapped her fingers— "like that," she said.

Miraculously, a stewardess finally appeared.

"I'm not doing anything," said the girl, suddenly sulky, wandering away.

I told the stewardess about Rozzy, feverish with panic. She furrowed her brow. She was young and blond and pretty. "OK," she said, and suddenly she was wonderful. She took me to one of the desks and figured out the possible flights and then checked the passenger lists. She even got me to the correct gate. "Will you be OK now?" she said.

There was a pay phone by the colored plastic seats and I called Bea and told her that Rozzy was pregnant, and coming home, that she had left Stewey, who was baffled, and that she was in a terrible state herself.

"What? How could this happen?" said Bea. "It's right out of the blue, isn't it?"

I rubbed at my temples, trying to press in a growing headache. "Rozzy will tell you what she wants you to know."

"*Damn* her," said Bea, and then sighed. "Well, this is her home and she can stay here for as long as she likes, until she decides what to do."

I heard Ben's voice, muffled in the background, heard Bea say something, and then his angry undercurrent of sound.

"You bastard," said Bea, "she's your *daughter*."

When Bea came back on the line to me, her voice was even. "You bring her here, and then we'll see. And you call if you need me. When's she due in?"

"Half an hour," I said, "if it's on time."

Rozzy came in on time. She was all bundled up in a bright red coat and a black felt hat that flopped over her eyes. She looked lost and tired and there were big stains of sleeplessness smeared under her eyes. When she saw me, she smiled. "I knew you'd be here," she said simply.

"You did, huh," I said, moving to her.

She didn't want to talk about anything. She said she had to sleep first. We cabbed back to my dorm and she threw herself down on my bed, still in her coat, and fell asleep. I sprawled out on the floor, on the rug, beside her.

In the morning, she was still sleeping, so I scribbled her a note and went to breakfast, bringing back boxes of yellow raisins for her, some cereal, and a carton of juice. When I put my key in the lock, balancing her breakfast, Rozzy was up. She looked white and frightened.

I sat on the bed while she ate. "I called home," I said. "They want to see you."

"Forget it," she said, stabbing a spoonful of dry cereal into her mouth. "No milk?" she said.

"Bea will pay for a doctor, you can live there, have the baby."

"Can't I stay with you? I won't be any trouble."

"Of course you can. I can even move in with David and you could have this place for yourself."

"No, I can't be alone. Please."

"OK, fine, but if we don't go and see Bea, you know she'll be calling and calling and maybe even showing up here. That would be worse, wouldn't it?"

She didn't want to go, but she dressed and we took a cab, and the whole way over, she bit her nails and complained about her stomach hurting.

Bea was waiting in the living room, reading a magazine, confident we'd be by. When she spotted Rozzy, she leaped up and hugged her. She kept touching Rozzy's face, her trembling shoulders, the thick mane of black hair so like her own. "Come in, come in, honey," said Bea. "Everything's going to be fine."

"Of course it is," said Rozzy coldly, pulling back, twisting around to catch my eye.

She wouldn't take off her red coat and she wouldn't sit still. She paced, picking up the plants and putting them down, silent and uneasy. "You want to talk about it, any of it, baby?" said Bea gently.

"No," said Rozzy.

"Ben's here, should I go get him?"

"You don't have to," said Rozzy, but Bea was gone.

"Oh, shit," said Rozzy, looking helplessly at me.

"It'll be over with soon."

Ben's face changed when he saw Rozzy standing unsteadily in the room. He looked from her stomach to her face, to me and then Bea, and back to Rozzy again. Rozzy stood white and terrified by the fireplace, holding her hands over her stomach, pressing her back to the brick, waiting like some sort of trapped animal.

"You're going to have a baby?" he said. Rozzy nodded. "Do you want it? Are you going to raise it, you're not going to abort?"

"It's mine," said Rozzy, "I love what it is."

Ben sighed, then he held out his hands to her for the first time since she was little. She didn't move. She was frozen. He walked right over to her, peeling her away from the fireplace, placing her in his embrace. She stiffened, and then she relaxed, weeping, taking gulps of air, trying to speak. Her words kept snagging into sobs, and soon she stopped trying to tell him anything.

"It'll be OK," he said. "We'll get you a good doctor, you can even go back to school, you always had a good mind." He pried her face away from his shoulder and forced her to meet his eyes. "It will work. It's different now."

Bea stood by the door. She watched Ben leading Rozzy into the kitchen, talking to her about herbal teas, about foot soaks. "I don't believe it," said Bea. "It's all I could do to get him to even stay here when he knew she was coming home."

"Did you tell him she was pregnant?"

Bea shook her head. "I thought one shock at a time was enough. At first, anyway. I told him about ten minutes before you arrived. He just got up and went into Rozzy's old room and shut the door.

"You'll call Stewey," she said.

"What do you mean, *I'll* call him. Why, what for?"
"Bess, don't you give me a hard time, too."

In the next hour, it was decided. Rozzy would stay at home where Ben could monitor her pregnancy. "I thought you wanted to stay with me," I said to Rozzy. "What happened to that idea?" Rozzy gave me a blank, drugged look. "It's different," she said quietly.

"Sure," I said, looking at her, and then at Ben, who was digging out his old collection of *Prevention* health magazines, looking at all the old photographs of Rozzy when she was a baby, and smiling to himself.

CHAPTER ELEVEN

I was glad I wasn't living at home, that I had a place of my own at school. Being home made me feel fuzzy-headed, as if time had thickened and pushed me backward. I visited Rozzy on weekends. David had quickly decided that the best way to ensure seeing me was to drive me out there and then pick me up. He never came in because Rozzy disliked him, but he didn't seem to mind. He seemed content to spend his time waiting for me, always waiting.

Rozzy was always drinking something pastel and sludgy. She sipped, making faces, slapping the glass down on the table, dripping, speckling the cloth with liquid. Bea sniffed at it and took a tentative poke with her finger, touching it to her tongue. She grinned. "Why, this is what Ben made me drink when I was carrying you, honey." I leaned forward for a taste, but Bea whisked the glass away, popping it into Rozzy's limp unwilling hands.

It was hard to have Rozzy all to myself. Ben was always taking her to the doctor's, to the health food store, to the market. Sometimes, waiting in that lonely house, I called Stewey. He couldn't believe Ben was doting on Rozzy. "She'll never come back to me now," he said. He was convinced that Ben was filling her head with lies about him, telling Rozzy that she was better off without him, that

Madison was no place to raise a child. "He probably believes her when she says it's not my child," he said glumly.

"I don't think she told him that."

"She will," he said.

I never could speak long with Stewey, because Bea was always coming back in, and if I was forced to share Rozzy, I wouldn't share Stewey.

It wasn't until another week had passed that I managed to get Rozzy all to myself. We walked up to the old school yard up in back of the house and sat on the swings. "What's it like?" I said.

Rozzy frowned.

"Being pregnant," I prodded.

She bit off her thumbnail and then looked at me. "Well, it's like having swallowed something. Like having eaten something that's big and huge and alive, and having that thing stay right there in your stomach. It's a little uncomfortable, like the whole digestive process has gone screwy and instead of you digesting it, it's digesting you, taking your calcium and your blood, and your food." She took my hand and placed it on her stomach. "It'll kick soon, won't it?"

Rozzy threw out her legs, making the wind push the swing forward. "I'm three months, now," she said, "and Stewey hates me. Don't try to tell me he doesn't. I know you talk with him, but you don't know him. You haven't lived with him, with his accusations."

"He loves you."

"How could he?" she said.

"Maybe it somehow is his baby."

"It doesn't even matter, does it?"

We walked home and Ben's car was in the drive. Rozzy brightened. "He said he was bringing home special lemon grass for tea," she said. "I love lemony things."

When I got home, I called David and told him I had a

headache and wanted to sleep and then I called Stewey. But he was suddenly bitter, angry, hostile to me. He rampaged. He had been going through Rozzy's things, setting them in order, when he found a journal of hers. When she was too shy to discuss something she would write it out in her journal and leave it around where he could find it. So he read. "Men," he said, in disgust. "She had so many men. Every damned page was about a different one. Nights when she said she was too sick to come out and meet me while I studied all night in the library, days when she was supposed to be seeing her doctor.

"Love," he said bitterly. "Did you ever worry about coming home because you were afraid of what you might find there? I'd get nauseated wondering what she was doing."

"She needs you. It's not good for her here, with Ben."

"You don't understand, do you?" he said. "It has nothing to do with her being pregnant, don't you see? Now it's changed. It has to do with all the incidents, with all the things that were going on every single day that I didn't even know about. I can't go through life just giving support to her, even when she does the most heinous things imaginable, and never getting any support myself for my own fairly simple problems." He paused. "No, you don't understand. Why should you?"

I lay flush against my bed, looking at the ceiling, wishing for those shooting stars Rozzy had once wanted to paste up there.

"I understand, Stewey."

"No, you don't. You're her *sister*."

"I'm glad she left," said Stewey abruptly. "I never want to see her again. I never want to hear about her again. I'll give her money if she needs it, but that's it."

"She doesn't want money."

"You know, when I heard your voice, I thought it was

Rozzy," he said. "I'm getting an unlisted number. And don't you write me because I won't read any of it. Words, nothing but letters strung together." He was crying, his words drowning. "What am I supposed to do, Bess?" he said, and then he hung up, the swift clean silence enveloping me like a shroud. I tried not to think much, to just breathe and sleep and have that day over with, transformed into memory, and forgettable.

Rozzy never mentioned Stewey, and I kept that pain to myself; I carried it much the same way Rozzy did her fetus.

One evening I heard Ben and Bea arguing in the kitchen. I had come home for dinner, but Rozzy was still at the doctor's. Bea was clanging dishes around, threatening to break them. Ben was whirring something in the blender, shouting over the noise. "She needs to know she has a choice," Bea shouted. When I walked into the kitchen, she clamped her jaws shut.

Bea later told me she had tried to convince Ben that abortion was an alternative. Rozzy might not be a stable mother; what would happen to a baby that needed feeding and washing when its mother was hearing voices? It was the first time Bea had experienced one of Ben's sulks firsthand. He acted as if she weren't really there at all. At dinner he ignored her, and he slept on the far side of the bed or in my old bed in the other room. If she touched him, he would contract his body away from her. She tried to be friendly, she told him about a new French farce that was playing at the Orson Welles Theater in Cambridge, but in the middle of her speech he yawned and picked up yesterday's newspaper and read it avidly.

Bea was stubborn. She asked Rozzy to talk to a doctor. Rozzy's face clouded. "I'll go see Leffler," she said, "just to prove you wrong."

She went to the doctor by herself, not mentioning it to Ben, and when she came back, she was triumphant. "Leffler thinks it's a great idea," she said. "He said not to take any medication right now, but if I need to, he can give me stuff that won't harm the baby."

"Leffler said that? You didn't misunderstand?"

"He said to make an appointment for next Thursday, and he found me a doctor—a baby doctor."

When Bea saw that Rozzy was determined to have the baby, she tried to talk with her about adoption. She left magazines around open to articles about how families were crying for healthy babies. Rozzie skittered from Bea. "You think I couldn't handle a kid?" Rozzy said. She'd start to weep and then Ben would emerge from his sulk long enough to yell at Bea, to ask her why on earth she did that, why couldn't she be supportive?

"Oh, *please*," said Bea bitterly. She saw what was happening, saw how Rozzy was avoiding her, how the girl kept watching her mouth as if Bea's next words were going to condemn the child to an unknown family. Bea couldn't stand it. Her husband, her daughter, the two of them were lined up against her. She went over to Rozzy and sat gingerly beside her. "OK," she said, "whatever you want, I'm behind you."

"No," said Rozzy calmly, "I'm in this alone."

Something flickered in Bea's face.

"It's OK," said Rozzy.

Sometimes Rozzy would come swimming with me. She was starting to swell and she really liked looking at herself. "I look like a beached whale," she grinned. She dawdled in the showers, letting the spray run over her stomach. She wouldn't use the special hot-air dryers on her hair, fearing the ends would split, but she liked to stand naked under the dryers, letting the hot air push down on her. "It feels Texan," she said.

She began talking more and more about Texas. When Ben insisted that she talk to the fetus (he even rested his head on her belly, much the same way he had with Bea, while Bea stood, leaning against the door, watching, a queer set smile on her face), Rozzy would call it the little Texan, she would tell it how life was going to be in the humid sticky heat.

"What do you want to go out there for?" Ben said. "Stay here. I'll put you through school, whatever you want. What does Texas have to offer a child?"

"Everything," said Rozzy.

"Here, read a baby book," said Ben. He was bringing her home two new books a day. Rozzy spent days listing different names, looking up their meanings, and she was even considering going to a medium.

"My baby and I will go everywhere, just the two of us."

"No man?" said Ben, amused.

"Babies do things to relationships," said Rozzy, and Bea, hearing that old ghost phrase of Walt's, dropped a glass, cutting herself. She drew a thin red thread of blood on her thumb.

Ben decided that Rozzy should be exercising, so he enrolled her in classes at the museum. She wanted to try ballet. "You can't dance with a child," Ben said. "You'll hurt it. Don't be silly, Rozzy. Try something else." But Rozzy was stubborn. She went into town to the museum and spoke with the ballet teacher, a tall thin woman in her forties, who suggested that Rozzy wait until the child was born. When Rozzy persisted, the teacher shrugged. "You won't be able to do much," she said, "and I won't pay you much attention."

"I don't care," said Rozzy.

"You say that now," said the teacher, "but what about

later, in class? How will you learn? How will you accomplish anything at all?"

"I just will," said Rozzy.

"It's your money," said the teacher.

Rozzy couldn't wait for class to start. She had a week's wait, and she used the time to check out books on the ballet from the library, to comb the stores for dance posters that she could hang in her room. She was more interested in the look of dance than dance itself. She went out and bought herself different colored leg warmers—black, brown, pink, red, and tweeds. She had warmers which pulled up waist-high that she rolled down to her hips, she had short leg warmers that came to her knees. She bought dance slippers in both leather and canvas, and sweaters that wrapped around her waist. She had cashmere tights and silver combs to knot her hair up high on her head. She didn't care that her body pushed out from her, that there was a subtle swelling to her, denying her the hard flat stomach of the other dancers. She took out the toe shoes she had worn to the wedding when she met Stewey and brought them to class with her, stringing them over one shoulder. She worried about the correct way to wear her leg warmers. Should she pull them down over her shoes or keep them at the ankle? Should she wear two pairs at the same time, letting a ribbon of color show at the top? She went to the dance department at one of the colleges and studied the dancers, prowling the studios. She saw the sweat flickering off their faces and hitting the floor as they whipped around in a turn, she saw them cutting away the tops of their T-shirts and leotards, the way some of them wore their tights over their leotards, or wore baggy shiny pants. She saw the girls daubing on perfume, and when she asked, they said it cooled them, so Rozzy swiped Bea's best perfume and walked into her class smelling of lemons, making the girls behind and in front of her at the barre wrinkle their noses.

Rozzy lasted for three lessons. It hurt. She'd see the other girls comparing their aches and pains, collecting torn muscles like medals. She felt like weeping, as if she were trapped in her own body. "Your posture is terrible, the worst I've seen," her teacher told her, standing in front of Rozzy, critically watching her. "I think you should crawl."

"What?" said Rozzy, fidgeting with the tie on her sweater.

"Crawl. One hand, one leg, right, left," she said.

Rozzy dipped to the ground and tried to crawl, but something was wrong with her coordination. She looked up at the teacher. "Don't look like that," the teacher said. "You want to dance, you have to suffer."

Other girls did. In Rozzy's last class, a girl ripped a muscle. She pinwheeled over into a ball, weeping, while two other girls rushed to her and rubbed her back. Someone peeled off a heavy brown leg warmer and wrapped it around the hurt back. Rozzy's head reeled. The teacher didn't seem alarmed. Rozzy got up and walked out of class.

"Ballet's not for me," she told me. She never danced again, but she wore her leg warmers over everything. She pulled them up over her arms as a makeshift sweater, she layered her leotards and tights, complaining only when she had to strip down out of all those layers to go to the bathroom.

Rozzy tried yoga and even photography. "All that walking around to get the perfect shot is exercise," she explained to Ben. But after two classes, she gave up. I picked up the camera Ben had bought her, a Nikon. "Take it," she said, "there's still a roll in it."

I took the camera and the little booklet that explained how to use it. I wasn't very good at first. I simply squinted, held my breath, and clicked. David was a great help, and he liked coming out with me, explaining about angles, being listened to and appreciated. He kept telling me that I would be his photographer in Africa when he went to do his field work on monkeys.

"It's too hot there," I said, crouching to get a shot.

"We'll have air conditioning."

"Outside?"

He ran his hand through his hair. "What are you going to do with your life, then? You told me you were getting disgusted with the art department, that you didn't want to be a painter. What are you going to do, wind up swimming for a living?"

"Fuck you," I said, standing up, angry.

"OK, I'm sorry. What do you want? Want me to study snow monkeys in Alaska? I'll go and study snow monkeys."

"I don't want to talk about it."

"You never want to talk about anything important."

"Could we drop the subject, please?"

We spent the rest of that day combing the streets, snapping people. Sometimes the expressions on their faces when they knew they were being photographed were far more interesting than when the shot was a candid. Later, at times when I couldn't afford film, I would go out with an empty camera and snap anyway, just to see all those faces.

I never took pictures of anything other than faces. David surprised me by setting up a tiny darkroom for me in his apartment, and gradually I began to get better.

I fell in love with photography. I could do more with it than I ever could do with a paintbrush, and I began to mount some of my best shots. One day David borrowed a little shopping cart from a friend and we loaded it with my photographs and wheeled it around Harvard Square, peddling each shot for only two dollars. Within a few hours, we had sold every picture, and I was feverish with delight. "You're famous now," said David, ruffling my hair. "Do you realize how many people now own a Nelson? A Bess Nelson?"

I reached up and kissed him. "How many people?" I said. "Tell me how many over and over."

"Maybe you'll be a photographer instead of a painter," he said. "It's still art."

"I'm not taking classes in it, though. That seems to spoil everything."

I began photographing Rozzy. She was never satisfied. She would take the contact sheets and study the pictures, shaking her head. "I look disgusting," she said.

I took only one picture of the whole family, including myself. I set the whole thing up with a timer, placing the Nikon on a tripod, and I had to rush to be included in the picture, settling down into a hasty crouch in front of Bea and Ben. Rozzy was squeezed in the center, her hands tucked into her lap, the fingers curled under so you couldn't see how raw and bitten the nails were. Her head was dipping down, half hidden by a sheet of dark hair. Ben had his arm thrown around her, his fingers resting on the edge of Bea's shoulder. Bea was laughing, her head thrown back.

I still hate that picture. It's undefined. Faces seem to be melting into other faces. Something about that photo always disturbed me and I never made copies of it. When Bea asked me about it, saying we had never had a family portrait and she wanted one, I told her the negative had been ruined.

I did take one perfect picture. Of David. He was sleeping. He was the only person I had ever met who could sleep with his mouth closed. He liked the picture, but he kept urging me to take pictures of his monkeys at the zoo. I was never interested.

Rozzy got a little larger, and I kept track with the Nikon. She was getting restless, itchy to leave, and when Ben saw her leafing through the yellow pages for airlines, he went out and found her an apartment, making her a special present of a one-year lease, tying it up with an olive ribbon that Rozzy would later wear in her hair. Rozzy accepted the lease silently.

"I guess I can't keep you here forever," Ben said, "but I'll still check up on you every day, see how you're doing, if you need anything. And if you like, I can even pick you up on my way home from work and you can spend your evenings here." Ben grinned. "You'll forget all about Texas when you see the place I found for you. It's wonderful, clean, bright. Close to the house, too. And it's only a one-year lease," he said hopefully.

We all went to see the apartment. Bea brought along a notebook so she could jot down things Rozzy might need to make the place her home. Two days later, Rozzy moved in.

No one could forget anything in that apartment. It had no sense of life, no living wood or high ceilings. It was flat and square and had red tiles in the hallway. It was only a three-room apartment, ten minutes away by car, and Rozzy was almost never there. "It's hideous," she said. "I'd rather just stay in my old room, or be in Texas. I can't believe Ben thinks I like it."

"Tell him, then," I said, staring moodily out the window, tracing the dust with my finger.

"Come on," said Rozzy.

She never decorated any of the rooms, but she went out and bought a baby crib secondhand, and painted it white. "But it's bad luck to have the crib before the baby," Bea protested, but Rozzy just laughed at her. Ben made out lists of things for Rozzy that he thought the baby would need— all of Beethoven's symphonies, some Mozart, Bach, some Italian opera, all of them to be played the moment the baby came home. He went into the Harvard Coop and bought a few large-sized prints of various masterpieces to be hung at the baby's eye level, and he bought books with print so small Rozzy had to squint to see it. "You think a baby can read?" she asked sarcastically.

"This one will," said Ben happily. "*You* did when you were small."

Ben and Rozzy didn't argue much. He was delighted that she refused to wear maternity clothing and lived in a pair of Indian wrap pants and T-shirts. The only sore point between them was Rozzy's refusal to allow Ben to meet her obstetrician. He couldn't see why she got so flustered, and when his sudden sulking didn't prod her into acquiescence, he dropped the subject.

"The baby is Rozzy's, not yours," Bea reminded him, but he tuned her out, he refused to listen. His family was Rozzy now, and her baby. When I came home with a bright red silk baseball jacket as a gift for the infant, Rozzy whooped and held it up against her swelling stomach, but Ben took it into town and returned it for a white Harvard University sweatshirt; "Class of the Future," it said.

Rozzy spent most of her time at the house, and when the weather was bad, Ben encouraged her to stay over. I saw Rozzy when I could.

One morning I noticed her glancing at the clock in Bea's kitchen and then carefully writing down the time on a piece of paper. When she saw me watching her, she shielded the paper with her fingers, and gave me a dark, secretive look.

"You feeling OK?" I said.

"Why, aren't you?" she said, standing, tucking that paper into the pocket of her T-shirt.

All that day, she kept checking that paper, slipping it out of her pocket and then sliding it back in again. I kept looking at Bea or Ben, but they didn't seem to have noticed anything, so I let it drop. We ate a silent dinner, and when Bea set out dessert, bowls of fruit, Rozzy said there was this program on TV that she had to see, and escaped. "I think I'll go watch, too," I said.

"Clear the dishes first," said Bea.

When I got to Rozzy, she was sitting cross-legged in front of the TV, which was a blank green stare. She was animatedly talking to herself, twisting shapes out of the air. I turned around and went into the kitchen and got a piece of ice and held it to my head.

"Head hurt?" said Bea, coming into the kitchen.

"It's Rozzy," I said.

"What do you mean, 'it's *Rozzy*'?"

Bea followed me into the room, but when we got there, Rozzy was sprawled on the floor, asleep. "She's perfectly *fine*," said Bea adamantly.

"Don't you notice anything?"

"Only that you're very paranoid about your sister. Now stop before you make me that way, too."

It took a lot for me to ask Ben, but I did it. I went into the living room, where he was avidly reading a baby book, and asked him if he had noticed that Rozzy was hearing voices, that she was talking to herself. He put the book face down in his lap, marking his place with his finger, and frowned at me. "It's just tension," he decided. "Carrying a life can make anyone extremely nervous."

"Is Rozzy seeing Leffler? She won't tell me."

"She doesn't need to see him."

"Do you know?"

Ben shrugged.

"You'd see her bills, wouldn't you?" I persisted.

"Look, I give her a large sum of money to do with as she pleases. And she's *not* sick, she's fine."

He might have thought she was fine, but two nights later he went for a long walk with her up around the school, and when they came back, Ben was grinning. "We had a good long talk," he said pointedly.

He kept close to her the next few weeks. I couldn't manage to speak with Rozzy alone, and since she seemed happy,

I edged away from my fears. In fact, I wasn't the one who discovered Rozzy sitting on the bathtub talking to herself, running the water and holding one hand under the flow. It was Bea.

When Bea came into the living room, where Ben and I were sitting, her face was white with anger. "She's talking to someone," Bea said. "That girl is hearing voices."

"It's nerves," said Ben.

"Nerves?" said Bea coldly.

"I told her that."

"You told her all right. You told her to talk to the fetus, listen to it. You helped her along, you did it. You helped her to hear those voices." Bea was panting with anger. "I should have listened to you, Bess, you told me something was wrong."

"No, I didn't mean—" said Ben, standing. "Where is she? What's she doing?"

"She's *talking*. In the bathroom."

We all went to find Rozzy, but she didn't even turn around. Her ears were picking up other sounds. "Rozzy, honey," said Ben, touching her, and she turned, giving him a loose, dreamy smile.

"I never heard voices," said Bea, softly, angrily. "You told me to listen, too, don't you remember? How you used to sit there and rub my belly and talk right into it just like it was some damned telephone. I never heard one damned thing. I just said I thought I was communicating with the fetus to please you. Because it was so important to you. Because it meant so damn much." She spat out the words.

Ben looked at her, and then at Rozzy, and then left the room. "That's right, *leave*," said Bea, but he was slipping out the front door. We took Rozzy into her old room and put her to bed. "Can you sleep?" I asked her, and she drooped her lids shut, obedient. Bea stood at the door, her hand braced against the wall, slowing her breathing, trying to match Rozzy's. "She's seeing Leffler tomorrow," said Bea, "if I have to take her myself."

I slept in the room with Rozzy, on a cot by her bed. It wasn't until very late that I heard Ben come back in.

When I woke up, Rozzy's bed was empty, the covers thrown back. I stumbled into the kitchen, finding her sitting at breakfast, lazily spooning dry corn flakes into her mouth, Ben across from her, studying her. He told her to put some milk on the flakes, that she needed the calcium.

"You feeling better?" I said, slumping into a chair.

Rozzy dipped her head. "I feel ashamed," she said, "and kind of dopey, too. I'm not going to hear anything anymore, I'm *not*."

Ben drew back a little when I looked at him. "She called Leffler," he said. "He can give her something that won't harm the child."

"Where's Bea?"

"I was up before her," said Rozzy. "She kept watching me, staring, until I said something, and I guess because it was coherent, she figured she could communicate. She told me about last night, though I remember it, told me she was calling Leffler, and I told her I already had. I don't know where she is now, but she left the car, said for you to drive me, Bess."

"I can take you," said Ben.

"Let Bess."

Rozzy was silent during the ride into Boston, and she wouldn't let me come into Leffler's office, so I drove around, aimlessly picking out pathways for myself until it was time to go pick up Rozzy again. She bounced out and hopped into the car.

"OK?" I said. "Does he want to see you again?"

"I'm perfect," she said. "Ben was right. It was just nerves. He gave me a prescription to fill. And an appointment."

She wouldn't let me stop at a drugstore, but insisted on

driving home to tell Ben. Her easy smile pulled Ben and Bea
into a truce. When Ben asked to see the medication so he
could look it up in his *Physician's Desk Reference*, Rozzy
balked. She said she hadn't filled it yet, and anyway, she
wasn't a child, what medication she took was as personal a
matter as what she said to her doctor. "That's absurd," said
Ben, but Rozzy was silent.

Rozzy developed a slight stutter, and sometimes she
seemed a little hazy, her movements slowed, but she said it
was simply a side effect of the medication, and it really
didn't bother her in the least. Ben kept urging her to take
less of a dosage than Leffler put on the label and to drink
more of his special vitamin drink, but Rozzy merely smiled.
She was sometimes very tired now, and she wanted to be
alone in her apartment more and more.

I was there one night, leafing through an old magazine
and talking to her. She was lying on the bed smoking. "You
shouldn't be doing that," I said. "Bad for the baby, and it's
disgusting."

I was reading, sucked into the deep hynotic pool of
words, when I smelled something burning. I looked over.
Her cigarette was still lit, burning her shirt, forming a growing jagged black hole. I lunged at Rozzy, clapping my
hands down on her chest, over and over, brushing the cigarette off, the ashes. She had a tiny burn over her left breast,
and she looked up at me curiously. "Is Stewey here?" she
said, detached.

"I'll be right back, don't move," I said. "I'll just be in the
kitchen." Rozzy flopped gracelessly onto her side. I clutched
at her purse, thrown into a corner, and went into the
kitchen and dialed information for Leffler's number. But
when I was put through, the nurse curtly told me the doctor
was busy. I didn't care whether Rozzy heard or not, I was
hysterical, incoherent, so much so that the nurse must have
thought I was one of the patients on the verge of suicide,

and so she put me through. I stammered out the story to Leffler.

"What pills?" he said. "I haven't seen her in months."

I fumbled in Rozzy's purse, throwing the candy wrappers, the linty pieces of Kleenex, the untubed lipsticks onto the floor until I found two pill bottles. "But those are old prescriptions," he said angrily. "Who the hell filled those for her? What's the name of that damned drugstore? I'll have them sued." He sighed, exasperated. "How many pills did she take? Count them. Count from both bottles."

I counted, all the time clutching that phone as if it were an artery connecting me to life, to reason, to something safe that could direct me step by step. My fingers seemed dead, they plucked at the pills. I finally got a count.

"Oh Lord," said Leffler. "Why didn't someone in your family call me?"

"She said she was *seeing* you."

He sighed again. "She's pregnant, too. Does she have an obstetrician—but never mind about that, she might not have seen him either. Well, she'll see me now, she has no choice. Can you get her dressed and to St. Elizabeth's in Brighton?"

Questions hammered inside my head, but I was afraid to ask, fearful of knowing. I occupied myself with detail, with pulling Rozzy upright and into a fresh blouse, with calling a cab so I could sit in the back and hold on to her. She looked lazily around her, and when we got to the emergency room, she allowed me to hand her over to a nurse.

I sat in the waiting room, not calling Ben or Bea or David, not knowing any longer how to move or what they might be doing to my sister. It was very late, and I stretched out across three plastic chairs and fell asleep.

CHAPTER TWELVE

It was Leffler who told me that Rozzy's baby was dead inside of her. He introduced himself to me with a frown, saying he had heard many things about me from Rozzy, and that it was a real shame that we had to meet like this, on such an occasion. They had done sonar scans, he said, which showed the fetus was dead, and he had given Rozzy some medication to calm her down, to stop the sounds racing through her head. He had also called Rozzy's obstetrician, getting the name and number from a card in Rozzy's purse, but the doctor said she had only seen Rozzy twice and then had assumed Rozzy had switched doctors. "It happens," she had told Leffler.

Leffler said that the sonar showed the baby was badly deformed. "She was taking powerful drugs," he said. "They went right through the placenta to the fetus." He said he thought that Rozzy's medication had probably depressed the fetal respiration to such an extent that the fetus virtually smothered. "With those deformities, it's a blessing in disguise," he said.

The terrible thing, said Leffler, was that labor would have to be induced. She couldn't go around carrying a dead fetus inside of her. But he was afraid of what labor might do to her just now; he was more concerned with the things she was hearing. "It can wait three or four weeks," he said. "I know of one case, documented in all the books, of this seventy-year-old woman who complained of stomach pains and when she had an X-ray it showed a calcified fetus inside of her. All that time. Imagine." Leffler pulled out a prescription pad and scribbled something. "It doesn't matter what medication she takes now. Someone's going to have to make certain she takes all her medication, that she swallows it and doesn't just stockpile it under her pillow or something. This stuff will make her pretty dopey for a while. All she'll want to do is sleep."

"She can go home then?"

"I don't want her in a hospital. I think it would make her worse. Hire a nurse if you have to, but she'll get better faster in normal surroundings."

"What made her sick?"

He looked at me. "It could have been anything. A chemical reaction in the brain. An event."

"Did you tell her about the baby? Should I?"

"Let's deal with those voices first. I'll want to see her in a week, at my office. Cab her over. The obstetrician will want to see her. She isn't aware right now. She probably won't remember the sonar scan or anything else."

"Should I take her home now?"

"I'd let her sleep out the rest of the night here. Come tomorrow."

Ben took the news very badly. "The baby should have been *perfect*," he railed. He called Leffler up and then the obstetrician and demanded another explanation for what had happened; he even tried to threaten both of them with malpractice suits. The patient way Leffler buffeted his attack angered Ben, the complacent silence of the obstetrician made him bang down the phone in fury. Ben paced the house, he cursed, and after a while, he shifted the blame a bit, put it right back where it had always seemed to rest— on Rozzy.

Bea wept a lot. "In a way," she said, wiping her eyes, "it's good this happened. What would she ever do with a child, a girl alone? Maybe now Stewey will take her back. Someone should contact him." She refused to believe that Stewey had disappeared, that he didn't want to be found. She called information and when they had no listing, she sat down and wrote him a letter in care of the university. When I brought Rozzy home from the hospital, her hair slack and dirty on her neck, her eyes drugged, Bea reached out and stroked Rozzy's hair in a manner Rozzy never would have tolerated had she been aware of it.

My sophomore year was over and I moved back home. I was in constant panicky motion, winding my way from David's to Rozzy and back again. I couldn't stop worrying about how Rozzy would react to her baby's death. I tried to take up smoking, but the cigarettes always made me cough, so I began to simply suck on them, inhaling nothing more dangerous than air. It relaxed me.

Rozzy was too ill to notice Ben's absence, how infrequently he looked in on her. He didn't want her in the house. "It's a drain on you," he told Bea, "and it's not good for Rozzy, either. That girl should be in a hospital, with a nurse. It's ridiculous. You have to siphon out her pills into little cups, you have to stand over her half the time and just watch her."

Bea was fixing up a tray for Rozzy, ladling onion soup into the prettiest bowl she could find, digging out her silver from one of the drawers, and even using a navy damask napkin. "She does not belong in a hospital," said Bea. "Leffler said that would be the worst thing for her, that she's better here." Bea hesitated, and then she filled a wine goblet with orange juice. "He says she's getting better. We may not notice it because she seems so drugged, but she is. He should know. Bess packs her in blankets and gets her there every week."

I was cracking the ice out of the ice cube tray, and I looked up when I heard my name.

"Look at you," said Ben. "Are you her maid? She needs a nurse." He picked up the goblet. "Crystal. She won't even notice. It could be a goddamned Dixie cup."

"Take the tray in to her."

"I'm going to the office."

Bea stopped and looked carefully at him. "She could have other babies someday," she said quietly.

"I used to think she could have anything," said Ben. "I thought she *had* everything." He ran his hand over his face and then straightened. "I won't be home for dinner. I'm working right through it," he said.

Ben wouldn't even step into Rozzy's room. He'd stalk by it and carefully shut the door, and Bea, walking by, would jerk it right open again. Rozzy never knew the difference. When she saw him walking by and shutting her door like that, she assumed he had been sitting with her and was just now leaving. She sometimes thought he had been holding her hand, speaking, but she couldn't remember what he said. Even when I took her to Leffler's, leading her into that familiar brown office and waiting outside, Rozzy seemed to have no sense of time. She would suddenly seem to bolt awake. When Leffler led her back out to me, she would frown at him. "Did I say anything?" she'd demand. He'd take her back inside his office for a minute to tell her, but she'd always forget again.

The whole house was so fragmented that I couldn't wait to see David. As soon as I was in his overheated car, I'd push my hands inside his jacket, into his sweater neck, touching his flesh, feeding on its warmth. Sometimes I made him pull over on some deserted section of road, and we'd climb into the back seat and make love. I wept when I came. "I'm a good lover, aren't I," said David, pleased.

I carried my Nikon everywhere. I would take quick shots when the light was bright enough to do without a flash, at dinner with David where we would swap the camera back and forth to capture each other's image, and at home where the taking of pictures soothed some of the tension. Bea began carrying a tube of lipstick in her pocket and when she spotted me coming toward her, she would flash it out and paint her mouth. Even Rozzy was aware enough to primp a little, although she liked to study her pose in a mirror first before she would grant me permission to shoot. I never bothered developing these posed shots—it was only the candids that interested me.

Rozzy quickly began to get better, began to emerge into the world. She still had no idea her baby was dead, and it was painful to watch her talking to it, patting her stomach and glancing out into space. "You'll take the baby's first pictures," she told me. "Were you this big?" she asked Bea, and Bea fumbled with a dish towel. "You excited about being a grandpa?" she teased Ben, and when he stalked past her, she called after him that she was only kidding, she didn't think he was old at all, not really.

Leffler reduced Rozzy's medication, and she began taking long walks around the neighborhood with me, bundling up in layers of wool and cotton, pulling on heavy boots to tramp down the snow.

She made an appointment to see her obstetrician. I heard her explaining to someone over the phone why she hadn't been in in so long. She had been traveling around the country, she said, and hadn't thought regular visits were needed, and yes, she now realized how stupid she had been. Rozzy even began to see Leffler by herself.

But then, abruptly, her mood changed. She wouldn't get up in the mornings anymore, but lay in bed, her hands dead on her stomach, waiting for Bea to put orange juice into them. She called for Ben to come and talk with her, but he cut her off, and she would shrink down into the covers.

"She needs Stewey," said Bea, but Bea's letters to the university kept boomeranging back, "address unknown" neatly stamped in the corner.

Rozzy asked Ben what was wrong, why wasn't he talking to her; she asked Bea, and she asked me. "Ben's just Ben," I said. It was on a Thursday, when we were walking in Boston, on our way to Leffler's, that Rozzy blurted out, "It's dead, isn't it?"

"What's dead?"

"It doesn't kick inside of me anymore. It doesn't move. When I went to the obstetrician, I saw how it was. All those young silly nurses teasing the mothers-to-be, patting their bellies, asking them if they wanted little boys or little girls, asking about names, giving all kinds of loony advice on things they probably know absolutely nothing about. The nurses don't tease me. They don't ask when it's due or give me one of those baby magazines. The doctor just prods me and takes blood and says she's in touch with Leffler. When I ask her about the baby, she says there's plenty of time for questions later. And Leffler, that bastard, he wants to know everything I think about, and he never asks how I feel about mothering. He just says the baby is something we'll have to talk about very soon."

I wrapped my scarf tighter around my neck.

"That's why Ben hates me, isn't it?" she said.

"You want to sit down somewhere and talk?"

Rozzy looked at me. "If you tell me I'll have lots of other children, I'll scream."

"Will you be OK?"

"Can we take a bus the rest of the way?" she said. "Please?"

We were crowded on the bus. An elderly woman with blued hair noticed Rozzy's swelling stomach and touched her. "Have a seat, honey. You need it more than I do." Rozzy sat down, her smile wobbling, and then she hid her face in her hands. I bent toward her, but the woman tapped me.

"It's always that way when you're pregnant. You should

have seen how I carried on. Don't you worry. It's all perfectly natural."

I reached out my hand and Rozzy convulsively clutched at it, holding tightly to me until we reached our stop, Leffler's, and her truth.

Rozzy accused Leffler of keeping information from her, of being in league with the obstetrician. I was sitting in the waiting room, leafing through a magazine, and I heard her shouting at him, screaming names and insults. When she barged out of his office, her face was gray. She wouldn't talk on the way home, and when the obstetrician called and asked Rozzy to come in so she could explain the procedure of induced labor, Rozzy refused. "I don't want to understand anything," she said flatly, "ever." Rozzy paraded past Ben at night, guzzling Coke from the bottle, eating Fritos.

Rozzy had to check into the hospital a few days later. They gave her a private room, away from the maternity ward, because Leffler was afraid the other mothers, the babies being carted back and forth, would prod Rozzy back into illness. Leffler came in to see her, so did the obstetrician, but Rozzy kept her face stubbornly to the wall.

She had an easy labor. When she came to, she placed her hand on her stomach. It was flat, alien territory instead of flesh.

Rozzy wouldn't allow the baby to be buried. She wouldn't mourn and she wouldn't listen to anyone who tried to talk to her about caskets and tombstones. She wouldn't even give it a name and she didn't want to know its sex. When a nurse, unthinkingly cruel, told Rozzy it had been a little girl and that downy black hair had already sprouted on its tiny head, and that she herself had always considered deformed children "special" children, Rozzy screamed and screamed until they had to give her a sedative. Two orderlies had to pin down Rozzy's flailing arms so the nurse could jab in the shot.

Rozzy gave the baby's body to the medical school, to the medical students to cut into and wonder over. No one said anything to her about it. When Leffler came in to talk to her, she clamped her mouth shut. He sat there beside her bed, leaning against a hard-backed chair, waiting for her to open up. Sometimes he asked her questions, but she remained mute as stone.

Rozzy was in her private room for three days. Bea and I both went to see her. Rozzy slept as much as she could. When she was awake, she panicked, she would immediately squeeze her eyes shut again, blotting everything out.

Bea fiddled with her hands and peered at the other faces that passed by Rozzy's door. Sometimes she got up and wandered around, asking questions of the other people: who were their doctors, what were their problems? She gave sympathy, she offered advice, but when anyone asked about her, she gave a helpless smile and averted her face. She phoned Ben, pleading with him to come and see Rozzy, and when she got off the phone, she wouldn't meet my eyes. She fished out rolls of Life Savers, chewing gum, anything sweet. She was always sucking on something, trying to make it last.

I picked Rozzy up from the hospital when she was ready to come home. She didn't want to see Bea and she didn't want to go back to that house, so we cabbed back to her apartment. She looked listlessly around her and said she wanted to shower and then rest. "You won't go, will you?" she said.

"No, I won't go."

She was in the bathroom for so long that I went after her.

She was sitting in the tub, her head resting on the rim, letting the water massage her, her eyes open and staring. She let me help her up, let me wrap a towel around her and get her into bed, and almost immediately she slept. I called Bea to tell her Rozzy was home and better and that it would be a while before she might want to talk to anyone or see anyone, and then I called David and told him I was staying with Rozzy for a while.

The baby crib was still in the apartment, but when I tried to haul it down the stairs and put it out with the trash, Rozzy balked. "I *want* it," she said fiercely. "You leave it right where it is."

"But Rozzy—" I began, but the look on her face stopped me.

"I just want it here," she said quietly. "I can't explain why."

Rozzy went to see Leffler every day, and gradually, he reduced her medication even more. One day, she came home with two Siamese cats, one tucked under each arm. "I couldn't resist," she said sheepishly. "This girl had them in a brown box on Newbury Street and I just bent down and scooped the last two of them up in my arms and brought them back."

Rozzy loved those cats. She named them Litter and Box, interchanging the names at will. I photographed them for her and blew the pictures up into poster-sized prints, which she hung on her wall. She dragged the two of them into bed with her at night, rubbing them into submission. They were not really friendly cats; when I bent to pat one, it bit me and then hissed, arching its back. Rozzy never bothered to buy cat food, but let them eat the remains from her own plate, feeding them Chinese food and Italian food, making them international animals. The only time I ever saw her get angry with the cats was when they both got into the baby crib. Their cries were human. Rozzy grabbed them by the scruff of their necks and flung them to the floor, where the cats indifferently washed their paws and stretched. "They have no right to sound like that," said Rozzy, "no damn right at all."

Rozzy sometimes just listlessly sat in her apartment, staring. "You know what?" she said, sputtering suddenly, starting to laugh. "I should go back and ask for that fetus, for that clot of blood and life, and put it in my old museum." She rubbed at her eyes, starting to cry. "How's that for an artifact of existence?" She bunched over, hiding her face. "That's really funny, isn't it?" she said.

She picked up Litter and buried her face in the cat's fur. Litter yowled, and pounced down on the floor, zipping into another room, ignoring Rozzy's baleful yearning.

The more Rozzy brooded over what had happened to her, the more she began to dislike the cats. She plunked them deliberately into the baby crib to keep them in one place. It bothered her when she didn't know where they were. She began imagining that they were going to jump on her face at night and smother her, and she began to dread going to sleep, putting it off until her eyes were lidded with iron and drooping despite her. Rozzy got so obsessive that any kind of fur began to bother her. We went shopping one day and Rozzy let the saleslady, a pushy middle-aged woman with stiff yellow hair, talk her into trying on a mink coat. As soon as she felt that fur on her skin, she panicked. She let the coat slide right off her shoulders onto the dirty floor and then she was running out of Bonwit's, swinging her purse, banging it against her thighs as she ran.

I got rid of the cats for her, the same way she had found them. Everyone liked Siamese cats and they were easy to dispose of. I sat in the park and waited and, soon enough, two young kids ambled by, holding hands, and took the cats.

Rozzy thought about Stewey again. She even tried to call him. "His line is disconnected," she told me, painting her toenails with bright red polish. She shook her head, concentrating on her big toe, licking it with red, like blood. "He could be anywhere," she said. "He could even have another woman friend. But he'll have to contact me when he wants a formal divorce, won't he? I'll get to talk with him then." She was very calm, and I sat down and watched her meticulously daubing at her toenails with Q-tips, swiping up the excess polish. She looked up at me. "Who wants him anyway?" she said. She reached forward and suddenly flung the bottle of polish across the room, spilling red globules of shimmering scarlet on the wall across from her. I jerked up, but she thrust out her hand. "Don't. Don't you dare clean it," she said. "I want it that way."

She stood, half her toenails bright red. "I want you to go. I want to stay here by myself."

"I'm staying."

Her shoulders tilted forward. "No, I'll call you if I need you. I promise. Now, please, please, just go."

So I left. But it was lonely without Rozzy, without Stewey's phone calls marking out the time for me, and I began to cling to David a little. "Oh God," said Rozzy when I told her I spent most of my time with David.

"I could move back with you," I said, but she shook her head. I made Rozzy a big blue sign with David's phone number scribbled on it in white paint and had her tape it by her phone, telling her to call anytime she wanted me.

She did call, at all hours, jangling us awake at dawn, at midnight, nine seconds before the alarm at eight. Sometimes she was having nightmares, other times she just wanted to talk. A few times she was so hysterical I would have to get up and have David drive me to her place. He held my hand in the car, claiming a kiss for himself before I leaped up, before I gave myself up to Rozzy. There was never that much terribly wrong. Rozzy was lonely; she wanted someone to share hot chocolate with. I couldn't be angry with her for long, not when those really were the best times, when we could giggle and talk and loosen up like when we were kids.

Rozzy phoned me at David's more and more. She would never speak with David himself, except to curtly spit out my name. If I wasn't there, she would snap down the receiver, cutting him off. She disliked him so much that when I was at her place and she answered her own phone, she would wait, silently, until a voice identified itself. If it was David, she handed the phone to me, still mute. David tried with her. He'd blurt out on the phone, "Why don't you like me? What did I ever do to you?" but she simply hung up on him.

"Can't you be civil?" I pleaded with Rozzy. "I really like him."

"I don't," said Rozzy.

"But why not?"

She shrugged.

"You could at least be polite," I said, but she bent over, humming some pop tune under her breath.

I spoke with Bea a few times. She never discussed Ben, but she did want to see Rozzy. "Can't I take the two of you to lunch, my treat? You talk to your sister, she won't listen to me."

When I spoke to Rozzy, she balked. "Why should I have lunch with her?"

"She loves you."

"Oh, come *on*," said Rozzy bitterly.

"Please. Just do it. Get it over with, otherwise you know she's just going to nag and nag and never let up. Please."

Rozzy set the phone in my lap. "You call," she said, "but I don't want to go out. We can eat here. I'll dump something together."

Bea came for lunch two days later, dressed in a bright green suit, carrying a bunch of red roses wrapped in a blue wax cone. "What a nice place," she said. She handed me the flowers and a brown bag of groceries she had bought, despite my insisting that we were handling lunch. "Oh, you can always use extras," said Bea mildly. She hugged Rozzy, one hand trying to lean Rozzy's head onto her shoulder, but Rozzy jerked back from her.

We ate in the living room, facing the windows, all the food on paper plates because Rozzy refused to do dishes. "Everything tastes marvelous," said Bea brightly.

"It's just mushroom quiche and it's no big deal."

"Well, it is to me," said Bea, "so there." She kept up a shiny patter of conversation, never mentioning the baby or Ben, but encouraging Rozzy to think about going back to school.

Bea got up and served us more food, until Rozzy had to cover her plate with her hands. Bea fussed and took the plates and dumped them in the trash, and while she bustled, Rozzy and I exchanged glances. Bea called out that she was going to "look around," and she was silent for so long that I got up to drag her back in. She wasn't in the kitchen, but was in the bedroom, staring at the white baby crib, her hands planted on its sides. She looked helplessly at me. "Come on, Bea," I said. "Rozzy's waiting." I pivoted, listening for her footsteps following me.

Bea didn't stay long after that. There wasn't much to do. She didn't like sitting around, she kept perching by the window sills and looking out. Conversation dwindled until the three of us were lost in our own hazy dreams. "Well," said Bea, glancing at her watch, "I'd best be getting home and seeing to Ben."

"How is he?" I said, ignoring Rozzy's darting glance.

"Oh, you know," she said. "Next time, lunch is on me, darlings."

When she left, Rozzy stood by the window and looked down at her, at the green fleck getting into the car, moving away and disappearing. "That ought to hold her," she said.

It was a week later that Rozzy made her decision. She would go back to school, in Texas, and she began applying. Occasionally, when she was plowing through catalogs that had come through the mail, she would look up at me and ask wistfully about Stewey. "He loved me, don't you think?" she said.

My junior year began, and Rozzy began coming to classes with me. She was bored with sitting around the apartment. We left everything up to chance. If she came to a class, she came, if she didn't, she didn't, but she was almost always there, settled into a seat, holding a place for me. She copied my schedule and tacked it to her wall and learned where the buildings were located. She always sat in the front and she became angry when kids talked. She'd turn right around and shush them, she'd grab cigarettes from lazy hands, take a puff and put the cigarette back, ignoring the aghast looks. The professors loved her. She was alert, she asked questions, she shamed everyone with her restless mind. She led discussions, and no one, except for me and for Rozzy, knew she was not a student.

She not only did the reading, but she did the papers, too. I'd put my papers off, spending afternoons at David's, reading his magazines while he studied. "I can't work with you about, it's too distracting," I'd tell him. Meanwhile, Rozzy would be furiously typing on a rented machine, the windows in her apartment thrown open, catapulting the jammering sound out into the street. She wanted grades. "Can't you put your name to it?" she said. "No, I guess you can't. Would they grade it if I asked?"

She went around to all my professors. One coldly told

her she was freeloading and he didn't want to see her in his class again. She had to bite her lip to stop from crying, and it tore, bleeding, staining her chin. Only two professors agreed to grade her papers, and they were delighted by such initiative. I felt humbled. In my lecture classes, where I was one of two hundred, the professors knew Rozzy by name.

It surprised me when Rozzy started applying to technical schools. "God, you're so bright, go to regular college," I told her.

"There's too much pressure," she said.

"What do you think you're coping with now?"

"This is different," she said. "You never saw me the way I was at school."

"What way, how were you?"

"I don't want to talk about it," she said.

Rozzy always came to class. On the day of an exam, she would set her alarm and race to class. One day, David's alarm broke and I woke up late. I flung a dress over my head and ran barefooted to the car. I stumbled into the class an hour late and grabbed an exam. It wasn't until the exam was over that I noticed the angry stinging burn of my feet, the terrified stare Rozzy was giving me. I walked back to the car leaning on her shoulders. When I got home, David rubbed my feet and set them in a pan of cool water while I wept in self-pity and pain.

In addition to her schoolwork, Rozzy went through a book a day. She prowled the bookshops, there was nothing she wouldn't read—a cereal box, a TV listing, a novel. She carried paperbacks with her, and when she finished with a book, she left it on mailboxes, on doorsteps in Beacon Hill, in an empty shopping cart at the supermarket. "Someone else will pick it up and read it now," she said, "someone who might not have ever thought to buy it." She used to revisit the places where she left her books. If the books were still there, she would move them to another place, but usually they were gone, and that always put her in a good mood for the rest of the day. In fact, she was in a good mood more and more now, and for a while I thought everything was fine.

CHAPTER THIRTEEN

Bea began calling me. At first, she never mentioned Ben.
She simply nagged at me about why I never came home.
"You and that sister of yours," she said, "you always do just
what you damn please. So independent. You've always been
a problem."

"What are you talking about?"

"Isn't that nice, two daughters less than ten minutes
away, and I have to make an appointment to see them."

"Bea, come on, what's the big deal? It's not as if I'm
forty miles away."

"Forty miles, four seconds, what's the difference, you
were always unreachable."

"OK, I'm hanging up."

"Wait," said Bea, "it's Ben."

She unwove the story. Ben hadn't said much when Rozzy
gave her baby away to the medical school, but it did something to him, it changed him. He began narrowing his life,
closing up his outlets; and at the same time his mind was
shrinking, his flesh was expanding. It was suddenly as if
he had never been a gourmet, had never been health-con-
scious. *Prevention* magazine slapped uselessly into the house,
his stockpile of vitamins grew stale and impotent on the
shelves. He never checked labels on cans anymore. He'd

come home from shopping balancing four heavy bags in his arms and would set them down on the table for Bea to sort.

She said she couldn't stand it. He had boxes of cheese crisps, cans of Spam and deviled chicken, packets of soup and bags of frozen peas. At breakfast she would find him teasing his omelet with a fork, giving it up to eat Fruit Loops straight out of the box. "What is it?" she begged him, but he just glanced at her and went back to his cereal.

He wouldn't mention Rozzy at all. "Let's go visit," she kept saying to him, but he always had work, he always had to be in court, he never once said simply that no, he didn't want to go.

"I could have gone to see Rozzy by myself," said Bea, "I know that, but there was something about Ben that scared me. I was afraid to leave him alone in the house, afraid he might need me. Evenings I knitted in the living room, some tasteless ragged-looking sweater I would probably never even wear. I didn't have the patience to knit well, and when I dropped a stitch, I clumsily knitted it back up. I kept hearing music from Ben's study—Bach—but his door was shut against me. One evening I knitted for an hour and then went into Ben's study to ask him if he'd like to see a film. His desk was clean of work, and he was asleep, snuffling into a pillow on the couch." She had shut the door, a shiver of irritation running through her. She sat up by herself very late that night, looking out of the picture window at the suburbs and idly rubbing one finger against her wedding band.

She said she began watching him, waiting for him to speak to her. He stopped reading and came home with a little Sony TV, no bigger than a hat box, and every single night he propped it onto his stomach and watched whatever was flickering on. "I hear the worst kind of drivel from that set," Bea told me, "the talk shows, the movies, and he never shows any response at all, not a laugh or a snort or a burp out of him, and at twelve, he snaps it off."

She wanted the old Ben back. She saw him disappearing, swallowed up by pounds, as invisible as Jonah in the belly of his whale. But she wasn't sure how to go about getting him back. One day, she ran around Boston buying fresh basil from a little Italian store in the North End, dodging the little old women in their shapeless black dresses. She bought pesto from someone who yammered Italian at her, and she peered into a live lobster tank and pointed a finger at a green one scuttling toward the back.

"Dinner that night took me five hours to prepare," Bea said. She cringed when she took the lobster out of the paper carton they had boxed it in. It was still alive, and although its claws were pegged shut, she was afraid. She set it on the table, fearful it would slide off, and went to fetch a pot. She didn't have a pot big enough, wide enough, she couldn't find anything in which to boil this poor sea creature alive. She flipped through her Julia Child. You could slice them, she found, could sever the spinal cord in one neat move for a quick and easy death. The book even said it was more humane to do it that way, and at least she wouldn't have to hear the creature rattling against the sides of the pot as it boiled. Bea went and got her butcher knife that Ben had specially ordered for her one year, and with one hand she carefully positioned the lobster on its back on the table. She felt as if she were officiating at some sacrifice. She sliced, and the lobster moved. But it didn't die. She looked at the knife. Bea had to slice that lobster four times before it died, bludgeoning it, murdering it. She got it into a baking dish and into the oven, but she had lost all her taste for eating it.

Bea made a stew with the pesto, a salad with a mustard dressing, small green onion tarts, and for dessert a chocolate mousse spiked with brandy. She set the table with her best linen cloth and her silver that she almost never used and the carved wooden animal napkin holders from Africa. There was even candlelight.

That evening, though, Ben ate silently, using his fork as a shovel, dripping lemon butter sauce from the lobster onto the tablecloth. When he was through, he put the flat of his hand on the table and pushed himself up, and with a start, Bea saw him, saw how he was. His hair was graying and pulling away from his skull, his belly protruded against his shirt, and his eyes focused on nothing.

"I told him to talk to me," said Bea, "to wait, not to go. He only patted me on the shoulder and said he had some work to do. He went into the den and I could hear that damn Sony clicking on, that damn brackish canned laughter assaulting me."

Mornings, she got up and ran, hoping to shame him, but he stayed in bed, and by the time she got back, exhausted, her hair damp and slick against her back, he was gone. She continued to plot. One evening, for his dinner, she bought the cheapest kind of TV dinner she could find, roaming up and down the frozen foods section of the supermarket. She had always avoided these aisles, and her cart began to look just like the carts of the women she and Ben used to mock and pity, women with pink sponge rollers twisted in their hair, women with tight doubleknit red pants pulling at the seams over their spreading rears. Well, if this was the stuff Ben chose to snack on, she reasoned, let him have a feast of it, a whole dinner, see how he liked it then. She bought a loaf of soft white bread and a three-course spaghetti dinner with peas and tomato soup, and apple crisp for dessert. She bought one stick of white oleomargarine. She felt vaguely embarrassed at the checkout stand, and kept looking around for people who might know her. Bea dipped her head. She wanted to apologize to the girl ringing up her order.

"I couldn't bear to cook the stuff," Bea told me. "I turned my face away and breathed through my mouth when I had to peel off the foil to pop the TV dinner into the oven." She knew the spaghetti would look like white worms, that the peas would have a faint perfumy odor, a gangrenous color. She certainly didn't intend to eat this stuff herself, so she made a *salade Niçoise*, cut up some cheese, and uncorked some wine, setting it out to breathe.

Ben sat down to dinner without even looking at her. She handed him a plate with two soft white slices of bread, smeared with oily margarine. At his place was a can of iced tea. She put the TV dinner out in front of him, still in its compartmentalized tin. Ben never even noticed that he wasn't eating what she was; she sipped good wine instead of sweetened tea. He polished everything off in ten minutes, then he got up and went into Rozzy's old room to watch TV. She got up and followed him, leaning in the doorway.

"He didn't even hear me say his name," Bea told me. "I had to repeat it, and when he finally looked up, I asked him if we could take a vacation, go to France. 'What for?' he said. I asked him if he would like to go riding—and you know I hate riding, hate the smell of the horses, the way the damn leather saddle rubs me raw. He said he didn't want to go riding, and then he very politely asked me to shut the door when I left. The worst is," she said, sighing, "that today at work, he collapsed. They took him to the hospital and when I got there, some young punk doctor was yelling at Ben about high blood pressure and diet. I swear you wouldn't know your father anymore. He's ballooned right up there and apparently he's taken his blood pressure right along with him." She was very quiet for a minute and then she asked me if I could get home for the weekend.

"He won't want to see me," I said.

"It's not for him."

"I don't think Rozzy will come."

"That's OK," she said. "That would make it worse."

When I told Rozzy, she said, "So Ben's sick, probably a vitamin thing, or just in his mind."

"Don't be mean," I said. "If you need to get me, you can call. Or if you feel uncomfortable, call David and he'll call me."

"I can take care of myself," she said coldly. "What time are you leaving?"

When I got home, Bea was in the front yard, crouched down, pruning the low green bushes by the side of the house. It would be snowing in a month or two, and the green would be powdered white until it disappeared altogether. Seeing her gave me a queer fishy feeling. She had cut her hair short, had styled it into two stiff wings on either side of her head, making her look as if she might take flight any moment. When she saw me, she fingered her hair defensively. "Does it look funny?" she said. "I had it done today." She stood up and hugged me. "Why don't you come home more often? What's the matter with you?"

"Why did you cut it?" I couldn't get used to how she looked. Her eyes were smaller, her face more lined. She suddenly seemed like someone else's mother, a little used.

"It was Elizabeth Arden who cut it, not me," she said. "I wanted a drastic change, and they kept thrusting pictures at me of all these gorgeous young models with short hair."

"But you've always had long hair."

She dusted some dirt from her hands onto her jeans. She had on an old flannel shirt of Ben's with one fraying sleeve, and she wore no makeup. "Actually, baby, it was for Ben, to shake him up. I sat in that chair and I cried when they clipped it. I wouldn't let any of it touch their floor. They had to line the whole area around me with tissue paper, and then they had to wrap up all the hair they cut and give

it to me to take home. My head feels so funny now, so light."
She shook it for a moment. "Ben didn't say anything. He
just looked at me and then at the tail of hair in my hands and
said that whatever I did was fine by him." She fingered her
hair. "It feels so odd," she said. She stared off into space,
teasing the wisps with her fingers. "I want it back," she
said suddenly.

"I love you," I said.

"Why, baby," she laughed, "I love you, too. Let's go
inside and see Ben." She turned around again. "I look fine,
don't I?"

"You don't look like Rozzy anymore."

She laughed. "Why should I?" she said.

Seeing Ben was even more of a shock. He was bloated,
shuffling, stopping in the hallway to lean one leaden foot
heavily in front of the other. "Bess," he said, patting my
shoulder. I leaned forward to kiss him. His cheek was
papery and dry.

We all sat in the living room. Ben began chain smoking,
not even half finishing a cigarette before he stabbed it out
and lighted another. "When did you start smoking?" I
asked him, but he only shrugged. Bea kept removing the
ashtrays, setting them up high on the mantel, and when he
lighted yet another cigarette, she snatched it from his hand
and tossed it out the door. While she was throwing it out,
he flicked the ashes from a new cigarette behind the couch.
He took the raisins from the candy dish and dumped them
on the table, and used the dish as his new ashtray. "Jesus,
Ben," said Bea, coming back in, but he looked at her as if
she were addressing someone else, someone he didn't know.

It wasn't funny. I knew it wasn't funny, but sometimes
it's those unfunny things that get you going. I had struck
a laughing vein and I began nervously giggling. It was like

all those times at the dinner table when Rozzy and I were young and for no reason at all one of us would erupt into giggles and start the other one off. Our sides would stitch up, we couldn't eat without spattering our food on the tablecloth. Ben used to send us away from the table, banishing us to our room. He was looking at me now, as I stuttered over my laughter, but he wasn't enraged as he once would have been, he was merely disinterested.

"How's Rozzy, the poor thing?" said Bea.

Ben stubbed out his cigarette and lighted another.

I choked on a snort of laughter. "In the spring, she wants to go off to school."

"I wish she'd take up with Stewey again," sighed Bea. "He loved her, didn't he? I always liked him." She squinted at me. "What on earth is the matter with you? Is there something funny that I should know about?"

Ben suddenly straightened up. "And what are *your* plans, Bess, what are you going to do with *your* life?"

The laughter stopped, frozen inside of me. "I like taking photographs," I said slowly. "I want to be a photographer."

"That's a hobby, not a vocation," he said evenly. "What am I paying all this money for? First it was art, now it's something else. If you want to be a photographer, fine, be one. I'm not paying for grad school in something like that. I'm responsible only until you finish being an undergraduate." His face was bruised with blood. Bea got up and put a hand on his shoulder.

"I'm going to bed," he said abruptly. "I have court tomorrow." He left the room. Bea looked curiously at her hands. "I used to have such nice hands," she said. "Now look at them, my skin is so cracked and lined. I remember my mother's hands looking like this."

We didn't stay up very long. Bea was suddenly silent and the only other thing to do besides watching television was to go to sleep. It felt funny being in my old room, sleep-

ing in my old bed. It didn't feel like it belonged to me anymore. It didn't even smell like it used to, the old familiar
combination of inexpensive perfume and the dimestore
makeup that used to rub off on the sheets. I lay in bed and
looked around the room, but I couldn't sleep.

The house was silent. I blinked at the darkness, for a
moment drifting into the past, when Rozzy was in the room
beside me, when the thought of her could comfort me to
sleep. I threw off the covers and pulled on a robe, and went
into the kitchen for a piece of ice to cool my thoughts.

Ben was straddling a chair, eating an enormous chicken
sandwich, sloppy slices of red tomato oozing out of the
sides. Beside him, on the kitchen table, was a carton of
vanilla ice cream with a spoon jabbed into it. Ben gave me
a sharp look. "Go back to bed," he said, spooning some ice
cream into a dish. I got myself a clean glass and filled it
with water and sat down beside him. "You'll have nightmares eating that," I told him, but he simply nodded at me,
and picked up his ice cream and his sandwich and padded
out of the kitchen. I sat sipping my water until I had drained
the glass, and then I went back to bed, passing by Rozzy's
old room, where Ben was sprawled on the couch, an old
yellow army blanket thrown over him, his feet sticking out,
bare and enormous. He didn't notice me and continued
sucking the ice cream from his spoon.

In the morning, though, Ben was sleeping on the living
room couch, the same tatty army blanket tossed over him.
I showered and when I came out, Bea was whirring something in the blender and Ben was gone. "Don't ask me where
he went," said Bea, "but I have to be out of here in an hour
to go and get something done to my hair."

"I thought you just had it cut yesterday," I said. "What's
wrong with it?"

Bea fussed with the feathery ends. "I don't know. *Something*." She put out two glasses and poured me some orange liquid. "Orange juice and strawberries," she said, sitting down beside me. "You know, I think it really threw your father having you sleeping in your old room like that. Usually it's one of his nightly stops. Don't look so surprised. He sleeps in at least four different places each night." She heaved a sigh. "God," she said, "God, *God*.

"You know, he wouldn't even see a doctor at first. I had to threaten him with divorce; I even had to contact a lawyer, one of his associates, in fact, so he'd know I was serious. So he went to a doctor and got this special diet, but what good does it do? Just look in his pockets—candy wrappers, pretzels, cigarettes. If I scream that he's killing himself, that he's killing me, he's still untouched. He goes to work and he comes home and he eats."

Bea began to bustle, getting ready to leave. "You want to come? Get a pretty new haircut?"

The front door slapped shut. "Ben," she said.

"I think I'll hang around," I said.

I heard the TV snap on, the blur of voices. "I'll be back in about two hours or so, depending on what they do."

"Don't come back a blond," I said.

"Now, that's an idea," she said, rushing out the back door.

I waited a bit and then I went and changed into cut-offs and a sweatshirt. It was warm enough to go running. I followed the murmur of voices until I threaded my way to Ben.

"Come run with me," I said, kicking off the TV with a sneakered foot.

"I don't run anymore. Turn that back on."

"So we'll walk. Come on. Please."

He looked up at me.

"I want to do something *with* you," I said.

Ben stretched, then he stood up and rummaged around in the closet for his old expensive running shoes. He had once been able to bend straight from the waist and tie his shoes, but now he had to sit down, a movement that had neither grace nor style.

He was cheerful at first. We walked, and I was jittery with energy. I wanted to sprint ahead and race until I was out of breath, but instead I slowed my steps to match my father's. We held the kind of pace lovers keep, even and steady and long, or maybe it was more the pace of old people. We didn't talk and by the third block, Ben began to pant. His feet stuttered on the small stones seeded along the walk. "This is ridiculous," he said.

"One more block and then we'll turn," I said, but Ben started to cough, a sharp hacking ripping from his chest, and he waved me back. He hunched into his coat and then turned back to the house. He stopped coughing, and stood a little straighter, but he continued homeward.

I ran. As fast as I could, away from Ben, away from the house, eating up the curving blocks with each step of my feet, retracing the routes Rozzy and I used to prowl, sweating and panting. A collie dog bounded out of his grassy yard and nipped at my heels, keeping pace with me for a few more blocks before another dog claimed his interest.

I was dripping with sweat when I started back and my thighs hurt, my feet burned. The first thing I heard when I got back into the house was the TV. Ben was in the room, staring at the blinking images in front of him, his running shoes thrown back into the greedy mouth of the closet. He didn't look up.

I showered again, and then read magazines until Bea came home, her hair a bit shorter, the wings gone. "Better?" she said self-consciously.

"Better," I said.

Ben stayed in that room watching the TV all evening, and when it was dinner time Bea brought him in a tray.

Every few minutes I looked up at the clock, wading through the hours until I could go back to school. Bea and I ate in the dining room, a quiche she made and some red wine, and she chattered about the weather, about the freaky high and low temperatures, the sudden dips. "It makes people funny," she said. "One minute they're smiling, loosening up their collars, shedding jackets, lolling on the streets—the next, they're ready to bite your neck in two."

We both went to bed early. I didn't night-walk. I could hear Ben padding around the house, opening and closing the freezer. I could see the thin slice of light from the kitchen. I lay in bed and wished on one of those stars Rozzy had always wanted to paste up on the ceiling.

I was the last one up the next morning. Ben was already out of the house and Bea was taking chocolate cookies out of the oven. "I thought you'd like some to take back with you," she said. She had a streak of flour on her neck. "I got up at five to make these."

"You didn't have to do that."

"Couldn't sleep," she said apologetically.

I waited around for Ben, to say my good-byes, to tell him that I hoped he felt better, that I was glad to have seen him, but he didn't return. "He might not come back until midnight," said Bea. "He gets that way. There's nothing you can do about it. I can tell him good-bye for you."

Bea drove me home around six. "Do you think Rozzy would ever come home to visit?" she said.

"Maybe."

Bea swerved around a stone in the road. "At least you didn't say never," she said, attempting a smile.

I phoned Rozzy that night and told her about Ben, about Bea. "They were always that way," she said slowly, "forever dying like that. I always noticed it. Only you didn't see."

It was Monday again, and class, and I had three minutes to get to the lecture hall. It was a five-minute walk that wound all the way around several buildings, a walk made even longer by the snaking crush of students. I hated being late, so I decided to skip class and hang around the student union. I had a friend who worked the information desk there; she gave out student phone numbers and addresses, whiling away the boredom by knitting scarves for almost everyone she knew. When I walked into the union, she waved at me and called that there was someone looking for me, that she had given my number.

"Male or female?" I said, pulling up a chair. "Female, I bet."

"Unhunh. This one was male."

"What did he look like?"

She shrugged. "Jeez, I don't remember. Blond, I think."

I didn't give it much thought. I sat and talked for a while longer, then started home. It was probably someone in one of my classes looking for notes from a class he had missed, or it was a friend of David's who wanted me for something. As soon as I got inside the apartment, I headed for the shower, but the water pressure was down, and I felt irritable. I washed my hair and thought about dinner.

I didn't get a phone call until the next day, just as I was dashing out the door to class. I yanked up the receiver. "Yeah—"

"I'm here," said a voice. "I need to see you."

"Stewey?" I shut the door and sat on the floor, leaning my back against the wall. "Oh God, you're *here*."

I couldn't talk on the phone, not when he was in the same city. We made immediate plans to meet at the Blue Parrot in Cambridge. We would talk then.

Stewey was already seated by the time I got there. He

stood up, smiling, and I wrapped my arms around him, buried my face against his shoulder, wanting to weep, to shout, to never let go of him. "God, I *missed* you," I said.

Stewey pulled back, tilting my chin up. "You know, you're still the second most beautiful girl around."

"The second?" I said, and we both sat down.

"Well," he said, grabbing my hand between the two of his.

"Well," I said. "Where's Rozzy? She must be delirious."

Stewey's face clouded. "I haven't seen her yet."

"What?"

"I was afraid to call her, afraid she might hang up when she heard my voice. I knew you'd see me, though, that you'd tell me how she was." He ran his hands through his twisted black curls. "I slept in the union last night on a couch in the back. No one bothered me." He looked at me. "I'm scared, Bess. Maybe Rozzy thinks I died along with the baby. I know about that, about how it happened. She wrote me letters. I got them all. She never said she wanted me back in any of them though. I tried to read between the lines, to find any trace of loneliness or need. That's all it would have taken, but all she ever wrote about were the general things—there was never any emotion. I don't know if she wants anyone anymore, if she wants to see me or not. Not now."

"She wants to see you."

"I still love her," he said helplessly.

"I wasn't sure whether she was writing you regularly," I said, "but Stewey, I know she wants to see you. I know it."

"Will you come with me?"

"You know I will."

"Wait, don't get up. Not yet. I have to—you know—feel *ready*. Can't we just sit here and talk for a bit? I haven't seen you in so long."

"Sure."

"It was funny how I got the letters from her. Madison has a terribly thorough post office. Although I left no forwarding address, a guy who works sorting the mail remembered me. Actually, he always had this crush on Rozzy. He used to save the prettiest stamps for her, he'd even tell people who specifically asked for special stamps that he was out, just so he would have more to give Rozzy. He wanted to see her face when he planted them in her hand. She got so excited, just like a little kid. Anyway, he knew I was an architecture student because he used to kid Rozzy about marrying me when she could have married someone with a never-ending supply of stamps. When he saw her name, her jangled handwriting, he put the letters aside, he wouldn't brand them with that 'address unknown' sticker —not Rozzy's letters. He reasoned that if Rozzy were writing me there, I must be somewhere in Madison, and sooner or later I'd have to come in and buy stamps. I wasn't in school. I was living in a tiny place, working on my thesis, and when I did come into the post office it was to mail a package to my mother. This guy handed me the letters, glaring at me as if I were some criminal or something. When I saw Rozzy's name, I wanted to throw those letters out, but that guy was watching me. I could just see him swooping down on those letters and reading them himself, and I didn't want that. As it was, he was asking me all kinds of questions—where was Rozzy? why had she left so suddenly? were we still married? I fielded them and left.

"I took those letters home and ripped them up, still tucked in those awful strawberry-scented envelopes Rozzy seemed to like. Then I stood there and looked at the pieces scattered on the floor, a paper storm. I went and got the scotch tape and sat on the floor and taped those letters together again. God, you have no idea how long that took, how much it hurt. I strained my eyes. I had headaches the size of North America. It took me days to do it."

"You never called," I said. I fiddled with my chocolate drink, staring into it.

"I couldn't. I couldn't respond to anyone. But I had to see what she had written. I thought she was lying when she wrote about the baby, that it had died." He sipped his chocolate, his hands quaked. "You know, my friends were delighted when she left, isn't that funny?" She'd always been so sullen with them, but really, she was just shy. And there was something else, too. After she left, my friends came to me with all these stories about her. They'd tell me about when they had seen her nuzzling some strange man, when they spotted her accepting roses from a boy who kissed her." He sank deeper into his chair, so I reached out and hooked my little finger around his. He gave me a watery quick grin. "No one came right out and said they had seen her go into a hotel or anything, but they hinted. I kept getting these dinner invitations, too, and sometimes I would go just because I couldn't bear being alone in my place. Without Rozzy, my oxygen was missing. So I'd go to these things and there would always be some girl there, someone really pretty, very bright and stable and interesting, and just not Rozzy at all." He unhooked his finger and downed the last of the chocolate. "Who the hell *needs* this?" he said.

"I went back to the post office once more, but there were no more letters. The guy wanted to know how Rozzy was, he assumed I had fixed things up, so I lied. I made him happy and told him Rozzy was fine. I couldn't stand it. Without her letters, I didn't know how she was, if she was even alive or not. Who was listening to her voices the way I had, coaxing her, prodding her, loving her?" He sighed. "That's the bottom line. I love her. Do you think I'm a fool? That I'm ridiculous? My friends do."

"No, I think you're wonderful."

"OK, I'm ready to go see her."

Stewey had parked his familiar green Chevy on a side street. "It took forever driving here," he said, "and you know, I was glad. I needed the time. I think it relaxed me." The whole ride over, Stewey slumped over the steering wheel. "What's wrong?" I said, but he only shook his head at me.

When we got to Rozzy's, he stood outside her door, rocking on his heels. "Well, *knock*," I said, "go ahead."

"Fuck," he said, "fuck," and then he knocked, jittering on his feet.

Rozzy pulled the door open, tousled and sleepy, in nothing but a blue T-shirt that said that Danskins were made for dancing. She was holding a red hot water bottle over her belly, and she rubbed one lazy foot over the other, extending her toes into a fan.

"Is the missus in?" said Stewey, his face pained and white.

Rozzy blinked and then she began crying. He immediately pulled her toward him, outside on her porch, and the two of them wrapped themselves up into one tangle of arms and legs.

"You're *here!*" cried Rozzy. "Oh God, everyone has to come inside and help me wake up. I'll make coffee. Come on, Bess, you're part of everyone, aren't you?"

We all sat on Rozzy's dusty wood floor, sipping instant coffee from cracked blue mugs, grabbing cookies from the box. "When do we leave?" said Rozzy, breathlessly looking from Stewey to me. "I can be ready in two minutes." She put her coffee down and hooked her arms around Stewey, twisting her body around him like a cat. She kept sniffing at his shirt, burying her nose into the crook of his elbow, into his damp warm neck, into his hair, inhaling him, letting her breath out only when she could hold it—and him—no longer. He grinned at her, pleased, and stroked her hair. "Whatever you want, I'll do, anything, anything," she said.

He crouched over her and kissed the top of her head. "Was it very rough?" he said.

Something flickered in her face. "We can talk about that later," she said, "but not now. Please. I just want to feel that you're really here."

"I'm not going anywhere," said Stewey, and Rozzy relaxed.

"Uh, I think I should, though," I said, standing clumsily, separating myself.

"No, not yet," said Rozzy.

"We should all celebrate tonight," said Stewey emphatically, "the three of us, like old times. Sit down, Bess, come on."

"I even have some special things we can wear," said Rozzy, leaping up, returning with two red velvet dresses she had plundered from Cambridge thrift shops, and a top hat which she popped on Stewey's shiny curls.

We paraded in Boston that night, hooking arms, prancing on the sidewalks, winding in and out of bookshops and cafés, taking the eating tour of all the old familiar streets. Rozzy was exuberant with energy, she shimmied as she walked, and she couldn't stop beaming. She lit up the faces we passed; strangers would stop to watch her slip past them, a flash of quicksilvery warmth.

"I want it to always be like this," said Rozzy, "you and me and Bess."

She wouldn't let me go back to David's that night, but insisted that I camp out on her living room floor. "But you and Stewey should be alone," I stammered. "You should talk."

"We'll be alone," said Rozzy. "We'll be in another room altogether. Stewey doesn't mind, do you?"

"Do you, Stewey?" I said, my eyes probing his face.

"Now what kind of a question is that?" he said. "I thought you knew me, Bess."

When I phoned David to tell him I wouldn't be coming home to his place that evening, he became morose and sulky.

"Rozzy needs me to be here," I said.

"I guess it's unavoidable," he said gloomily. "What's the problem this time?"

"No problem," I said.

"Well, you call me if you feel blue."

"OK," I said, already turning from the phone.

We all became hermits in that apartment. I skipped classes and even Rozzy forgot her papers and her books that were lying open around the apartment, their pages inked up. We sealed up our existences in that place, emerging only at night. The old familiar triad was rebuilt, and if there was a question of privacy being intruded upon, then it was *our* privacy that might be invaded, and not just that of Rozzy and Stewey. I felt no guilt about David. He was used to my absences.

"We've got to start clean this time," Rozzy decided. "Everything we ever blamed one another for, we'll write down on strips of paper and then we'll burn them in the gas flame, a ritual cleansing." We sat on the kitchen floor and tore up strips of cheery yellow paper and then scribbled "blames" on the strips with colored Flair pens. We balled the strips up and then ceremoniously dumped them, one by one, into the licking blue and red flames of the stove. "This will probably screw up the stove, but who cares?" said Rozzy. "We're leaving anyway."

"What did you write?" Stewey teased her, wrapping his arms around her waist, swaying her like a blade of tall grass.

"It's in ashes," said Rozzy, smiling.

I got out by myself a little, to bury myself in a darkroom at school, to swim, to give them some time alone. They had never been quiet lovemakers. At night I lay on a narrow green blanket in the living room, listening to the sounds shivering the night, moving the darkness. I always missed David then, but it was a false anguish.

In the morning, Rozzy called for me to come in, and I went and crawled into her bed beside them, falling asleep again. I fitted in between the two of them like sandwich filling and the whole bed began smelling of warmth and sleep and family. Sometimes Rozzy woke up and disengaged, padding into the hall in her T-shirt and underpants, twisting on the shower. I'd wake up with my head on Stewey's shoulder, his arm thrown over me. Rozzy would come in later with a plate of jellied and buttered toast, and the three of us would sit up in bed and eat, littering the sheets with crumbs. Rozzy's wet hair would make pinpoints on my T-shirt, on Stewey's, as she swooped toward each of us.

"I want you to come to Madison with us," Rozzy said.

"I can't."

"You could transfer," she said, picking at her nails, pulling at the ridges of skin around the base. "Is it because of David, is that why you won't think about coming? I wish you liked someone other than him."

"I liked him," said Stewey.

"You didn't know him," said Rozzy. "If you liked someone that I liked, too, then it might work, the four of us. Wouldn't that be wonderful?" She brightened.

"It would be something," I said.

I called David that evening, but he was short and irritable. Bea had called him wanting to know what was going on, why she hadn't heard from either Rozzy or me. "I felt like a fool," he said, "I couldn't tell her anything, and it was obvious she didn't believe me. Would you call her, please?"

"Stewey's here," I said.

There was a gaping silence, and for a moment I thought he might have hung up.

"I want to see you," he said, his voice hard.

"Time's so funny for me right now."

"Set up a time, then, make a date."

"David, come on," I said. "Rozzy's leaving soon."

"Maybe I will be, too," he said, slamming the phone down.

I wandered into the living room and slumped down beside Stewey, who put his hand lightly on top of my head, flickering his fingers through my hair.

"Look, Bea wants you to call her, Rozzy," I said. "She wants to know what's going on."

"You call her," said Rozzy, "and don't tell her you're calling from here, please. I don't want to talk to her."

"I do," said Stewey.

"Kiss me first," said Rozzy, lifting her head.

I wasn't sure how Bea would react, but she was delighted. "I knew he loved her, I knew it," she cried. "I knew he wouldn't just let her disappear from his life. You tell those two to come for dinner. You come, too, and bring David."

"Matchmaker," I said, hanging up.

"What did she say?" called Rozzy.

"Nothing. But I could tell the news really made her day."

"Oh, *please*," snorted Rozzy.

"You won't come to dinner?"

"Why should I? So she can pry and ask questions? So I can be ignored by Ben?"

"She worries. She wants to be sure you're really happy."

Rozzy flung back her head sharply. "I changed my mind. Dinner's on. But not because I want to see them. Because I want to get some of the stuff I left at the house, I want to pack it and take it to Madison."

I slouched against the wall. Everyone was leaving. Stewey. Rozzy. The old Ben had already left. "Do you think I should transfer?" I said wistfully. Rozzy's face slowly bloomed into smile.

CHAPTER FOURTEEN

When I tried phoning Bea to set up dinner, there was never any answer. I called for days. I would idly dial the number when there was a lull in the conversation with Stewey and Rozzy; I would sprint into the pay phones in the subway stations, holding my breath against the sharp tang of urine; and I fed dimes and even quarters into the phones at the movies. It took me one full week, and then, finally, Ben answered, his voice cramped, and he told me Bea wasn't in.

"Where is she?"

There was a handclap's pause and then Ben said, "She'll be here tomorrow. You can call her then," and he hung up, severing our connection. I immediately fidgeted a dime out of my jeans pocket and called back, but the line clicked in a busy signal.

The next few days I kept calling, but the phone rang and rang, never catching. "That takes care of dinner, then," said Rozzy. But I was disturbed. Bea usually managed to call me every few days, and although those calls usually irritated me, their absence was unnatural. It only underlined the falseness of everything around me, the unstoppable way things were sliding apart. I rummaged around in Rozzy's cluttered medicine chest, ravaging the hotly colored pill bottles for her blue ten-milligram Valiums, and teased one out into my palm. I swallowed it surreptitiously, without water, something I had taught myself to do when I was in high school and so hyperaware of Rozzy's pill diet that I had to disguise the few times I took aspirin. Rozzy wouldn't miss one Valium. Stewey was the drug keeping her sane now.

The Valium diffused things. I slid down along the wall to the floor and watched Rozzy and Stewey organizing, gathering the things Rozzy would take with her to Madison, discarding the rest.

"No one knows where Bea is," I said, interrupting Rozzy as she hooked her fingers through the handles of some of the plastic mugs that were lying around. They were sticky with juice residue. She'd dump them into the tub and run the shower on them to clean them.

"Dinner will be postponed then," said Rozzy, absently stooping to curl her pinky about one last mug. "The later the better, as far as I'm concerned," she said. Stewey was stuffing the dirty laundry that had avalanched on the baby crib into a pillow case. Neither of them would ever acknowledge the crib as crib.

"Where could Bea have gone?" I asked Stewey.

"Don't worry about it," he said. "You know how she runs around." He called over to Rozzy to ask her if she thought she might like her old job at the student pharmacy back, if she'd like to move closer to campus.

I started going to class again, steadily moving toward Christmas break. "Why don't you and Stewey wait until next fall to go back to Madison?"

"How? On what?" said Rozzy, exasperated. "In Madison, Stewey has money to live on, has a place to live. The university will take care of us. Why can't you come there?"

"I can't."

"Why? Why can't you?"

"I just can't," I said miserably.

I ran into David one day at school. He had on a new

pair of green suspenders and he was laughing to himself about something, but when he spotted me, his face turned stubborn. "What's the matter with you, Bess?" he said coolly. "You don't look very good."

I told him that I was tired, that I was depressed about Rozzy and Stewey leaving so soon, and then I told him that no one seemed to know where Bea was.

"That's crazy," he said. "Are her things still at the house, did she take a suitcase?"

"God, I don't know. I didn't even think of that."

"See," he said, taking my arm, suddenly cheerful, "you *do* need me. Let me drive you over to your house. You'll feel better."

But when we got to the house, it was silent and unkempt. Dishes crusted with food were jumbled in the sink. Dust balls floated like tumbleweeds across the wood floors. The beds were unmade, the towels damp and tangled on the floor. A suitcase was gone, and a large part of Bea's wardrobe. Panic sprouted in me like a green plant, taking hold.

"We'll go to your father's office," said David. "He has to know something about what's going on here."

Rozzy and I had both been to my father's office as children. It was something Bea thought we should do, and I always brought a book along with me so I could settle into the chair by Ben's desk and read. Rozzy liked to roam around. She always sought out the janitor, who gave her sugar pops, putting his fingers across his mouth to hush her into secrecy. She only got to lick the pop a few times before Ben caught her and snapped it out of her mouth, making the hard candy click unpleasantly against her teeth.

Ben worked in the Prudential Building, on the third floor. David sat in the brown carpeted waiting room while I pushed past the secretary into the office with Ben's name on it. He was slumped at his desk. He loomed, fat and pale and tired. "Where's Bea, what's going on?" I said.

"Shouldn't you be at school?" he said.

"Why are you being such a bastard?" I cried.

He blinked at me. "Why don't you ask your mother where she went?"

"I will. Tell me where she is and I'll call her."

"I don't know. Leave me alone, I'm busy. There's nothing I can tell you about that woman, about what she does."

I sat in a stuffed black leather chair, stroking the arms, picking at a tiny rip in the leather. "Where is she?" I said.

I don't think he would have told me anything except that I kept sitting there, glued to that chair, staring at him while his phone buzzed. He abruptly picked up the phone, pressed a button and told his secretary to hold all of his calls, unless it was his wife. He didn't look at me while he spoke.

He said he had come home on a Thursday. The house smelled of his dinner. It was in the oven, bubbling and crusting over, yellow with cheese, red with paprika. The table in the dining room was set for one, at his usual place. His cot and the bed were turned down with sheets so new and fresh that they snapped at the corners. There was no note, and he went to sleep expecting to see her in the morning, expecting the breakfast smells to rouse him. The next day, when the house was still empty, he called the police. They humored him, they pacified him with tidbits of information, they said it was too early to worry, that cases like this were routine. "Nothing about Bea is routine," he said.

I stood up, one finger still teasing at the rip in the leather. "Will you call me if you hear anything?" I said.

"I promise."

"Are you all right?" I said abruptly, pushing my hands into my pockets, stretching the fabric. He looked at me for a moment and then clicked on the intercom and told his secretary that she could put calls through now. Turning back to me, he said evenly that it was always good to see me.

"Stewey's here," I blurted. "Did Bea tell you? He and Rozzy are going back to Madison."

"Fine," he said. "Now I have work to do."

When I left the office, I had a bad taste in my mouth, a film that stretched and smeared over the whole day. David was eased in a chair reading a magazine, but he stood up when he saw me and threaded his arm through mine. "He doesn't know where she is," I said, burying my face in his neck.

"Maybe she just went someplace to think."

"About what?"

David wanted to take me back to his apartment, but I lowered my head. "To Rozzy's?" he said, sighing.

I shook my head. "No, not there. Could you drop me off in Cambridge? I just want to sit in the movies by myself. It'll help me relax."

He bent and kissed me very lightly on the chin. "Sure," he said.

I couldn't think in that theater, and I couldn't think in my classes the next day, or at Rozzy's either. Every time the phone rang, it was an assault. I don't really know at what point the burden of family shifts, at what point the child transforms into the parent, but I began worrying about Bea, about where she was. I fretted about Ben eating and choking, about him rotting away in that house, already stiff before he was found. I kept calling home, but he never answered, and when I phoned him at work, he put me on hold until a busy signal split the connection.

Three days later the line to our house bloomed open. Bea answered. I was suddenly an open palm, twitching to strike. "Where the hell were you?" I spat.

"Kansas," said Bea evenly, "and you can just drop that tone of voice with me."

"You worried everyone sick."

"There were reasons."

"What reasons?"

"I'll tell you, but not on the phone."

"Don't do me any favors."

"Would you like me to hang up? I think you should hear me out. You're old enough to understand."

We set up a place to meet, but rocking back and forth in my mind, never stilling, was the implicit danger of what being old enough to understand meant.

Bea met me in a Boston café. She was already seated, her smile set, her hair curling. I tugged at my white sweater, at an old jacket of Stewey's thrown over my shoulders.

I slid into a seat. "Is Ben all right?"

"It's very difficult to talk to anyone with that kind of look on her face," she said, smoothly handing me a menu. "Your father's just fine, thank you. I told him I went on a vacation to think things out, that I was worried about how he looked, the way he had changed."

"That's why you left? Really?"

Bea flipped a menu page, frowning before she looked up. "No, *not* really. I didn't plan on leaving, it really started when you told me Stewey had come back. He came back because he *had* to. Certain people are meant to be together, aren't they? He must really love her. The two of them just seem to keep banging together like magnets, despite everything."

The waitress appeared and we ordered salads and iced tea, and Bea didn't really begin talking again until the food arrived. "After I got off the phone with you, I went in to tell Ben, all delighted, but when I saw him, the delight changed into something sticky. He was snoring on the couch. When I first met Ben, at the beach, his muscles slithered under his skin. He was like some stalking jungle animal. I lifted up the cover Ben had thrown over him, and his arm was just lying there, flaccid and pale, on his belly. His breathing was so noisy, so rumbling and uneven. I pulled back the cover and pushed in beside him. There wasn't much room. I raised myself up to look at him and his eyes were half open. 'Ben,' I said, but he didn't move, so I got up and went into the kitchen."

I fiddled with my salad. I kept glancing up at her, hearing her speak, seeing her mouth move and shape each word, but I was unable to connect those words with Bea, my mother.

"The phone company has a special number you can call," she continued. "They have these tapes, one for every disease, and you just tell them what number you want and they ping it in for you. I listened to the tapes on high blood pressure, on obesity, on divorce. Look at these hands," she said, showing me her palms, and then the backs. "Not one age spot. Not one."

It was then she told me the details about Walt. I knew, like most children, how my parents had met, who had been there before Ben claimed Bea. I knew the child's version of those happenings, and now I was hearing the adult story. As I listened, I felt as if I were on a fun house train—the more Bea opened up and sped toward me, the further away she got. "Stop staring," she said. "You knew about Walt. I've told you that story plenty of times."

"I thought it was just part of your past."

"There's no such thing as just part of the past," she said.

She told me she had dreamed about Walt. He was a giant bird, weaving and dipping. She was way down on the ground, a pinpoint, waving to him. He stretched his talons and started moving toward her, his wings pulsating. She jerked awake. It hurt. She got up and looked at herself in the mirror and then she got into the car and went to the all-night supermarket and bought a box of cookies and some hair coloring, something to put highlights in. She did her hair in the shower, and she let it dry with a towel wrapped around it. She coated her face and body with Vaseline and spread the bed with towels and lay down, waiting for something, for anything, to happen.

"It got worse," she said. "One night Ben's snoring woke me. He wasn't even sleeping with me. I couldn't roll over a quarter turn and shove him awake or move him onto his stomach. I couldn't even tell which room he was sleeping in, where the sound rumbled from. I got out of bed. He was in Rozzy's old room, snuffling and snoring on her bed, fully clothed, his face to the wall. The bed sagged under his weight. I shut the door and went into the kitchen. I don't know why, but I started calling information for Kansas City. I got every number that might turn out to be Walt's. There were ten of them. I didn't know what the time difference between Kansas City and Boston was, and I didn't care. I dialed each of those numbers, one right after the other. What did I care that people might be sleeping, might be making love, what did I care that Ben might overhear? The people must have sensed something in my voice, because no one got angry when I jangled them awake for someone who wasn't even living there. Finally, with eight names inked out, I got Walt. I knew it was him as soon as he spoke. I'd always remember that voice, how the cadence touched me. As soon as he said hello, I hung up. I was afraid. I called the operator back and got his address. They're not supposed to give out that information, but I got it. I sat down and wrote Walt a letter saying I was planning to visit the area and would he like to see me, and then I mailed it, airmail, and I waited.

"I got an answer back almost immediately. Yes, he said, yes, come see him. I thought of what to tell Ben, reasons why I might take a trip, but they all felt alien and hard in my mouth, so I just packed and left."

"Why are you telling me this now, if you didn't think

to tell me before you left?" I said. "Why am I suddenly your confidante?"

"Who do you want me to discuss this with?" she said. "With Rozzy, who won't even see me? With Ben, who's buried under fat and ill health? You're family. And you're an adult now. It isn't as if you were living at home and this would affect you personally."

"This doesn't affect me?" I said, incredulous. Bea was suddenly silent. She stirred some sugar into her tea, not looking at me. "So you were at Walt's," I said.

"Things hadn't changed that much," she said. "He was still married, a little older, no children—as he always said there wouldn't be. He trailed me around the house, he kept me up all hours talking, toying with ideas. I told him you and Rozzy were adults now, on your own. Jess, his wife, was pleasant, friendly. One night, after she went to bed, Walt offered me a job in one of his book places. He said he could find me an apartment nearby." Bea grinned. "You know, I liked Jess. I really did. She spent time with me mornings before she had to go to cap some kid's teeth. She had all these funny stories about her patients, and I laughed so hard I almost wet my pants. She said Walt was a real baby when it came time to fill a cavity, and sometimes she had to give him gas because the needle for the Novocain scared him. She didn't mind when Walt and I went in his battered VW to take a ride and talk. Walt told her I was thinking of leaving Ben and she was as understanding as my own mother. She made herself available to me."

"Bea," I said, carefully searching for words, but she waved her hand at me.

"I still love him," she said. "You never forget your first love. He cried when I took the plane back. He couldn't understand. Jess kept hugging him, telling him they could come and visit."

"Are you going to divorce Ben?"

She paused. "I don't know." She sipped at her coffee and then asked me abruptly whom I would choose to live with, if they did divorce and I were living at home. Just as abruptly, she said never mind, that that wasn't a fair question.

Unfair, but considered. Rozzy and I *had* played that game once, when we were kids. Each parent would have one of us, and we would be at opposite ends of the country, never to see each other. "Who would you pick to go with?" we demanded of each other. I never could say one name, Bea or Ben; guilt would set against my teeth like tin foil. Rozzy always said Ben, and then, bitterly, as if it would hurt him, she pronounced Bea's name, like a judgment.

"What happens now?" I said.

"I don't know." She gave me a funny smile.

Something small leaped within me. "You don't know?"

"That's right, baby, your mother doesn't know."

"When do you think you'll know, what are you going to do, how will you decide?"

She shook her head. "Something will tell me. I know I sound like a simpleton, but it's the way I am. It's always been that way for me."

"What did you tell Ben?"

She lifted her straw from her water, creating a vacuum by putting her finger over the top of the straw. "He doesn't know about Walt. Nothing's changed between your father and me. Ben wasn't angry when I came home, why are you? Why are you suddenly so righteous when it comes to him?" She sighed.

"Rozzy doesn't even know you were gone," I said.

Bea looked up abruptly, lifting her finger and letting the water from the straw slide back into her glass. She flashed me a sudden smile. "You know, Walt's a little afraid of Ben. He won't call. I call him. Stop looking at me, what do you want of me? Do you expect me to worry myself sick over a situation that might not even happen? You don't understand love, do you?"

"Let's go," I said. "It's getting late."

"I'd still like all of you to come for dinner," she said, fishing her money from her purse. "Things are still good with Stewey and Rozzy, aren't they? Nothing's gone wrong?"

"Things are fine," I said, standing.

I didn't want to tell anyone about Bea. I avoided David at school and I didn't answer the phone. I wouldn't even have told Rozzy, except that, like Bea, it was not a question of want anymore, but of need.

"Call them up right now and say we want to come to dinner on Wednesday," said Rozzy, her mouth set. "It's not the same thing at all, Stewey coming for me, and that Walt and Bea." She looked down at her fingers. "Is it?" she said.

A cold spell had set in when we started driving toward home. Rozzy was bundled up in an old wool sweater, a hat pulled down over her brow. She shivered and complained and moved so close to Stewey that it was difficult for him to drive. We listened to the radio on the way over. They said there hadn't been a chill like this since 1905, and snow might even be expected. "I can't bear this," said Rozzy. "God, but I hate winter. It's an unnatural season."

We pulled up into the drive around two. Bea prodded the heavy front door open, holding out her hands, smiling. She grabbed for Stewey, pushing back his hair, while Rozzy stood there, her own smile stiff. "Come inside, all of you," Bea said. "Isn't this weather something?"

She called for Ben. We were all sitting on the couch in the living room when Ben plodded in. He moved as if he were sleepwalking, his hair pulled away from his scalp, and the buttons on his shirt had tugged open. Rozzy dug into her pocket and lighted a cigarette. "Hey, you quit that," said Stewey, trying to take the cigarette from her, but she pulled her arm back fiercely and took a defiant draw, blowing out the smoke in circles.

"Here's Ben," said Bea pleasantly. Only Ben's eyes were the same. They took Rozzy in, and then, just as swiftly, discarded her. He thrust out a hand to Stewey. "So you're back," he said.

"Hey, where's David?" said Bea. "I thought you'd bring him."

"He's not home," said Rozzy.

We all sat in our old places for dinner, even Stewey, who got the mismatched kitchen chair. No one talked very much, except for Bea. All through dinner, Rozzy kept glancing at Ben, at the way he was taking third helpings of everything. Whenever Bea got up from the table to refill a water glass, he would heap his plate again, glancing at all of us, condemning us to secrecy. He gulped down his fish; he swigged down wine. Rozzy ate very little and drank three glasses of water.

In the middle of dinner, when the candles started to drip red wax onto the tablecloth, Ben got up. He tossed his cloth napkin into his plate, drawing the wine sauce from the fish into the cloth and staining it a shade deeper. Ben lumbered off toward the bathroom, and then there was the sudden sharp sound of choking, a gagging which ripped into the air. Rozzy's eyes stayed fixed on the hall, on what she couldn't see. Bea began noisily clearing dishes, stacking plates and cups into a clattering pyramid.

The bathroom was suddenly silent. "He has a doctor," said Bea flatly. "He has medicine."

Ben didn't come back to the table. Bea whisked away the dishes and the old tablecloth, and reset the table for a dessert of fresh fruit and cheese. "Such silence," said Bea. "Do you like my hair this short, Rozzy?"

Bea clicked on the radio by the window. The weather report boomed on. There were storm warnings, and Bea clucked her tongue, shaking her head. "You stay the night," she said.

"No, we won't," said Rozzy, but Stewey touched her arm. "There are those things you wanted to pack up, remember?" he said. "You don't really want to do it tonight, do you? We can do it in the morning and leave."

"What things?" said Bea. "You can leave anything you want here. It's your home."

Rozzy looked out the window. "Well, if it wasn't so cold—" she said moodily.

Bea gave them Rozzy's old room, and I was to have the couch. Bea went to bed early, and then Stewey went to their room, yawning, wanting Rozzy, who insisted that she had to stay up and speak with me.

Rozzy and I sat in the kitchen, eating cookies from a box we had found tucked under the sink. "Bea looks awful," said Rozzy, biting into a cookie. "Do you think she'll leave Ben? Anything could be a sign for her." She got up and took the milk out of the refrigerator and poured a glass for each of us. She dipped her cookie into the milk until it was soggy, and then popped it into her mouth. "Ben could die any day, couldn't he?" she said.

"He's pretty sick looking, but I don't think so," I said.

"I don't know," said Rozzy. "Men drop like flies when they get to that age. Fifty is the death age."

"Not all of them die."

"Do you remember when were were kids and we played

the heaven game, how we made up what heaven would be like and I ran into the house all excited to tell Bea that in my heaven you built your own house out of gold bricks and wood, the gold for all the good things you did, the wood for your sins? The prettiest houses would be for the people who were the prettiest inside. But Bea said that wasn't it at all, that when you died, you died, and that was it, and the only thing inside you was worms, winding their way through dinner. I was five," said Rozzy bitterly. "She was my mother. Why would she lie? I ran and hid outside in the bushes and then I went and dug up the doll we had once buried, only it wasn't there. I thought it had turned to dirt because of the worms. I didn't know that Bea had probably thrown it out, dug it up and thrown it out because she thought it was a bad sign or something." She looked wistfully out the window. "I never could play the heaven game after that. It was ruined for me."

"Come on. Let's go to bed," I said.

It was snowing when we woke up. The front steps were powdered over. We all got up and Stewey tried to start his car but the motor wheezed and died. We all ate breakfast together. Bea would stand behind Rozzy, fingering Rozzy's hair until Rozzy would jerk forward. Bea gave a little laugh and then her restless hands strayed over to Stewey, who beamed.

Ben crouched over his eggs, sucking in air and hacking it out again. Rozzy looked sharply at Bea, who was clearing away speckles of toast with a damp finger, her rings glittering, catching the morning light. When the phone rang, Bea picked it up in one swift move. "Who is it?" demanded Rozzy, but Bea waved her aside. Rozzy sat perfectly still, hushing Stewey when he tried to talk with her. She waited, listening to Bea's monosyllables. "She looks embarrassed," said Rozzy. Ben got up from the table and went into the other room, and Rozzy suddenly followed.

Bea hung up the phone. "Such a look she gave me," said Bea. "She's not hearing voices again, is she?"

We finished breakfast, and while Stewey perched on the kitchen stool and kept Bea company as she did the dishes, I went to find Rozzy. She was in the den with Ben, sitting opposite him. "You look so terrible," she was saying to Ben. I pulled back from the door, listening.

"Are you going to be OK?" she said.

"There's nothing wrong with me."

"Hey," said Rozzy, "remember when you went to Haymarket and bought me all those green peppers when I was sick?"

"That was a long time ago."

"When I touched you when I came in here, you thought it was Bea, huh?" she said, and then she stood up, making the leather on the chair whistle, and left the room. She didn't notice me, pressed along the wall.

Stewey, Rozzy, and I spent the morning in the basement going through Rozzy's old things. Rozzy touched everything, the musty books whose pages were skittering with silverfish, the dresses she hadn't worn in years, the old unworkable toys. She dumped everything into big white garbage bags to take back to the apartment with her or to throw out. "You want this?" Stewey lifted up a frayed Beatles sweatshirt. "If it's mine, I want it," said Rozzy.

She worked frenetically, by herself, taking huge armfuls of things into a corner, keeping her back to us. Stewey and I teased and jolted against each other. Stewey kept trying to convince me that there were huge hairy wolf spiders lurking in the corners, and he'd tickle my legs when I wasn't expecting it, which made me jump.

Bea came down the stairs with Ben once, to show him something about the furnace. As soon as Rozzy heard them clumping down the stairs, she stopped her rummaging and came over to Stewey, wrapping her arms around him, kissing him. She stroked his back with her bitten nails. "Rozzy—" he said, embarrassed, trying to ease her away, but she clung even tighter. Bea glanced over, but Ben saw only the furnace. It was only when they went back upstairs that Rozzy disengaged. "No more, you had your fill," she said, and she returned to her corner, showing us her back once again.

We were through around three, and settled back upstairs. "Try the car again," said Rozzy, "just go out and try. I can't hang around here all day."

"Why not, what else do we have to do that's better?" said Stewey.

Rozzy flopped down on the rug, laying her head in the crook of her arm.

"OK, I'm sorry. Don't be mad at me," said Stewey.

He went to stand by her, planting a foot on either side of her head. She flexed her fingers and gripped his ankles. "Can't we walk to the bus and get home? You could get the car later."

Stewey looked toward the window. The pane was speckled with flakes. "I'm game to go," I said, bored with the house, with doing nothing.

"Bea will be upset," said Stewey.

"Oh, *please*," said Rozzy, sitting up. She looked up at the mantel, at Bea and Ben's wedding photo, flanked by two brass candlesticks. "You think if we had had a wedding picture, it would be there, too?" She stood up and took down the picture, giving it a curious stare. "Stewey, are you happy?" she said.

"I'm married to you, aren't I?" he said, with a loose, easy grin.

Rozzy was suddenly preoccupied, she didn't seem to see him. "I'm so crazy sometimes," she said. "Once I made up this list of people I knew, separating them by who was happy and who wasn't, who showed they were happy, who showed they weren't." She smiled wryly. "Oh, Stewey," she said.

Bea came into the room, wearing a red cooking smock, her face dusted with flour. "I thought I heard you kids in here," she said, and then she looked sharply at Rozzy. "You look tired. You had better rest up. You know how you get when you don't rest."

"I don't get any way," said Rozzy, annoyed.

"We're going to walk to the bus to get home," said Stewey. "We'll pack Rozzy's stuff in the car and I'll get it later. The motor's just cold."

"I can drive you home," said Bea.

"No," said Rozzy, "we'll walk."

"Rozzy, are you sure? You really want to walk? It's cold and it's snowing. You won't like it," said Stewey.

"What makes you experts on me, on how I act, what I like?" said Rozzy angrily. "I'm going to change and gather my things, then I'm going, whether you are or not." She stormed out of the room.

"Oh, my," said Bea. She winged her flour-dappled hands out to her sides. "Come hug me, Stewey," she said, "and I want to see you before you and Rozzy leave."

"Is Ben still here?" I said, and Bea shook her head.

"At court," she said dryly.

It was cold outside, although it had stopped snowing and nothing had really stuck to the ground. I could see my breath. The ground was soggy and water kept slipping inside my boots, making my steps slow and tentative. Rozzy lagged behind, panting, kicking up angry clumps of dirt.

"I'm *cold*," she said.

"Well, if you move faster, you won't be."

"It doesn't get this cold in Texas," she said.

"It gets colder in Madison."

There were a few cars skidding on some slippery patches of road, whining their motors. "Why do we have to go to Madison?" said Rozzy. "It's cold there, I won't be happy. Why do we always have to do what you want?" Her words came out in tufts of frozen breath.

Stewey stopped walking and waited for Rozzy to catch up with him. Then he wrapped his arms around her and kissed her. "Come on. I came all the way out here because of you," he said.

"It was for you, not me," she said, wrenching away.

He grabbed her again, trying to still her. He stroked her through her heavy coat. He tried to tilt her stubborn face toward him so she would have to look at him, have to see what was in his face.

"Do you care if I just spend today with Bess?" she said. "Would you go back to the apartment alone?"

He released her. "Rozzy, is everything OK? Talk to me. Please."

"I just asked you a simple question. Will you go to the apartment?"

"Sure. I'll go."

"You really don't care? Really?" She looked at him cautiously.

We had another ten minutes to walk. Rozzy continued to lag behind, to complain loudly to herself about the bony coldness of the air, the terrible softness of the ground. She was haranguing the weather so loudly, gesturing so wildly, that when I glanced back at her, I sputtered with laughter. "Quiet," whispered Stewey, "she gets mad if you don't take her seriously."

When we got to the bus stop, the bus was just pulling in.

Rozzy gave Stewey a cool peck on the cheek and indifferently waved him onto the bus. He had the whole bus to himself and he sauntered to the very back, and pressed his face against the large back window, flattening his features, making faces at Rozzy, trying to entice a smile from her. She was stubborn, she kept her face stone. She ignored Stewey until the bus pulled away and his face faded with the distance.

"You all right?" I said.

She whipped around. "Why does everyone keep asking me that? *Christ.*"

We caught a Cambridge bus ten minutes later. Rozzy wanted to walk around Harvard Square, to prowl. We went past Holyoke Center where we used to sit on sultry summer days, waiting to be picked up. The granite stoops we used to lounge upon indolently, the broad walkway where we sashayed, were covered with slush. There were lots of young kids tramping around. Rozzy kept staring at faces, her eyes devouring, sprinting from one face to another, snagging. She was caught by detail, by fringed leather boots, a lacy shawl knotted over a black woolen coat, felt hats dripping with feathers, the quick puppylike kisses the young lovers exchanged.

"Oh God," said Rozzy, "look at them. They're so young."

"You're not exactly old," I said. "Twenty-three isn't over the hill."

Rozzy began shivering and we went into a paperback bookstore to warm up and to browse. We wandered around every section, riffling through the bins of unbacked posters, the table of already dated art calendars, the poster books. Rozzy examined everything, and her blatant curiosity was infectious.

I had always been secretly and shamefully addicted to trash. As much as I feasted on good literature, I hungered for pulp. I indulged my passion in airport magazine stands and in terminal shops, in drugstores late at night when no one I knew was likely to be about. When I went to the supermarket with David, I read all the magazines I could slide out from the wire shelving, while David grinned wickedly.

I was looking for the magazine section, when I noticed Rozzy staring glumly at a shelf, not moving. I wistfully glanced around for periodicals, and then went to Rozzy. "Look at this," she said, "three whole shelves devoted to self-help books. Skinnies can get fat, fatties can get thin, and shy people can be as much of a bastard as anyone. Ben would like this section." She paused, frowning. "At least the old Ben would. The new Ben doesn't give a damn one way or the other, does he?"

"Rozzy," I said, "these books don't work. If they did, there wouldn't be so many fat, thin, shy people waltzing around."

"But they must work," said Rozzy. "People buy these books all the time. Some of these things are in their fifth printings."

"Well, maybe the books work for a while, maybe people trim down and then toss out the book. Then they just get fat again, so they go and buy another book."

Rozzy was scanning titles, crouching down to see the lowest stacks. "Everything's circular," she said. She lifted up a book, smiling: *Menal Health Through Will Training.* "Let's get out of here," she said. "I feel claustrophobic."

We ended up at one of the Pewter Pot chain shops, a muffin and coffee place where the waitresses dressed up in black vests and red skirts and encouraged you to share your table with strangers. Rozzy and I were lucky enough to get a small table to ourselves.

Rozzy was still gloomy. When her fudge muffins came, black and shiny as her hair, she picked at them, mashing them, slicing them with her fork. She kept looking at me expectantly, and then she'd stare down into her plate again.

"What?" she blurted, her eyes tense.

"I didn't say anything."

"You didn't say a long sentence and then my name, you didn't say 'Rozzy'?" She stopped smashing down her muffin.

"Rozzy, it's noisy in here. I don't know about you, but I can hardly hear myself think. You probably just heard someone else say something that sounded like your name."

"Sure, the noise," said Rozzy, her voice flattening. "You like this purse? It's new. I almost bought you one, but they didn't have another." She held up a fringed buckskin pouch, and then set it into her lap again. Her hands moved under the table. At first I thought she was going to reach for a comb, which irritated me a little. She didn't take anything out, not that I could see. She yawned, covering her mouth with both her hands, and when she took her hands away, she was swallowing something. Her head moved forward a bit.

"This used to be my favorite place," said Rozzy. "When I was sixteen I used to come here and imagine that I'd bump into Joan Baez or Bob Dylan. I even thought I might be sitting in a chair Baez had sat on." Rozzy straightened. "Don't you ever wish you could go into the past and stay there? Everything you like always changes completely, and everything you don't like gets worse with repetition." She sighed. "I think dread is the worst emotion of all. I used to think loneliness was, but now I think dread."

"Hey," I said, "come on."

"I'm fine," she said, giving me a weak smile. "Did you think I was getting sick again? Everyone else seems to." She glanced at the rim of her plate, smeared with the chocolate paste of her muffin. She shrugged into her coat, buttoning it, getting ready to leave. "I want to call Stewey," she said.

We walked toward the subway. "Are you going to marry David?" said Rozzy. "You'll marry him and I'll never see you. He'll be the kind that won't let you take a vacation by yourself."

"That's not true. And anyway, I'm not marrying David."

"Do you think Bea will marry Walt?" she said, shivering. "Oh God, *everything*, everything's changing except for me."

"I'm glad you're not changing," I said, taking her arm, stopping her from rushing forward. "I love you."

She looked at me for just a moment, before she darted her head to the side. "I'm not glad," she said. She started looking around for the phones. "You're lucky," she said wistfully. "You'll probably be a great photographer, have a rich and famous life. You do whatever you want and it just works out right."

I touched her shoulder. "Rozzy, I can't believe you think that."

Rozzy dug out a dime from her purse. "Maybe Stewey will meet us for dinner downtown," she said. She slid into one of the phone booths, cursing at the sharp smell of urine. I leaned against the glass, breathing on it, tracing out pictures with the tips of my fingers.

Rozzy was only in the booth a few minutes. She placed the receiver gently on the hook. It toppled off, dangling, and she slammed it back on. "No answer," she said.

"He probably just ran down the street for a paper," I said, "or maybe he's in the shower."

"Sure," said Rozzy. She put her thumbnail into her mouth and chewed, and when I tugged her hand away, she smiled at me.

We went down into the subway, ignoring the young kids hawking *Boston After Dark*, the bums begging for quarters, the kids clotted under the stairs smoking dope. The subways were always jammed, and now the place smelled of wet wool and leather boots.

We moved toward the front, where the platform stopped and opened up into the dark pit where the subway ran. People were already jockeying for position, guessing where the doors might open, maneuvering for a prime spot to get a seat. A woman in front of me was talking to herself, using her arms like a spatula to clear out some space. Rozzy stared at her, frozen, until I touched Rozzy and then she looked down at the filthy ground, at the litter of shiny gum wrappers and Coke cans. When I said her name, she ignored me and kept her head down.

"Rozzy," I said, but her eyes remained unfocused. "*Rozzy*—" I pulled at her purse, and she turned, her face slowly taking on expression. "Let's get out of the subway, let's go walk upstairs for a while, get outside again. Come on."

"I hear the train coming," she said, smiling a little. She handed me her purse. "Hold this for a second," she said. "Please." Then, while I was watching her, curious, waiting, she stepped over the white warning line, falling, disappearing as the train screamed over her.

CHAPTER FIFTEEN

Everything happened very quickly after that, so quickly that it didn't have time to really solidify into memory. Sometimes I think I know what happened. I'll get these tugs deep within me, pictures as vivid as breath flickering suddenly; the panic will start, but then I'll lose it. I wonder sometimes if anything happened at all the way I remember it.

You can't go by what the papers said. They all had stories about Rozzy. The evening news even had a film clip. I don't know how they get around so quickly, how they film things; but even film can lie, and you couldn't see all that much in the clip anyway, except for the crowds and the smart young reporter. Some of the papers hinted that it wasn't an accident, that she had been pushed. The prose got a little purple, the accusations absurd. People even began getting panicky about taking the subway. Bea told me that for months afterward, no one would go near the white warning line, no one would approach a train at all until it had moaned to a complete stop. People eyed one another suspiciously. Everyone was suspect. There were stories about people being pushed in front of trains by packs of kids, but the newspapers were silent. The stories continued to seed themselves.

There were things I do remember, that I'm sure of, though. The whine of the ambulance. The men rushing into the subway with a stretcher. The crowds, the confusion, the eyes feeding on me, vampirish. A cop asked me something over and over, but my mouth wouldn't open, my mind wouldn't work. The cop took Rozzy's purse from me, unclenching my fingers, one by one, and he took my purse from my other hand, and looped them both over his arm. He kept one arm linked through mine while he fiddled in both purses. "Which one is yours?" he asked, but I couldn't answer. I let him lead me up into the street, while the crowd gazed at me. We rode in the ambulance with Rozzy to the hospital. I tried to ride in the back with her, but the cop wouldn't let me. He kept patting my arm.

And then I remember the hospital, how blindingly white it seemed, as sudden and white as the snow, as unnatural. The cop sat me down and was gone. Rozzy was gone. Bea later told me the cop had phoned them, but he didn't know who was alive and who was dead, he read her both ID cards, mine and Rozzy's, and told her the name of the hospital. Bea said for a while she thought both of us were dead. Maybe that accounted for the look on Stewey's face when he rushed into the hospital. Stewey's eyes banged into me. His body shook. He was flagged by Bea and Ben. There were hands, faces close to me, arms pulling me up, words. Throughout the ride home, I kept touching one of my hands with the other, pinching myself, forcing myself to feel, making every cell in my body recognize the life that moved within.

The three of us were there, sitting in a church. Rozzy had done it again, had thrown us together because of her. Only Stewey seemed a little apart. But for him Rozzy had died so many times that I don't think he needed any ceremony to make it final.

I couldn't look at him. I was afraid of how he might feel seeing me against the backdrop of Rozzy's coffin. I was afraid of reading something in his face. He was in a black suit and he flinched when Bea tried to hold him. He moved back as if burned.

I didn't cry. I didn't feel. It was Ben who said, "Oh Rozzy—" who made her name an anguish, and who tried to throw himself onto her coffin, tried to wrap it protectively in his arms. Bea had to get up and pull him back to his seat, hold him to her, her arms retainers. She kept whispering to him, wiping his face with her white lacy handkerchief. Her mascara was smeared down her face, twin black stains.

There weren't many people, mostly friends of Bea's, Dr. Leffler, David. He didn't belong there. Rozzy never liked him.

I didn't see Rozzy buried. I was there, but I didn't see any of it. I wasn't standing in the cold getting slush in my shoes watching my sister be buried. I was in a haze, in the kind of half-dream before you shake awake, when your mind is there before your body. When Bea took my arm to lead me back into the dark mouth of the limousine, I opened my eyes only enough so I wouldn't stumble. I never focused; edges blurred.

People came to our house all week. We were never alone. Bea made up a special room for Stewey, and I stayed in my old room. "You're in no condition to go to Madison, yet," she told him. She even called his parents for him and told them about Rozzy. She said later that they were very nice, that his mother had even started crying and had said that Rozzy had been a beautiful girl, a lovely wife. I sat in the kitchen and listened. Stewey's mother spoke very loudly. You could hear her voice climb right through the wires. Stewey wouldn't get on the phone. He sat in the room that Bea had made up for him and kept the door closed, not talking to anyone, not acknowledging the hesitant knocks of people who came to the house, who wanted to tell him how sorry they were. Stewey and I hadn't really looked at each other once since leaving the hospital.

Bea and Ben popped tranquilizers like party nuts. They were joined to each other by a held hand. Our house that never invited people because Ben was so antisocial was now crowded with relatives I hadn't seen in years. An Uncle Jason, fat in checkered jacket, raced toward me, telling me I was a little doll even as he clapped me against him. "Such red hair," he said. "Where's the fire?" A friend of my mother's came over and told me I looked anorexic. "We brought all this wonderful food—honey cakes, pies, meats—and you don't eat. I get hungry just thinking about it." My cousin Trina, married and heavier, lifted up the hem of my skirt to check the label, muttering to herself. Women told me about their sons. "It's terrible, isn't it," said Trina, "that such an occasion should finally bring us all together like a family."

There it was, what Ben had feared when we were babies, why he hadn't wanted relatives visiting. People taking on the parts of your life that were yours and no one else's, people digging up your past and making it their own. No one said much, but people suddenly seemed to know what our lives had been like. I heard them discussing Rozzy, comparing her to friends of friends who had been institutionalized, who were worse off now, who got sleep therapy, water therapy, shock therapy.

"No wonder your father didn't want people to the house," said Trina, "the poor man."

I got up and went into the kitchen, running cool water over my hands, spotting my blouse. It was silk and it would be ruined. People were nibbling at the cakes, the molds. I wandered around. David was sitting patiently in the living room, although I had asked him not to come. He was talking pleasantly to someone, and when he saw me, he got up and came over. I averted my face, and he touched my shoulder. "Later then," he said gently.

Ben was listening to Trina's husband talk about his new job at a lab. Stewey appeared and sat beside David, who handed him his own cup of hot coffee. Stewey's eyes were tiny red stars in his face, dying. Instantly, people approached him, but he looked through them, he made them uncomfortable, and they flickered away.

"What an accident," said Trina, "and poor Bess was there."

"It wasn't an accident," I said.

"Baby," said Bea, "you were in shock, you don't remember. You said yourself you didn't remember."

"I was there. She handed me her purse."

Ben was watching me, his face changing. I looked over at him, lifting my chin up.

"You can't be sure," said Bea, taking Ben's hand, rubbing it. "In a crowd, people push."

"Jesus," said Trina. "Holy Jesus."

I didn't know half the people in the room. They were faces, looking at me. Only Stewey didn't seem surprised. He hadn't changed posture and when I looked at him, he gave me a faint, bitter smile. I got up and walked out of that house, ignoring Bea's chanting call. I walked up and down the blocks, taking the routes Rozzy and I used to follow when we were kids. I walked until the cold had become part of me, and when I came back into the house, everyone became silent. David had his hands in his lap, like dead dull fish. "You OK?" Trina said, touching my shoulder. Bea was harshly weeping against Ben. "I used to check her pills," she cried. "I hid the knives, the scissors. You ask anyone."

I went to find Stewey, brushing aside the hands that were fluttering at me like moths. Before I reached his room, someone tapped me. It was Betty West, an old friend of my mother's who lived a block away. She once babysat for Rozzy and me at her house, making us canned soup and jelly sandwiches, treats we never had at home. She hugged me. "It's been a long time," she said. "What, you're off to college, living away from home? Your mother tells me you have a talent for picture taking. You've grown into quite a beauty." She looked toward the kitchen. "Come sit down. Talk to me for a minute."

We both sat at the table, propping our elbows up. "I'm so sorry," she said. "It's so terrible that such a thing could happen. I always liked Rozzy. When I think about that girl, so young and beautiful—" She paused, shaking her head. "But really, who knows what would have happened to her? Maybe it's better that the pain is over right now." She glanced out our back window. "Pretty garden," she said, and then she turned back to me. "It was a terrible drain on all of you. I know it sounds awful, but it's better this way. Really."

I wrenched up from the table. "Get away from me. Why don't you go home? Who wants you here, you and your stupid, thieving opinions?"

Her features froze. "It's all right," she said evenly. "You don't have to apologize."

I went into the living room and took David's hand, yanking him up, pulling him outside. "What is it?" he said.

"Drive me somewhere, please," I said, "please."

He wrapped his arms about me and sat me in his car. We drove along the black stretch of highway, not talking, not even touching, and the silence calmed me. "This is what I needed," I said.

"Would you like to stay with me for a while?" he said. "You don't have to come back for this. I'll even leave, let you have the place to yourself, if that's what you want."

"No," I said, "it would still be your place."

"I don't understand."

I touched his arm. "I know you don't."

"Would you like to take a trip? Go camping?"

"No, I don't think so."

"You can call me anytime, you know. Or just show up. You don't even have to talk. I'll soothe you. I'm very good at that." He sighed. "I feel so useless, but I *love* you, Bess. Does that help?"

I leaned back against the seat, closing my eyes. "It's OK, David," I said.

Gradually, people stopped coming to the house. The phone calls petered out, dwindling to a few static rings, a few spurts of sympathy, of curiosity. Bea still had her hands full with Ben. She whispered to him, she fed him words. She kissed and touched him, making him real because of her. And he hung on her like a suit of clothing. No one even noticed when Stewey and I slipped out the front door, each of us carrying one of the plastic garbage bags full of Rozzy's things. We packed them into the car and went to clean out Rozzy's apartment. We huddled in the car with the bags.

Stewey walked into Rozzy's apartment first, loaded down with white garbage bags. Six brown boxes were banged up against the wall, all clumsily taped, Rozzy's scrawl identifying the contents.

"I'm not unpacking anything," said Stewey. "I'm going to throw everything into the fucking incinerator."

"Will it fit?" I said, dumping down one of the bags, leaning against the wall to rest.

"We'll make it fit. Help me carry this."

We picked up the boxes, Stewey at one end, me at the other, struggling, cursing, never meeting each other's eyes. The incinerator was at the far end of the hall, set up high so you had to stretch up and hoist whatever it was you wanted burned. Not all of the boxes did fit. Those cumbersome ones we ripped open just enough to flutter some of the contents in, and then mashed down the rest with our feet so they, too, would fit. Everything made a resounding whack as it hit the bottom of the chute. Stewey even went and got Rozzy's red bathroom scale and tossed it down. I could hear the glass on the dial breaking.

Stewey cleaned out the refrigerator, gathering the vegetables that had grown furry coats of mold, the sour milk, the butter. All that went down the chute. "No one's ever going to use Rozzy's things," Stewey said fiercely, "no one." He took the baby crib and kicked at one of the sides until the fragile wood splintered. Then Stewey took his buck knife and slashed up the bed. He tore the sheets apart with his bare hands, leaving ribbons of cloth trailing listlessly on the dusty wood floor. "We'll have to sleep on the floor," he said. "The trash truck will cart this away if we drag it outside."

We pulled the stuff outside and pushed it way in the back of the other trash bags and boxes in the alley. Then we came back upstairs and Stewey went in to take a shower. I sat on the floor of the living room, empty except for myself. I remembered when I was a little girl and an aunt had died. Everyone had wept, but I had gone into our kitchen and looked out the sunny bright window at the sky. I had thought that was a dramatic thing to do. The sky was where people went to live when they died. I had tried to feel sad, to feel terrible, but nothing had really changed for me, my life was the same. The only thing I felt was a flicker of guilt, and then resentment, and I threw those things off when I went outside to play, my heart beating youth and life within me. I looked out of Rozzy's window now and saw the smudged fingerprints where we had both leaned into the glass and made breath pictures. I got up and went into the kitchen.

I hunched over the sink and held on, waiting for the

sudden sharp tang of nausea to subside. It reeled and shivered within me, and then I was dry-heaving into the sink, being twisted inside out. I sucked in a gulp of air against that queasy current, and then Stewey was out of the shower, holding my head for me as I choked and gagged into the clean white sink.

Stewey and I were probably supposed to hold each other while we wept, to wipe away each other's tears, to make love—that old cliché about affirming life in the midst of death—but none of that happened. Not with us. We were dry-eyed. Sleepwalkers. The only conversation we had was small talk, about there being no soap to shower with, about the chill outside. We undressed at night and lay on our jackets, pressing our bodies together for warmth, waiting out the night and its shadows. There was nothing in our flesh, no energy or passion; it was simply flesh, as unmovable and unpliable as stone. Stewey didn't sleep. Every time I jerked awake from a bad dream, he was sitting up. He would listlessly pat my shoulder until I calmed.

In the morning Stewey got together the few things in the apartment that were his and had never been used or worn by Rozzy, and packed them in a spare box. "If I could do without it, I'd ruin the car," he said. "I can't stay in Madison. I'll go someplace else." We didn't make plans; we didn't talk. Really, what difference would it make if we wrote or called or ever did anything?

"Do you want me to drop you off?" he said. I shook my head. I could walk to the bus stop, and I wanted to be by myself. We walked downstairs to the car, and Stewey opened the door. I took his hand, ignoring the flinching movement of his body. "It wasn't because of you," I said suddenly. "She loved you."

He bent and kissed the top of my head. "I'm not going to think about that anymore. I won't believe it." He got into the car. "I'll see you, Bess Nelson," he said.

I never heard from Stewey after that. I didn't write him

or call him or contact his parents. Bea seemed to take his abrupt departure as natural, and she said nothing. Sometimes I imagined that he had another girl, that he was happy. Other times I wondered if he would eventually slash at himself, doing away with the last vestiges of Rozzy, the last memories that were himself.

EPILOGUE

People began getting on with their lives again. I sleepwalked through Christmas break, through the rest of my junior year. At first I waited to hear from Stewey, but then anticipation was transformed into dreamy wakefulness, into resignation. We were all playing a waiting game.

David said nothing when I applied to schools in California, in Oregon, in Europe. He put off his trip to Africa and began talking about taking a year off, but he didn't see how nervous that made me, how I pulled back.

Everyone kept yelling at me. "Put your past behind you," Bea said, "live your life." She didn't understand how my life could feel all lived out already, that everything was just repetition. Now I know what Rozzy meant that day in the Pewter Pot when she spoke about dread.

Bea and Ben adjusted quickly. He lost a great deal of weight and she got him to run with her. She said they were going on a cruise soon. I was home one afternoon when the mail came. I picked up a rectangular envelope postmarked Kansas, with Walt's name in the corner, and when I handed Bea the mail, I gave her that one first. She looked at it for a moment and then glanced up at me. She riffled through the other letters and then said quickly, "All junk mail.

Throw it out, would you?" She ripped the stack in half and handed the pieces to me.

I never went to Rozzy's grave. Bea and Ben went. In between their traveling. My room was dotted with their cards, but you couldn't tell anything about the places from their hasty scribbles, not the way you could with Rozzy's.

I had lunch with Bea one day. Her hair had grown out, spurting down past her shoulders. We had a good lunch, although we didn't talk very much, but then we never really had. Bea kept asking if I'd like to go on vacation with them. "You're too damned independent for your own good," she said. "We've always had that problem with you."

"What?" I looked up from my iced tea. "What are you talking about?"

"Call your father," she said. "He'd be so pleased if you would call the house and ask for him."

I looked helpless. "What would I say?"

"He's your *father*. Say hello, how are you?"

"*He* told you he wants me to call?"

Bea smiled. "Things are different," she said. "Call him."

Bea ordered lemon pie while I fiddled with my tea. "You still see David? I always liked him." She wiped some lemon filling off her mouth with the edge of the paper napkin. She never asked about Stewey.

"You're still not angry with me about Walt, are you?" Bea said suddenly. "Is that why you act this way?" She fumbled with her fork. "Oh, never mind," she said, and then she grinned. "We might buy a summer place on the Cape. Won't that be lovely?"

"I thought you hated the beach."

"That was before." She finished her pie. "Bess, are you going to be OK?"

"Why not?" I said.

I let David make love to me. I didn't participate, but he was so involved with his own passion, I don't think he noticed, or maybe he thought he could pull me along with him. That night, I dreamed I was being strangled. I jolted awake, coughing, scraping sound from the tubes of my throat. David woke up and shook me. "Can you speak?" he demanded. I nodded and he went to get me a glass of water. "What's wrong?" he said. "I knew you couldn't really be choking by the sounds you were making. You're really suggestible." He touched my neck and then rubbed it. "You need to cry," he said gently. "You'll feel better."

"Just like that. You want me to cry."

"I want you to do what you want," he said. "Do you believe I love you?"

"Let's go back to sleep," I said.

I was twenty-one, listlessly edging my way through my senior year, when Ben and Bea sold the house and moved to Wayland. I kept thinking about what Rozzy used to say about how we would one day come back and find our home repeopled, repeating our whole cycle of events. We would feel tugs of recognition. I went back to that house. A family was living there, but they had three scrappy little boys who threw stones at me when I came toward their walk, a big sheep dog, and no daughters at all.

I had no idea what I was going to do with my life. I was accepted to grad school in Oregon. I could become a photographer, still images, freezing time so it never moved forward, so it never got a chance to rot and spoil. Ben now said he would pay for any schooling I might want. He wanted to see me. He wanted me to come to dinner more often. When I told him I flunked an exam, he said to do better. He was encouraging.

Ben and Bea took me out to dinner once, but every dish, every spice, made me think of Rozzy. "Rozzy loved aspic," I said, ignoring Bea's harsh glance. "Look at the sweater on that girl over there," I said, "it looks like one of Rozzy's." I saw what it did to Ben's face, but I couldn't help it.

When the fall came, I didn't know what else to do, so I left for Oregon. David went a little crazy those last few weeks. He trailed me everywhere, his face a canvas of panic, and finally he became bitter, he wanted to hurt me. He accused me of abandoning Rozzy, he reminded me where her grave was. Then he said that maybe Rozzy wasn't the only unstable one in the Nelson family. Still, he was at the airport, standing beside Bea and Ben, his face pained and white as my plane rose into the sky. He wrote me for a few months, and then the letters stopped. I thought it was because I never answered, but then Bea sent me a clipping from the *Globe* announcing his marriage. There was a picture of the bride, a blond who had a degree in special education from BU. The article said they were honeymooning in Africa, where David was doing research on gorillas. Across the bottom of the picture, Bea had sprightly printed, "This could have been you." She was rabid on romance. She and Ben were planning their own second honeymoon, and she continually asked if I was seeing men.

There were men. There still are, but no one close. I sleep with men only so I won't wake up and realize how alone I am, so I'll hear other sounds besides the thud of my own heart.

I became a photographer for a small public television station. It's four years later and I'm still there. It's a job, that's all, and I'll stay until my restlessness propels me elsewhere. I am not famous.

I saw identical twins on the train the other day. I studied

them. They didn't seem to mind being stared at. They were about sixteen, with short curling dark hair, and they both wore these big sunny yellow tent dresses. The one on the left smiled pleasantly at me, and then she turned to her sister and kissed her on the cheek. They say that when one identical twin dies, the other soon follows. I was so jealously intent on watching the twins that I missed my stop. It didn't matter. There was no place to go. I watched them get off the train, stepping out into the crowd with an awkward kind of grace. I shut my eyes, not seeing anything anymore, letting the train mindlessly carry me.

It's difficult. I can't walk through a crowd without springing forward when I spot a flash of black hair, a heavy wool coat in the sticky summer heat. I once elbowed my way off a jammed bus to follow a girl with hair like ink spilling down her back. I raced after her for three blocks, and when I was two feet away, panting, my face wet, she pivoted and frowned. "'You want something?" she said. Her teeth were bad, her eyes dull. "You know me?" she said. When I turned away from her, apologizing, a headache was twisting behind my eyes.

The last time Bea saw me, my eyes were stained by circles, my color was ashen. It made Bea angry; she told me to stop dwelling on Rozzy, that she was dead, and better off, too, that she had never been happy living, "not that one." For Rozzy, she said, living was one agony after another, punctuated by brief spurts of joy.

Bea didn't understand, any more than Ben did, gardening in the backyard, trim and tan again, unpossessed of his demons. Bea has it wrong. I'm not so benevolent. I've always known I was selfish. It was always I who was desperate for the other's half, for the missing pieces. It was always I who needed Rozzy's needs in order to exist. It was I all the time.

Lately, I've been having these dreams, yearnings that

cling into my waking hours. I'm always part of a huge face-less crowd, and everyone is moving very slowly, except for me. I spiral through them, my glance fluttering like crazy trapped wings against each face, and then I'm searching, forever, endlessly searching for the only thing that can complete me, for Rozzy.